KU-742-104

MOST SECRET

It is early summer 1941 and Nazi Germany has
a firm grasp over much of Europe. Finn
Gunnersen and best friends, Loki Larson and
Freya Haukelid, have managed to escape their
native Norway and fly to Britain in order to
deliver vital information. Their astonishing
courage has not gone unnoticed. An enigmatic
man known only as X has recruited them into
a clandestine organization called Special
Operations. Under orders of the Prime
Minister, Winston Churchill, this most
secret organization is tasked with going
forth and setting Europe ablaze, to create
networks of agents in occupied countries,
and to help coordinate local Resistance
groups in the fight against Nazi oppression
and tyranny. It is extremely hazardous work.

Finn, Loki and Freya are now fully trained
secret agents. With their first mission into
France successfully completed they are ready
for action once again.

This story is inspired by real events.

Special Operations Personnel Files

MOST SECRET

NAME: Finn Gunnersen

AGE: 16

BACKGROUND: Born Trondheim, Norway. Father RAF Spitfire pilot (killed in action). Mother and sister arrested by Gestapo. Escaped from occupied Norway by stealing Heinkel 115 float plane.

(File note dated June 1941
Addendum: father officially reclassified as 'missing, presumed dead', based on advice received from Air Ministry.
Signed – Brigadier Devlin, Commanding Officer, Mulberry House – cross reference to file AirPMIA4)

ASSESSMENT: Basic training and assessment carried out at Mulberry House under Brigadier Devlin. Key observations: outwardly unremarkable. Taught to fly by father and keen to obtain his official 'wings'. Physically fit though not strong. Quick to learn and resourceful. Responds well under pressure though tendency to be rather reckless. Inseparable from Mr Larson and Miss Haukelid. A decent, honest lad. Brave but vulnerable. Far more courageous than he realizes. Keen to follow in father's footsteps.

COMPLETED MISSIONS:
Operation Death Ray (France)

RECOMMENDED
FOR ACTIVE SERVICE
IN THE FIELD
0619-3199-46

Special Operations Personnel Files

MOST SECRET

NAME: Loki Larson

AGE: 16

BACKGROUND: Born Trondheim, Norway. Father commercial pilot and member of local Norwegian Resistance. Escaped from occupied Norway along with Mr Gunnersen.

ASSESSMENT: Basic training and assessment carried out at Mulberry House under Brigadier Devlin. Key observations: a large lad and as strong as an elk. Taught to fly by father. Good with his fists. Might be prone to shoot first and ask questions later. A loyal and courageous chap who can be relied on in a crisis. Lifelong friend of Mr Gunnersen and close to Miss Haukelid. All function well as a team.

COMPLETED MISSIONS: Operation Death Ray (France)

Special Operations Personnel Files

MOST SECRET

NAME: Freya Haukelid

AGE: 16

BACKGROUND: Born in remote
part of Norway. Father arrested
for actively resisting Nazi
occupation. Mother deceased.

(File note dated January 1941
Addendum: father officially
reclassified as 'deceased', based on intelligence
received from agents located in Norway. Did not
survive wounds received during arrest.
Signed — Brigadier Devlin, Commanding Officer,
Mulberry House)

ASSESSMENT: Basic training and assessment carried
out at Mulberry House under Brigadier Devlin. Key
observations: an intelligent girl with tremendous
talents. Taught by her father, Freya is an
outstanding marksman (rifle) — the best we've come
across. Gifted at coding and Morse code, and learns
languages quickly. Physically far tougher than her
appearance suggests. Despite reservations about
sending girls into the field, Freya has proved
herself during first active mission. Survived
interrogation by Gestapo during capture (rescued
by Messrs Gunnersen and Larson).

COMPLETED MISSIONS:
Operation Death Ray (France)

RECOMMENDED
FOR ACTIVE SERVICE
AS W/T OPERATOR
0619-7639-25

Special Operations Personnel Files

MOST SECRET

NAME: Marieke Maartens

AGE: 15

BACKGROUND: Born
Scheveningen, The Hague,
Holland. Mother and father
drowned during floods in
Holland in 1937. Came to
England before outbreak of
war and lived with
grandparents near Oxford.
Has an older brother, Karel Maartens,
whereabouts and status unknown —
presumed to be still in Holland. Recruited to
Special Operations in November 1940.

ASSESSMENT: Basic training and assessment
carried out at Dovecote (Dutch Section) under
Major Gerrit. Key observations: English is
fluent, and coding and wireless skills have
reached adequate speed and accuracy. Excellent
organizational and communication skills. Prone
to let her emotions show but resilient. Below
average marksmanship — better in a leading or
co-ordinating role. Not short on courage.

Ready for active service.

APPROVED

REGISTERED
NO. 576834084-6

RECOMMENDED
FOR ACTIVE SERVICE
IN THE FIELD
0619-3199-62

Also available by Craig Simpson:

SPECIAL OPERATIONS: DOGFIGHT

'A fast-paced thriller' *THE TIMES*
'A full-throttle adventure'
SUNDAY EXPRESS

SPECIAL OPERATIONS: DEATH RAY

RESISTANCE

'A terrific romp . . . fans of films
starring Bruce Willis (or David Niven)
should love it' *TES*

A FINN GUNNERSEN ADVENTURE

SPECIAL **OPERATIONS**

WOLF SQUADRON

CRAIG SIMPSON

CORGI BOOKS

SPECIAL OPERATIONS: WOLF SQUADRON
A CORGI BOOK 978 0 552 56045 0

First published in Great Britain by Corgi Books,
an imprint of Random House Children's Books,
in association with The Bodley Head,
A Random House Group Company

This edition published 2010

3 5 7 9 10 8 6 4 2

Copyright © Craig Simpson, 2010
Cover artwork by Stephen Mulcahey
Map by Julian Mosedale

The right of Craig Simpson to be identified as the author of this work has been
asserted in accordance with the Copyright, Designs and Patents Act 1988.

Special Operations: Wolf Squadron is a work of fiction.
Any resemblance of characters to persons living or dead is purely coincidental.

All rights reserved. No part of this publication may be reproduced, stored in a
retrieval system, or transmitted in any form or by any means, electronic,
mechanical, photocopying, recording or otherwise, without the
prior permission of the publishers.

The Random House Group Limited supports The Forest Stewardship
Council (FSC), the leading international forest certification organisation. All
our titles that are printed on Greenpeace approved FSC certified paper
carry the FSC logo. Our paper procurement policy can be found at:
www.**randomhouse**.co.uk/environment

Mixed Sources
Product group from well-managed
forests and other controlled sources
www.fsc.org Cert no. TT-COC-002139
FSC © 1996 Forest Stewardship Council

Set in Bembo

Corgi Books are published by Random House Children's Books,
61–63 Uxbridge Road, London W5 5SA

www.**kids**at**randomhouse**.co.uk
www.**randomhouse**.co.uk

Addresses for companies within The Random House Group Limited can be
found at: www.randomhouse.co.uk/offices.htm

THE RANDOM HOUSE GROUP Limited Reg. No. 954009

A CIP catalogue record for this book is available from the British Library.

Printed and bound in Great Britain by
CPI Bookmarque, Croydon, CR0 4TD

Acknowledgements

A massive thank-you to the following people:

Clive Bassett, Harrington Carpetbagger Museum, for giving me permission to photograph items in his collection for inclusion in this book (parachutist's suit and suitcase radio set). Thanks also to Beaulieu for their kind assistance in allowing me special access to their exhibition on Britain's Secret Army, the Special Operations Executive (SOE).

I'm grateful to the management of the splendid Kurhaus Hotel, Scheveningen, Netherlands, for supplying me with extensive information on the hotel's and town's histories.

Last but definitely not least, my thanks to Sarah, Charlie and Carolyn for all their help, advice and support.

Have you ever wished for the seemingly impossible? Ever wanted something so much that it hurts inside, maybe even keeps you awake at night? I have, and it nearly got me killed. All it took was a glimmer of hope. It grew so powerful, so all-consuming, that I believed I could succeed against impossible odds. For once, throwing caution to the wind seemed best. Others called it reckless.

A courageous young Dutch girl once said to me that a life without hopes and dreams is no life at all. They were her final words to me. Her name was Marieke. Looking back, I think she was right.

Finn Gunnersen,
June 1941

Chapter One
The Messenger

Mulberry House, Special Operations Training School, May 1941.

'Stop it! Leave him be, you two. Can't you see you're frightening him?' Freya reached out and grasped my arm.

The boy was wrapped in grey woollen blankets and rocked back and forth on the edge of the brown leather sofa. His jet-black hair was matted and filthy, and his strange-looking clothes stank as if he'd been living in them for weeks. I could see that he was sick. His tortured breathing sounded strange, the short shallow gasps a bit like stifled hiccups. Loki and I stood barely six feet in front of him and bombarded him with questions. 'What's your name? Where are you from? What on earth happened to you?' His bewildered stare went right through us as if we weren't there. With Freya stepping in, Loki hesitated and we exchanged puzzled glances.

Dipping his head, our visitor began to mumble, softly at first but then with increasing volume and urgency. Loki pulled me to one side. 'Damn it, Finn, I can't understand a word he's saying. Sounds like Dutch to me.'

'Let's try out our German. Maybe that'll work.'

We'd learned to speak some German back home in Norway after the Nazis invaded our country, but on this occasion trying it out backfired. I'd barely uttered a word before a renewed look of terror appeared on the boy's face. He scrambled to the far end of the sofa, as far away from me as he could get, pressing himself into the leather and drawing his knees tightly up to his chin. Trembling, he suddenly looked me in the eye and shrieked, '*Asperge!*' so loudly it seemed to pierce the air like a rapier. Had the boy gone completely mad?

'Enough, Finn!' Freya shook her head at me in exasperation. Cautiously she stepped forward, avoiding any sudden movements, as if she were closing in on some cornered, wounded creature, all quivers and pounding heartbeat. 'What he needs right now is to know he's safe, that he's reached sanctuary. If we can get him to realize he's among friends he might calm down. We might even get some sense out of him.'

He watched her nervously, expectantly, ready to lash out. She thought better of it and backed away.

The arrival of our unexpected guest at Mulberry House had been announced in a telephone call earlier that evening, after which all hell had broken loose. Judging from the extremely alarmed expressions on our instructors' faces as they rushed to and fro gathering up files, maps and intelligence reports, something calamitous had occurred. By the time the car drew up outside and a stern-faced redcap – a military policeman – hammered a fist on the front door, the mayhem had been replaced by an uneasy calm that pervaded Mulberry like the pungent smell of boiled cabbage. Our chief instructor, Sergeant Walker, signed the policeman's clipboard, took delivery of the boy and ushered him into the lounge.

As usual, information was dished out by our superiors on a strictly need-to-know basis, and so we had no idea what on earth was unfolding. But whatever it was, it had to be big, as visitors were rare at Mulberry House – officially we didn't exist; Special Operations didn't exist! It was all top secret, very *hush-hush*. However, when Sergeant Walker poked his head round the lounge door I had the feeling all that was about to change.

'The doc is on his way.' The sergeant desperately tried to sound upbeat but he didn't fool me. 'Soon get you sorted, lad, don't you worry. You're as safe as houses now. I've asked Mrs Saunders to make you a nice hot mug of cocoa.' Edging back into the hallway, Walker caught my eye and mouthed the word *Trouble*.

What trouble? I mouthed back.

He didn't elaborate. Instead, jabbing a thumb over his shoulder, he said bluntly, 'The brigadier wants to see you three in his office. Now!'

Shrouded in a dense cloud of sweet pipe smoke, the brigadier remained seated behind his desk, his telephone glued to his ear. He looked up, waved us in and beckoned for us all to sit down. 'I share the prime minister's concerns, sir,' he said gravely to whoever was on the other end of the line. 'No, I can't think of any other way of getting at the truth . . . Uh-huh . . . Of course I appreciate that my suggestion is unorthodox, sir, but desperate times call for desperate measures . . . It is indeed a delicate matter and warrants the utmost secrecy . . . I agree the boy should remain here for now. A wise move given the circumstances . . . My team will deal with it, sir. You can rely on us. Thank you for giving me the green light. I've codenamed the mission Operation Salesman. I'll set the wheels in motion. Rest assured we'll get to the bottom of it all.'

The fiery-cheeked Brigadier Devlin was our commanding officer at Mulberry House. He was old-school army, stiff upper-lipped, and a fully paid-up member of the *charge the bastards with your bayonets fixed* brigade, stemming from his torrid time in the trenches of Ypres during the Great War. Now in his late fifties and in possession of a gammy leg filled with shrapnel that gave him hell whenever it turned cold, he had to be content sitting behind a desk and overseeing the training of those who'd do the Boche-bashing this time round on his behalf. We'd already learned that he was a shrewd man, capable of great warmth and generosity as well as a ruthlessness that made you quake in your boots. Such men shine brightly when their country goes to war. Carefully replacing the telephone receiver back into its cradle, he removed his favourite briar from between his teeth and tapped out the burned ash into an overflowing ashtray. 'So, how is our guest?' he enquired, lifting his watery gaze in Walker's direction.

'A few cracked ribs and suffering from exposure, I'd say, sir. Doctor's on his way.'

'I see.' Turning his attention to us, the brigadier gave a heavy sigh. 'Time to fill you in. According to his papers, the lad's name is Jan Keppel and he's fourteen years old.'

The name Keppel instantly struck a chord. While I tried to remember why, the brigadier continued, 'Having escaped from Holland, he was picked up at daybreak this morning in a small dinghy close to the beach at a place in Essex called Frinton-on-Sea. Poor lad's been through the wringer. Unsurprisingly, Frinton's Home Guard couldn't get much sense out of him. Delirious from his injuries, I expect. Anyway, all he kept muttering was a single word, over and over again: *asperge*.'

Loki's expression hardened. 'We heard him shout that word just now. What does it mean?'

'It's Dutch for "asparagus", Mr Larson. Our Dutch section has a network of agents in Holland. The circuit is codenamed Asparagus.'

Walker chipped in, 'It's our biggest operation. Our agents work alongside the Dutch Resistance, organizing parachute drops, sabotage raids and, most importantly of all, escape routes for aircrews shot down over enemy territory. Those lucky enough to have time to bale out of their aircraft and avoid capture the moment they hit the ground often find their way into the arms of partisans willing to hide them. Naturally it's our duty to try and bring them back home. Live to fight another day and all that. With Bomber Command's continuing heavy losses, the numbers are appallingly high, so the initiative is being given the highest priority.'

The brigadier finished up by adding, 'Various escape routes have been established across Europe. The Holland route is the most advanced. We've already had a couple of major successes. It's an important morale booster.'

The name Keppel continued to preoccupy my thoughts. During combined training sessions with the Dutch section of Special Ops, I was sure I'd met someone called Keppel. But it definitely wasn't Jan. I spotted his papers on the brigadier's desk and asked if I might have a look. The brigadier nodded. Jan's photograph was glued to the front, and all the official Dutch and Nazi stamps appeared correct and up to date – we'd studied them during lessons on forgery and I'd even had a go at making a stamp of an eagle by carving a piece of woodblock. On the inside Jan's name was followed by his date of birth, and above a slightly smudged thumbprint was a list of dates and addresses, the most recent being a place called Scheveningen. Loki was itching for a peek so I handed it to him.

'Scheveningen! I've got an aunt who lives on a farm not far from there. She left Norway when she married her Dutch husband,' he declared with a mix of surprise and delight. 'It's just outside The Hague, a few miles from the coast. I spent a summer there.'

Only half listening, I suddenly remembered where I'd heard the name. '*Bram* Keppel!' I blurted, thinking aloud. 'We trained with him a couple of times. He's with Major Gerrit's lot over at Dovecote.'

Teams of agents of different nationalities were often based at separate houses in the New Forest. Dovecote was a huge country pile hidden in woods about three miles from Mulberry and was used exclusively by the Dutch. Loki stared at me blankly.

'You remember. Tall boy, black hair. Crack shot. Jan could be his younger brother.' I looked to the brigadier. 'Am I right? Is he one of us too?'

The brigadier shook his head. 'Although Jan *is* Bram's brother, he's not one of us, Mr Gunnersen. He's an innocent civilian who's had the misfortune to get caught up in an ungodly mess.'

'Bram Keppel is, or at least *was*, the leader of Asparagus,' Walker informed me soberly. 'He was the first to be sent back into Holland.'

Fearing the worst, I asked, '*Was?*'

'Is or was, we simply don't know. That's the nightmare facing us.' The brigadier threw up his hands in exasperation. 'According to Jan his brother was arrested on the streets of The Hague three weeks ago – along with the whole damn Asparagus circuit, by the sound of it. Jan's convinced they must've been betrayed. The lad managed to get away by the skin of his teeth and escaped in order to warn us. If he's to be believed, we've lost all our agents, and months of hard work have been for nothing.' Slumping deep into the leather of his chair, he gripped the arms tightly as if he shared the pain of those captured.

Freya reached out and took Jan's papers from Loki. 'It sounds like you doubt his story, sir.'

The brigadier stabbed his pipe at wads of reports spread out on his desk. 'Have a gander at those. They're decoded messages, supposedly from Bram and his fellow wireless operators. Notice anything unusual?'

We each grabbed one. Mine looked routine – a request for more supplies to be dropped. Freya sat bolt upright and let out a gasp. 'Oh my, I see what you mean.' She pointed to the date and time of the transmission. 'This was sent only two days ago.'

I inspected mine again – it had been sent just one week previously. The penny dropped. If Bram had been arrested three weeks ago, then no way could the messages have been freely sent by him. I swallowed hard as my brain went into overdrive and I realized the terrible truth. 'Hell, this must mean the Germans have our codes and are impersonating our agents.'

'Or maybe German Intelligence is forcing Bram and the others to transmit with a gun to their heads, Finn,' Loki added sharply.

As I imagined the horrors our fellow agents might be experiencing at the hands of the infamous Gestapo, the brigadier bit hard on the stem of his pipe. 'You may be right, Mr Larson.'

Freya drew breath. 'But,' she said hesitatingly, 'it just doesn't add up . . .'

Loki cast down his message in disgust. 'Well, I think they must've been captured, just like Jan says. To doubt his story would be ridiculous. I mean, who else could he be? He's hardly likely to be a Nazi stooge or an enemy agent sent to feed us false intelligence.' He scarcely hid his sarcasm.

Freya responded quickly. 'Yes, but you know the drill. If we are caught and forced to transmit messages by the enemy, we deliberately leave out our security checks.'

She was right. Agents' messages were encrypted and then sent using Morse code. Crucially, as well as identifying themselves by their codename, agents routinely included deliberate errors or additional phrases in their messages – agreed with headquarters in advance – so that HQ could be certain it was them tapping away on the Morse key. Leaving them out or changing them automatically raised the alarm. It was standard procedure, drummed into our brains during endless hours of mind-numbing practice.

The brigadier's expression darkened. 'Quite so, Miss Haukelid. Unfortunately, according to Major Gerrit all his agents' transmissions have been normal. Nothing untoward. That's the puzzle, you see. On the one hand everything appears tickety-boo, and yet, on the other, we have Jan's distressing story.'

Loki glanced up at the ceiling and whistled.

'It gets worse,' Walker grumbled. He was leaning up against a set of filing cabinets and toying with a paper knife in a manner that suggested he'd love to have the chance to use it in anger. 'There are presently airmen waiting to get the hell out of Holland. It's critical we get them out as soon as possible. Unless, that is, they've been rounded up by the enemy as well.'

The brigadier rose from his chair and paced the room, flexing his knee and rubbing life back into his numb thigh. Irritably, he cursed both his discomfort and our predicament. 'It's a bad business all right. If Jan Keppel's correct, then the whole of Special Ops may have been compromised. We're supposed to be "Most Secret", for God's sake!'

'What are you going to do now, sir? Pull the plug on the whole operation?' Loki asked.

Freya's hand shot up. 'Surely you first need a way to find out the truth, one way or the other. Can't the local Dutch Resistance confirm the situation?'

'Afraid not,' Walker replied. 'Too risky. In the current circumstances we don't know who we can trust. We're totally blind to what's happening over there.'

The brigadier spun on his heels to face us. 'Miss Haukelid is quite right, though. All our efforts must be directed to establishing whether Asparagus really has been compromised or not. However, we mustn't do anything that might allow the enemy to get wind of our suspicions. If Jan's right and old Fritz gets a sniff that we've rumbled him, the consequences could be dire. Being of no further use, they'd have no reason to keep Bram and the others alive. Assuming, of course, they're still breathing. However, I believe there is a way, a cunning deception that might just work.'

'What kind of deception?' Loki asked.

The brigadier settled gingerly back into his chair. Searching the tabletop, he located a piece of paper and held it up. 'This latest message requests that we parachute in an additional agent. So that's exactly what I intend to do. I'm going to give them what they want: another agent, another wireless transmitter and another code book.'

'Sounds like a suicide mission to me,' Freya muttered under her breath.

'Quite right, Miss Haukelid. That's exactly what it is! That was X on the phone just now. After some persuasion he's given me the green light.'

Stunned silence filled the room. Had the brigadier gone doolally? I assumed not, as X had approved the scheme. X was in overall charge of Special Ops and reported directly to Britain's prime minister, Winston Churchill. Although we'd met him a few times, X's real identity was a closely guarded secret. As the brigadier's intentions sank in, a wave of confusion engulfed me. Scratching my head, I said, 'I don't get it, sir. What's the point of sending in another agent if there's every chance he'll be captured as soon as he arrives?'

A wry smile formed on the brigadier's lips. 'That's why we need to locate a rather special volunteer, Mr Gunnersen; someone willing to make an exceptional sacrifice, *someone expendable*! X wishes the matter to be handled entirely by our section, and so, Finn and Loki, you two will assist with the parachute drop. The need for your extra muscle will become apparent in due course. Tomorrow morning you'll receive a full briefing on Operation Salesman, and afterwards you must be ready to move at a moment's notice. Timing will be everything.'

Contemplating the idea of someone making an exceptional sacrifice, and figuring the brigadier probably meant the *ultimate* sacrifice, I exchanged fretful glances with Loki. Neither of us liked the sound of it.

Freya, meanwhile, struck me as being deeply puzzled by something. Not one to hold back, she asked, 'Why was Jan brought *here*, sir? Why wasn't he taken to Dovecote? That's where the Dutch are based. All this is surely Major Gerrit's problem to sort out. Why are we getting involved?'

The brigadier flashed Walker the kind of look that told me he'd been hoping to avoid such questions. Walker thought for a moment before offering an explanation of sorts. 'Jan's story would demolish the morale of Dutch agents based at Dovecote, miss, especially those next in line for returning home. They'd fear they might be parachuting straight into the arms of the enemy. Best the boy remains here for now.'

The brigadier seemed mighty relieved by the sergeant's answer. It was as if it had dug him out of a deep hole and avoided the need to reveal other reasons – maybe the *real* reasons – for our involvement and why Jan Keppel had been brought to Mulberry. Something else troubled me too. Where was Major Gerrit? Why wasn't he here, involved in our discussions about the fate of his team? I raised the point.

The brigadier squirmed and refused to look me in the eye. Without warning Walker sprang to his feet. 'Ah, I can hear a car, sir. Must be the doctor.'

We were dismissed. Our meeting was over, and although my question remained unanswered I'd read their body language. Major Gerrit's absence and the fact that Jan had *not* been taken to Dovecote were far more important than they were letting on. But why?

Chapter Two
You Only Die Twice

Emerging from the airfield's vast hangar, I grabbed the handles of the wheelchair and began pushing it across the grass. A week had passed since Jan Keppel's arrival and it was time to get some answers. The evening breeze was warm and brushed gently against my cheeks as I contemplated our peculiar mission.

On the far side of the airfield a lone Whitley bomber was waiting for us, her twin Tiger engines idling, the hot exhaust gases making the evening air shimmer, her de Havilland propellers spinning in a whining blur. Silhouetted against a fiery red sunset, she was an odd-looking beast, all straight lines, box-like, her ugly bulbous nose housing her forward guns. She was like some hideous black insect, the sort that could give you a nasty bite.

Loki jogged to catch me up, the carefully packed parachute slung over his shoulder and rhythmically slapping against his back. 'I can't believe we're part of all this, Finn. It doesn't feel right. I mean . . . *really* not right.' He gazed down at the man in the wheelchair and shook his head.

'Just be grateful it's not you sitting in this thing,' I replied. And I meant it.

According to the fake identity papers tucked inside

his jacket, our 'volunteer' in the wheelchair was one Paul van Beek, a travelling shoe salesman from Leiden, a small Dutch town midway between Amsterdam and The Hague. That was just part of his cover. He was no more Dutch than Loki or me. His real name was Private Clive Digby and he was as British as fish and chips.

I looked at the plane ahead of us again. With a wingspan of eighty-four feet, the Whitley normally carried a pretty hefty bomb load. That night, however, it was just Loki and me, Digby, and the Whitley's flight crew who'd be heading out across the North Sea.

Brigadier Devlin and Sergeant Walker had come to see us off. Leaning heavily on his steel-tipped walking cane, the brigadier inspected his watch and bellowed at us to get a move on. The worry and strain showed on his face and the sight hardly filled me with confidence. I gave the wheelchair one final shove and arrived next to the Whitley's fuselage, the backdraught from the propellers wildly scrambling my hair amid the sharp stink of burned kerosene and hot oil.

'Digby's supply canister is already on board,' Walker informed us, shouting over the deafening din of the engines. Turning, he waved energetically at someone in the cockpit to attract their attention and then, cupping his hands about his mouth, yelled, 'You can open them now.'

Clunks and whirs of the hydraulics operating the doors to the aircraft's bomb compartment struck up, and the gaping hole in the bird's belly slowly revealed itself. 'Manoeuvre the wheelchair underneath, Finn, and then climb inside. Loki and I will lift Digby up.'

Three minutes later, and volunteer Special Ops agent Digby was safely inside the plane. Walker and the brigadier wished us luck and retreated a safe distance across the airfield, Walker dragging the empty wheelchair behind him. The bomb doors swung shut and clicked into their locked positions.

The inside of the fuselage looked like a giant empty soup tin. To minimize weight it had been stripped of anything that might make our flight comfortable. As we settled down onto the hard metal walkway, our pilot, Captain Nils Jacobsen, ventured back from his seat in the cockpit. Smiling, he waved a hello. 'Everything all right, lads?'

We grumbled but nodded. Nils was a good friend, and with him at the controls I felt in safe hands. A Norwegian like us, he'd flown Spitfires alongside my father in the Battle of Britain the previous summer and had been called upon to chaperone us during our initial training in Special Ops. More recently transferred to the Moon Squadron, he was now responsible for ferrying agents in and out of Europe in the dead of night.

Mopping perspiration from his shiny brow, Nils hammered a fist against the airframe. 'This old crate isn't in the best shape but it's all they had at such short notice. It'll do the job though.' Bending down to get a better look at Digby, a shadow of disgust passed over his face. 'So this is the poor sod, is it?' He patted him lightly on the shoulder. 'Well, good luck, old boy!'

Digby couldn't reply because he'd already been dead for some hours.

Instinctively, Nils wiped the hand he'd used to pat Digby's shoulder on his tunic. 'Where on earth did they find him?'

'Salisbury Plain,' Loki replied. 'Apparently he bought it yesterday afternoon in a freak accident during training on an assault course. Broke his neck in two places. Died instantly. Just what the brigadier was waiting for. He commandeered the body and had him driven straight to the airfield in total secrecy.'

Nils shook his head in revulsion. 'Is there no limit to the depths people will stoop to? I mean, I know this war is vile, no holds barred, and all that, but . . . Christ! Anyway, what will dropping a corpse over enemy territory achieve?'

Nils's orders were simple. Having been given the map coordinates for Digby's drop, he had to fly us in and fly us out and try not to get shot down. He knew little regarding the background or purpose of Operation Salesman and so his distaste was understandable. I wanted to explain that Digby's injuries were entirely consistent with those a parachutist might experience should their silk canopy fail to open properly, that – sickeningly – it was this fact that made him the perfect volunteer for the brigadier's clever deception. However, Loki and I had been instructed to say nothing, and so reluctantly we kept our mouths shut.

Nils accepted our silence as being our sworn duty and didn't press the matter. Straightening up, he pointed to an instrument panel. 'Put on your helmets and hook up the intercoms to this unit. I'll keep you informed of our position and let you know when we approach the drop zone.' He gestured towards two naked bulbs. 'Standard procedure, lads. When the red light comes on, get Digby and his supply canister into position for the drop. He goes out through that hatch in the floor forward of the bomb doors. I'll switch to the green light when we're over the DZ. For God's sake remember to hook both static lines above your heads. Otherwise the parachutes won't open. Any questions?'

We shook our heads. Nils turned towards the cockpit but then hesitated. Reaching out, he placed a hand firmly on my shoulder. I sensed his awkwardness, especially when he peered at me with the oddest of expressions and I noticed a slight tremble on his lips. 'Listen, Finn – because of reports of enemy night patrols, our route takes us on quite a detour. We'll be flying over the spot where your father was shot down. I wasn't sure if it was wise to tell you. It's just that . . . well . . . I thought you might want to take a look. It'll probably be dark by the time we get there but you'll get a sense of where it happened.'

He'd taken me completely by surprise. It was like a punch to the face, arriving from nowhere, without warning, and it rocked me. As well as being startled, I couldn't suppress a huge lump in my throat. It almost choked me and snatched my breath away. Unable to speak, I could only offer a faint nod.

He smiled as if relieved. 'Good. I'll tell you over the intercom when we get there.' Partially unzipping his flying jacket, he reached inside and removed a small, neatly folded Norwegian flag. He handed it to me. 'I thought you might want this. A token of remembrance. You can say a prayer and then drop it through the hatch. I know it's hardly full military honours and there'll be no accompanying twenty-one-gun salute, but maybe this way's better, more personal.'

I thanked him, my voice feeble. Without another word he turned away and headed back to the cockpit.

Loki muttered, 'Are you sure about this, Finn? I mean, won't it just open old wounds?'

Leaning back against the fuselage, I pressed my eyes shut and counted slowly to ten, making myself breathe steadily, forcing myself to remain calm. When I opened them again, Loki was still staring at me. 'Nils is right. I *need* to see where it happened,' I said determinedly.

'Why? What good will it do?'

'I don't know,' I snapped. What I wanted to say, but couldn't, was that all I knew about Father's demise was what Nils had told me. During a frenetic dogfight Father had been outwitted by a Messerschmitt 109. There was no body, nothing to bury, no grave or memorial that I could visit and lay flowers beside. There was nothing. *Absolutely nothing.* It was as if he'd never existed. And that felt wrong. Father and I had been close. He'd taught me to fly – and to believe that there are things in life worth fighting for, like our freedom, our families and friends, our way of life. In part it was my attempt to follow in his footsteps that had brought us here, to Britain, to Special Operations. Maybe, I thought, just maybe seeing the location from the air might give me the connection I needed.

Minutes later we were taxiing across the airfield and then, with the engines screaming at full power and the Whitley rattling like a tin of nails, we roared down the runway and took off into the night, climbing steeply before turning east, towards the North Sea and eventually the coast of Holland.

We kept ourselves busy, wasting little time getting Digby's parachute onto his back. It had been carefully prepared so that, on opening, the cords would tangle, preventing the mass of silk from unravelling properly. It meant that after we'd helped him out of the plane, he'd hurtle several thousand feet down before smacking hard onto the Dutch countryside, making a horrible mess.

'I still find it hard to believe that all our Dutch agents have been captured,' said Loki as he checked and double checked the tightness of the straps before sitting Digby up comfortably against a rib of the airframe. 'I reckon Freya was right.'

'About what?'

'That Bram and the others would have warned us by leaving out the security checks in their messages. Perhaps Jan's mistaken.'

'Unlikely. He saw his brother and the others arrested.'

'Well, maybe he saw them arrested but maybe they managed to escape.'

'That's too many *maybes*. Still, you might be right.' Settling down opposite, I gazed across the poorly lit fuselage at Digby's boyish face. He looked no more than twenty years old and unremarkable, just a face in a crowd. And yet, plucked from obscurity, he was about to take his place in history. Digby didn't know it, but he was about to become a hero. He stared back at me, wide-eyed, and seemed to be grinning. He gave me the creeps. It was so unsettling I eventually leaned forward and pulled his goggles down. Even so, I felt he was still looking at me, studying me, questioning why he was several thousand feet up in the air and not buried six feet under the earth. 'I reckon there's *something* strange going on though,' I said. 'Jan's been with us a week, and not once has Major Gerrit visited him. If I were Gerrit, I'd have come knocking on Mulberry's door the moment I heard.'

Loki nodded thoughtfully. 'You're right. That *is* strange.'

Struck by turbulence, the Whitley suddenly dipped and shook horribly, throwing me hard against the fuselage and banging my head on the airframe. Briefly I saw stars in front of my eyes and had to sit quietly for a moment to recover, my head throbbing almost in time with the oscillating drone of the engines. Nils' voice crackled in my earphones. 'Sorry about that . . . Finn, we're more or less over the exact spot.'

Unhooking my intercom, I took a deep breath and eased myself on all fours along the fuselage towards the hatch. There I knelt, the flag in my grasp.

Loki joined me. 'Do you mind, Finn?'

I shook my head. We each sent up a silent prayer. Mine was a jumble of disconnected thoughts, flashes of happy memories, mixed with hopes and fears and the selfish belief that Father was looking down on me from heaven, and that he was proud of me for all the things I'd done. I also prayed for Mother and my sister, Anna, who were probably still in prison back home: they'd been arrested by the SS, but everything possible was being done to free them. When I'd run out of words, I opened my eyes, wiped away a solitary tear and leaned forward to slide open the hatch. Ice-cold air rushed in, smacking me hard, quickly numbing my cheeks. I reached down into the howling wind and let the flag unravel. It flapped wildly and tugged at me viciously. I let go. Whipped away by the wind, it disappeared instantly. I gazed towards the ground far below us. Dusk had turned to night, but it was clear and a crescent moon shed a little pale light on the world. Then it struck me with an electrifying jolt. All I could see below was water. We were over the sea! That wasn't right, was it? Although I'd been told that Father had been shot down close to the coast of southern England, for some reason I'd assumed they'd meant over land. I hurriedly slid the hatch shut and scrambled to hook up my intercom. 'Nils?'

'Land, sea, it doesn't make any difference, Finn.'

I was in turmoil. 'Yes it does!' I shouted. 'He might have baled out. He might have been picked up by an enemy ship or foreign fishing boat.'

Silence.

'Told you I thought it was a bad idea, Finn.' Loki was listening in.

'I'm really sorry, Finn,' Nils responded eventually,

after a long pause. He sounded distant, muffled. 'But that's impossible. I saw his plane go down. No sign that he baled out. Perhaps I shouldn't have said anything, after all. My fault. Blame me. I just thought it might help.'

Saw his plane go down! I felt in shock. Nils had never said to me before that he'd actually seen Father's plane go down. I held my head in my hands. I suppose he'd wanted to spare me the anguish and the horror. The revelation redoubled my sense of feeling crushed, and yet . . . What if he was mistaken? After all, in the mayhem of a dogfight you need to be looking in all directions at once, ever fearful of the enemy getting onto your tail. There surely wouldn't have been time for him to watch every moment of Father's plane's dive into the sea. Not *every* second . . .

Loki reached out and grabbed me. 'Are you all right, Finn?'

I nodded, but I was lying. I was far from all right. My pulse had quickened and my head felt as if it were spinning wildly, sparks flying in all directions. Was the impossible in fact possible? Could it be that somewhere out there Father was still alive? Loki could see what I was thinking. He was talking to me – I could see his lips moving – but I wasn't listening. Shaking his head, he lost patience and gave me a slap across the face. 'Don't be crazy, Finn. You heard what Nils said. He didn't bale out. He's dead, Finn. Dead as Digby here. Simple as that. Understand?'

Chapter Three
Dropping the Deception

Nils finally snapped me out of my trance. 'I can see the Dutch coast straight ahead, so it's only about twenty minutes to the drop. Brace yourselves as best you can because I expect flak from the coastal defences. Cross your fingers and say your prayers, because life's about to get a whole lot more uncomfortable!'

Nils wasn't kidding. When the barrage began, we grabbed hold of anything that felt solid and tightly screwed down. All around us distant dull thuds grew louder, closer, like a carpet of thunder. Flashes lit the night sky. Shells exploded, their deafening pressure waves smacking the Whitley hard, jolting us, making the plane rise and fall as Nils struggled to keep her level. The engine note altered pitch too, whining as if complaining bitterly. My ears popped and I felt like a marble being shaken about inside a jam jar. Curious pinging sounds made us flinch; they were tiny white-hot fragments of shrapnel from shell casings tearing right through the fuselage. It was like being attacked by deadly metal insects. We had to be on our guard, scanning the gloom for any signs of fire. Repeatedly banking to seemingly impossible angles, we equally abruptly levelled out again. I felt airsick for only the second time ever. Loki wasn't faring too well either, pressing his eyes tightly shut and singing our Norwegian national anthem at the top of his voice. I joined in: *'Yes, we love this country as it rises forth, rugged, weathered, above the sea— Ooooh, shit!'* More blinding flashes. We both swore blue under our breaths. Then, without warning, Nils threw the throttles forward, the engines screamed, and we climbed steeply. Digby slumped onto his side and began sliding down the fuselage towards the tail of the plane. I threw myself at him, managing to grab hold of his legs.

Between us we pinned Digby down. It was like some kind of hideous fairground ride, a roller coaster that was running wildly out of control. And I knew a horrible truth. A direct hit and we'd become a fireball, exploding into a thousand burning pieces of debris, each tumbling towards the earth like a flaming meteor. We'd not stand a hope in hell. A shell detonated so close it left my ears ringing. Our starboard wing dipped fully sixty degrees, the nose dropped, and we lost several hundred feet of altitude in seconds. The sensation was weird, like being in freefall, or trapped in a lift whose cable had snapped. I felt almost weightless. The contents of my stomach rose and I felt a spasm in my belly. There was nothing I could do. Unclipping my face mask, I puked, my spew showering against the fuselage and narrowly missing Loki's hastily withdrawn left leg. 'Jesus, Finn. Must you?'

I nodded and threw up again, one hand grasping Digby's leg, the other attempting to cover my mouth. I continued retching until my guts felt so sore it was as if I'd been turned inside out.

Despite the horror, Loki burst out laughing. 'Don't remember diced carrots being on the menu back at Mulberry, Finn!'

'*Shut up!*'

Five terrifying minutes later and we were through the worst of it. Nils announced that we were approaching the drop zone. The taste of sick was still sharp in my mouth, but I set to work. First Loki and I shifted Digby back along the fuselage and positioned him next to the hatch. Then we moved his supply canister, placing it next to him. Everything was ready.

'Jesus, Finn, you look like death warmed up.'

'I'm fine. Really!'

Loki punched me lightly in the shoulder. 'Well, if you have to chuck up again, for God's sake don't do it over Digby. He's all dressed up for his big night out.'

A gargantuan effort had gone into preparing Digby for his mission. Beneath his quick-release camouflaged jumpsuit – we called them 'striptease suits' because you could remove one in seconds – he was wearing civilian clothes: a smart, fashionable charcoal-grey pinstripe suit typical of a Dutch businessman. Expert tailors and seamstresses had worked through the night to make sure everything was perfect, stitching in labels of a well-known tailor in Amsterdam and rubbing the seat of his trousers and the elbows of his jacket to display just the right amount of wear and tear. Inside his jacket pocket lay a small, well-thumbed copy of a Dutch book about wildfowl called *Wilde Gevogelte*. Such a book was an agent's most precious possession. It was a code book used to encipher Morse code transmissions.

Digby's supply canister was almost as large as him and, as well as his disassembled wireless transmitter, it contained spare clothes, a small shovel for burying his parachute and gear, wads of cash, cigarettes, a Sten machine gun, pistol and ammo, a first-aid kit and emergency food supplies. There were also a dozen bicycle tyre inner tubes. The Dutch Resistance was always begging us to send them some as they'd become almost impossible to get hold of since the Nazi occupation: the Dutch loved to cycle everywhere. It seemed such a waste. If Jan Keppel was telling the truth, then it would all fall into the hands of the enemy. But Digby's cover needed to be perfect.

'Three minutes, lads.'

Feeling woozy and strangely hollow, I stood up and hooked both Digby's and the supply canister's static lines above my head. The red lamp came on, redoubling my sense of urgency. Wriggling forward on my belly, I grabbed hold of the catch on the hatchway and slid it open again. Cold air rushed in. The buffeting against my face made me feel loads better. I peered down. It was all black except for the occasional pinprick of light and silver slithers of meandering rivers and moonlit canals. Somewhere down there, somewhere in the invisible nothingness of Holland, was Digby's reception committee.

'Almost there,' Nils announced. 'Are you all set?'

'Ready and waiting,' Loki replied.

'Thirty seconds to go.'

Loki swung Digby's legs round so they dangled through the hatchway. 'Give me a hand, Finn.'

I scrambled next to Loki behind Digby's left shoulder. We waited impatiently for the green light. At last it came on. 'Action stations!' Loki shouted. 'On the count of three, Finn. *One . . . two . . . three . . .*' Grabbing Digby's arms, we pushed him forward. He slid through the hatchway, and in a blink he was gone. His parachute line snapped taut as the slack quickly got taken up. Then, once his parachute released, the line went limp and began whipping and jangling on the wire. I grabbed hold of it and drew the loose end back inside the plane. 'The supply canister, Finn,' Loki yelled. 'Quickly.'

With the canister gone too, our job was done. Almost immediately we felt the Whitley turn sharply. We were heading home. As we climbed to a safer altitude, I contemplated events unfolding on Dutch soil beneath us.

The outcome of Operation Salesman depended on who turned up to meet Digby, forming his reception committee. It was also essential that they assumed Digby had simply been unlucky. After all, parachutes did occasionally fail. It was an accepted hazard. That was the clever bit – the deception. Hopefully they wouldn't be suspicious. They'd locate his supply canister with all his gear and, on examining him, they'd find all the usual things, including his code book. Apart from Digby being dead, everything would seem to be in order.

We'd sent an urgent signal giving the time and location of the drop, our message enciphered using the code book carried by Bram Keppel and on the frequency corresponding to his radio set. So, if Bram and his Asparagus team were all OK and still operating freely, we'd expect to receive a radio message from them informing us that Paul van Beek unfortunately hadn't made it and that we'd have to send another agent.

The other possibility, the one we all dreaded, was that our message to 'Bram' had actually been decoded by the Nazis and that it would be they who were waiting for Paul's arrival. Finding his body, radio set and code book intact, they would surely find the temptation too great. They'd wrongly assume we had no idea that our agent had been killed and would reckon there was little risk in pretending to be him, sending back messages as though he were still alive. If that happened, if Digby came back from the dead, if a message claiming to be from Paul van Beek crackled over the airwaves, we'd know that Jan Keppel was telling the truth: that the Asparagus circuit had been crushed.

Chapter Four
A Message from the Other Side

We returned to Mulberry the following morning and were greeted by a most unexpected sight. After we'd passed the guards at the gates and driven up the long drive, the formidable brick edifice and towering chimney stacks came into view and we spotted two of our instructors, Smithy and Killer, in the midst of one hell of a set-to outside the front entrance. Smithy had Killer's head in an underarm lock while Killer had Smithy's vital parts gripped tightly in one hand, and together they seemed to be hopping and jigging about, neither willing to give an inch. Loki and I were out of the truck in a flash as soon as it stopped.

'All right, lads? Everything go according to plan?' asked Smithy, his voice rising an octave as Killer tightened his grip. 'Told Killer here that I could take him any time, any place, and now seemed as good a time as any.'

'Really?' said Loki sarcastically, a huge grin breaking out on his face. 'I think that was a big mistake.'

Corporal Smith knew a good scam or two and could get hold of anything you wanted for the right price. Though he was 'Smithy' to his friends, behind his back – and to his face – Sergeant Walker regularly called him an 'ugly little sod'. Without fail, the remark would draw a wide smirk across Smithy's lips and he'd throw back his head and roar with laughter. He didn't care. His hard upbringing in London's East End was ingrained in his face, not least in his crooked nose, which was so out of line it made him look as if he was turning a corner. At first glance Smithy was your typical corporal, but he had hidden depths that made him rather special. Somewhere amid the chaos and horrors of the mass evacuation at Dunkirk, Smithy had excelled, performing acts of heroism way beyond the call of duty, earning him the highest decoration, the Victoria Cross. He was both proud and embarrassed by it. I was just glad he was on our side. And what he didn't know about guns and explosives wasn't worth knowing.

Kip 'Killer' Keenan specialized in teaching unarmed combat and other generally painful stuff that might just save our lives in a tight corner. Nobody had a bad word to say about Killer – either behind his back or to his face – and that was probably just as well. Mrs Saunders, our housekeeper, called him 'salt of the earth' and reckoned that as long as Killer had breath in his body, Britain was safe.

The brawl, I realized, was just a game, all for the benefit of Jan Keppel, who'd ventured from his bed and was sitting bathed in sunshine on a bench beneath a mulberry tree. Freya was sitting next to him with her usual disapproving *boys will be boys* look on her face. On the other side of Jan was another girl with long brown hair. My heart leaped. 'Marieke!'

'Hello, Finn.' She smiled at me. The day had just got ten times better.

Marieke Maartens was one of Major Gerrit's team over at Dovecote. We'd met half a dozen times during combined training sessions. Something between us had clicked instantly. She was fifteen and had an elfin face hidden beneath a long fringe, and a smile that seemed to stretch from ear to ear. War had left its mark on her too – quite literally: a slender scar ran from her left temple, past her ear and ended on her neck. She'd got tangled up in barbed wire, and in her struggle to free herself had been badly cut. The scar wasn't that noticeable unless you were close up, but she was always conscious of it and had developed a habit of combing her hair across with her fingers to cover it.

The bout drew to a swift close, with Killer hoisting Smithy into the air, slipping his head out of the hold, and then dropping him from a bone-crunching height. 'Call it a draw?' a winded Smithy cried feebly from the ground as Killer placed a boot on his chest. Jan applauded. Killer flexed his muscles.

'Against Major Gerrit's advice, X sent Marieke over to us, Finn,' said Freya. 'Apparently X thought it would be nice for Jan to have someone he can talk to in Dutch.'

The doctor had diagnosed numerous cracked ribs and a bad case of exposure the evening Jan arrived at Mulberry, just as Walker had suspected. Rest was prescribed, and Jan had, until today, been confined to bed. With colour returning to his cheeks, he looked tons better – thanks, no doubt, to Mrs Saunders's sterling efforts as nursemaid. 'How are you?' I asked.

'All right,' Jan replied. 'Thank you.'

Jan's English wasn't brilliant, but he could understand simple stuff. He pointed to his chest and winced. 'Still hurts.'

'He's well on the mend,' Marieke said, rubbing a hand through his hair affectionately. Unlike Jan, her English was perfect, with only a hint of a Dutch accent. She once told me she'd moved to England to live with her grandparents in Oxford several years before the war. Her parents had drowned when terrible winter storms had breached the dykes and caused major floods in southern Holland.

An awkward silence ensued until Mrs Saunders hurried outside and, muttering something about the boy having had enough excitement for one day, took Jan indoors. 'Have we learned any more about what happened to him?' Loki asked, watching them disappear inside.

Marieke nodded. 'Yes. They escaped on a large fishing boat. The crew stowed them and their dinghy on board while moored in Scheveningen harbour and then set sail. Once far enough out to sea, the captain lowered their dinghy into the water and sent them on their way.'

'Them?'

'That's right, Finn. Jan escaped with his best friend, a boy called Patrick. Jan had been staying with him for the last few months, ever since Jan's parents were detained by the authorities for stealing food from a warehouse used by the Germans. Anyway, there was a storm. Their mast broke. Jan's friend got, erm . . . how do you say it . . . *lost overboard*.'

'Jesus. Is that how Jan injured his ribs?'

'No. Jan fell climbing out of a first-floor window to escape capture by the Germans. That captain should never have taken them to sea, not in their state, let alone set them adrift. It was madness. There was almost no chance of them making it to England.'

'Still,' said Loki, 'at least Jan made it. Pretty brave, if you ask me.'

'There is a fine line between bravery and stupidity,' Marieke snapped. Then her face softened. 'It's getting late and I must go. But I'll return tomorrow if that's convenient.'

'Yes,' I replied enthusiastically. 'I mean, I'm sure Jan would appreciate it.'

Captivated, I watched Marieke cycle off down the drive, her long hair catching the breeze. Loki sneaked up on me from behind and grabbed me in a bear hug. 'Quite a girl, eh, Finn? She's sweet on you too. I can tell.'

'Get off!' I struggled free.

Freya rose from the bench. 'So, everything went according to plan, then.'

'Uh-huh,' I replied, catching my breath. 'Does Marieke know what's going on?'

'She knows most of it. Jan's told her his story. I reckon she should thank her lucky stars. She was due to be dropped by parachute next week. Of course that's been placed on hold until we know the truth. The really scary thing is that she's the last of them. She's the only student left over at Dovecote.'

'The last one! But there were loads of them when we

36

last trained together. How's Major Gerrit taking it?' Loki asked. 'I wouldn't like to be in his shoes.'

'Badly,' Freya replied. 'Marieke suspected something was wrong because Gerrit's been behaving rather oddly over the past few weeks, coming and going from Dovecote at all hours. Been on a pretty short fuse too, by all accounts.'

'What's new? Doesn't take much for him to fly off the handle,' I replied sourly, recalling the last time our paths had crossed. Gerrit had chewed me out for not laying some explosive charges properly on a disused railway line. Calling me every name under the sun in front of all the others, he made me feel small and utterly useless. Smithy told me to take no notice, that *my* method would have worked just as well.

That evening I sat doodling on a sketch pad, dividing my idle thoughts between Marieke and Father while tunes sang out from our gramophone player. Weary from our mission, I closed my eyes and let my mind drift. What if Nils was mistaken about my father? I thought that I'd got over it months ago, moved on, accepted Father's demise as the price of war, but there was something niggling me. Father often appeared in my dreams and he seemed so real I'd wake up with the oddest, unsettled feeling inside, as if two universes had collided and briefly merged into one. Did I have a sixth sense? Freya believed that some people did; that if only we could understand it, it would guide us in life. Loki reckoned it was all rubbish, a bad case of wishful thinking.

Suddenly the telephone rang in the brigadier's office. Freya was attempting to teach Loki to dance; they froze mid foxtrot and I opened my eyes again, startled. Was this it? Was this the call the brigadier had been waiting for impatiently all day? Freya snatched the stylus from the record. The phone stopped ringing. The silence was unbearable. We all moved to the lounge door and listened out. Frustratingly, although we could hear the brigadier's muffled voice, we couldn't make out what he was saying. Walker, Smithy and Killer joined us in the hallway and we hovered expectantly.

The brigadier eventually appeared at the door to his office clutching a piece of paper torn from his notepad. 'That was X. Bad news, I'm afraid. The following coded message was received at nineteen hundred hours this evening. It reads as follows: *Landed off-target two miles but made rendezvous successfully. Asparagus in desperate need of more weapons and ammunition. Will send full list in due course. Will transmit again one week from today at same time – Paul.*'

'*Paul!* So, the dead have spoken,' Walker remarked grimly.

Smithy muttered something unrepeatable under his breath while Killer clenched his fists as if he were about to punch a whole new opening through the wall into the lounge.

Jan was telling the truth. Gerrit's team were in enemy hands and German Intelligence was playing a deadly game with us.

The brigadier gathered his wits. 'X will be travelling

38

down to Dovecote first thing tomorrow morning. We have been ordered to attend. Forgive my language, Miss Haukelid, but a truckload of shit has hit the fan and we're going to have to sort this mess out.' He removed his briar from his breast pocket and shoved it determinedly into his mouth. 'Now, Mr Larson, I want to bend your ear about that aunt you mentioned. You said she has a farm near Scheveningen. Come into my office. I want to know everything about her. And I mean *everything*!'

Chapter Five
A Question of Honour

Dovecote was a massive house with a labyrinth of wood-panelled rooms and passageways. Large French windows at the back led out onto a terrace overlooking manicured lawns that stretched down to the banks of a broad river. The place reeked of beeswax polish and our voices tended to echo. Although far more splendid than Mulberry, it somehow felt cold and less welcoming. A haggard Major Gerrit greeted us at the entrance. I don't think he'd had a wink of sleep: he was unshaven and reeked of stale tobacco and whisky – so much so that I reckoned if you struck a match close to him he'd spontaneously combust. At six foot five, Gerrit was an imposing Dutchman, his sharp, angular face giving the impression he was eternally furious about something. He also had an *I can do the* Times *crossword in under ten minutes* intellectual air about him. Rumours abounded that his posting to Special Ops had not been to his liking.

Sergeant Fitzpatrick was an altogether friendlier proposition. He was Gerrit's second in command and nodded a hello to us as we gathered inside. Simultaneously Marieke emerged from a back room clutching a handkerchief. Her eyes were red. I realized she'd learned the outcome of Operation Salesman, confirming the awful plight of her fellow Dutch agents. 'It's all so dreadful, Finn,' she whispered to me. 'I'd prayed like mad that Jan was mistaken. I feel so helpless stuck here.'

'Just be grateful you're safe.'

The front door crashed open behind us, making us all jump and turn. X stormed in, two redcaps hard on his heels. Acknowledging the brigadier and Walker with little more than a nod, X slammed down his leather attaché case, removed his trilby and hurriedly unbuttoned his coat, flinging it towards a chair. He approached Major Gerrit and angrily confronted him face to face. 'You've got some explaining to do, Major.'

Gerrit shrank before him. X snapped his fingers and the two redcaps took up positions on either side. 'Your gun, Major Gerrit, if you please.'

Fitzpatrick stepped forward in alarm. 'Sir, what is all this about?'

Gerrit held up a hand. 'It's all right, Sergeant,' he said calmly. 'I've been expecting this.' He reached down and slowly removed his pistol from its holster, surrendering the gun to X. Stiffening almost to attention, he held X in his gaze and said, 'So, what happens now?'

'Your office, Major. We know everything but I want to hear it from your own lips.'

Gerrit was marched into his office, X leading the way, the brigadier close behind. The door slammed shut and the two redcaps stood on guard outside. Fitzpatrick grabbed hold of Walker and demanded answers.

'Turns out your major's a rotten egg,' Walker hissed

angrily, tearing himself free. 'The lads in the Secret Intelligence Services got lucky and apprehended a Nazi agent operating out of Felixstowe. He was caught in possession of information that only Gerrit could have provided. *Intelligence about our activities in Holland!*'

Fitzpatrick swallowed hard. 'There must be a mistake.'

Walker shook his head vehemently. 'He's a traitor all right. Apparently, before the war Gerrit was based in Berlin, working as a representative of the Dutch government in their embassy. He settled there with his wife and daughters. When war broke out he was ordered to return to Holland. Believing that Herr Hitler had no desire to trample over Dutch soil, and that Poland was all just a storm in a teacup, his family remained in Berlin. Big mistake, of course. His family were arrested and imprisoned by the Gestapo. Gerrit is being blackmailed. The old story, I'm afraid: forced to feed the Nazi machine with our secrets or he'll never see his family again.'

It took a moment for it to sink in. 'What will happen to him?' I asked.

'Court martial and a firing squad, I expect.'

Shattered by the revelations, an open-mouthed Fitzpatrick leaned against a balustrade for support.

'He should have sought help from X,' Walker continued. 'He could have told us about his predicament. We might have been able to use it to our advantage and feed the enemy false information. But he didn't, and now our agents have been rounded up, their whereabouts unknown. Maybe they're all dead. And then there's the small matter of those airmen. Their lives depended on us. And the icing on the cake as far as the enemy's concerned is that they probably know all about us. Major Gerrit faced an impossible choice, but in my book he chose wrong!'

'Is there really no way this could all be a horrible mistake?' Marieke matched Fitzpatrick in her disbelief.

'Afraid not, miss. You see, X ordered me to re-examine all the original transcripts of the messages from Asparagus. Contrary to what Gerrit said, Bram and his team *did* try to warn us by leaving out their security checks. It appears Gerrit ignored them.'

'*Ignored them!* We're finished.' Fitzpatrick tore at his hair.

Marieke quickly disagreed. 'We can't abandon Bram and the others. They might still be alive. The airmen too. We must do something. We *must!*'

'She's right,' I said. 'They'll be relying on us. We're their only hope.'

'Well, that's for X to decide.' Walker's tone was blunt.

Reeling and visibly upset, Marieke stormed off and I followed her into the dining room. Like ours at Mulberry, it had been converted into a classroom, with neat rows of desks and chairs facing a large blackboard. Maps and charts covered the walls. 'What a disaster!' I sighed. 'Are you OK?'

'I hate this place, Finn,' Marieke replied. 'I want to leave. Right now. It wasn't so bad when all the others were here. We were a good team.'

'I know what you mean. Loki and Freya have been

my friends since before I can remember. We rely on one another. I doubt I'd cope without them. We've sworn an oath to stick together through thick and thin, to get through this war in one piece.'

With tears in her eyes, Marieke headed into the next room. It was as if she wanted to get as far away as she could from Gerrit's office. The room was an Aladdin's cave. Benches placed against three walls were piled with gadgets. As well as Sten machine guns, there were several tube-like pistols – single-shot guns that you could carry hidden up your sleeve. There was also a collection of equally impressive explosive tyrebursters in various states of disassembly, along with packets of incendiary cigarettes, bits of radio sets, waterproof haversacks and attaché cases with secret compartments. She stood in front of a window and gazed out across the garden. She was shaking.

Keen to change the subject, I picked up the nearest thing to hand – a piece of blank paper. It had the thickness and feel of the strong, waxy, lightweight paper you use when sending letters by air mail. There was a red edge to the sheet and it smelled strange. 'Is this one of Dr Witherspoon's inventions?' I asked. Witherspoon was a chemist with a vivid imagination. He'd shown us paper that you could write on as normal, but if you needed to get rid of it in a hurry you just dropped it into water and it disintegrated, or you could eat it, although it tasted disgusting. I tore off a corner and was about to put it into my mouth when Marieke reached out to stop me.

'No! That'll make you sick. Here, let me show you.' She took it from me, folded it and placed it in an envelope. Grabbing a pen, she poked a hole in the envelope and then reached for a box of matches. 'It's called nitrated paper. I can make it disappear as if by magic.' Still shaking, all fingers and thumbs, she fumbled and cursed in exasperation, but finally managed to strike a match. Allowing the flame to settle, she held the envelope horizontally and moved the flame towards the hole on the underside. The second the tip of the flame met the hole, I heard a strange sizzling *whoosh* and wisps of smoke crept out of envelope. Opening it revealed just a little ash.

'Amazing. It barely singed the envelope.' Astounded, I examined the evidence.

Raised voices emerged from Gerrit's office. We both looked towards the fracas and Marieke shuddered. 'What's this for?' I asked, quickly picking up the next nearest thing. It was a small device comprising two thin squares of plywood attached at each corner by screws and butterfly nuts.

'*What?* Oh, it's just my hobby, Finn. It's used to press flowers. My mother ran a small flower shop back home.' Taking it from me, she unscrewed it, all the while looking as if she wanted to throw it across the room.

Between the pieces of plywood were sheets of blotting paper, and between them were delicate flowers picked from the garden at Dovecote and the hedgerows in the lanes that surrounded it, each still vibrant with colour but squashed to the thickness of a wafer. I had the feeling they evoked strong memories for Marieke – good memories. Just as I thought that she'd calmed down, that her nerves had steadied, more angry shouts reached us. The press slipped from her hands and crashed to the floor. She threw her arms around me and cried, 'Take me away from here, Finn. Take me with you back to Mulberry. I don't think I can stay here a second longer.'

Loki appeared in the doorway. Spotting us, a huge grin filled his face. *Don't you dare say anything*, I thought, *or else* . . . Luckily he kept his mouth shut.

Freya followed him in. 'Did you have any doubts about Gerrit?'

Letting go of me, Marieke shook her head. 'No. I never liked him, but that's not the same as thinking he's a traitor.'

'What on earth are they going to do now?'

'Send us to Holland, I expect, Freya,' Loki replied. 'The brigadier spent hours questioning me last night about my aunt, Saskia. He wanted to know everything about her and where she lives, and whether I could trust her. He wouldn't have gone to all that trouble unless he was dreaming up one of his schemes.'

'But—' I began, just as X and the brigadier emerged from Gerrit's office. I was about to say that such an idea was crazy as we couldn't speak Dutch, but Marieke interrupted me.

'Your brigadier is right. We must go to Holland. We have to try.' She combed her hair across her face with her fingers, clearly deep in thought. Suddenly something occurred to her. 'Tell me, what do you know about those airmen waiting to use the escape route?'

We shrugged. 'Nothing. Why?'

'I have the feeling there is something special about them, Finn.'

'Special?'

'*Shush!* Keep your voice down.' She pulled me close to her, conspiratorially close, and beckoned Loki and Freya nearer. 'I think there's even more to all this mess than they've let on. When news first came through that Bram had made contact with the airmen, everything went crazy. Telephones started ringing every five minutes, Fitzpatrick and Gerrit were called up to London to see X and the prime minister, and I got the impression that something incredibly important was unfolding. It was really odd. You see, the first time the escape route was used successfully, all Gerrit got was a congratulatory slap on the back and cigar shoved into his mouth. This time it's different.'

I could see she was deadly serious.

'Keep your eyes and ears open. Try to find out what you can. I'll see if I can sneak a look at Gerrit's files. With him gone, it'll be easier to break into his office.' She saw the shocked look on our faces. 'I'm not being crazy, or overreacting. It might be important. If we're going to be sent behind enemy lines I want to know what we're facing and just who exactly we're risking our lives for, don't you?'

She had a point. 'But you said you wanted to get out of here. To join us at Mulberry.'

'I do, Finn . . . I know, I could come over to join you tomorrow. I'll break into his office tonight. Yes, that would work perfectly.'

Loki was staring at Marieke as if she'd flipped. 'If you get caught you'll be in serious trouble. I mean *serious* trouble.'

Marieke was willing to take her chances.

'First things first, though,' I said. 'We've got to get permission from X for you to join us. Come on – we best catch him before he heads back to London.'

We hurried through the dining room and into the hallway. The door to Gerrit's office was closed; X and the brigadier were loitering outside. It struck me that they were waiting for something or someone. 'Sir,' I called out.

As the brigadier turned towards me, a single gunshot rang out from inside the office, sounding like a champagne cork popping. Marieke raised a hand to her mouth and screamed. Equally alarmed, Sergeant Fitzpatrick rushed towards the door but the redcaps blocked his way. I suddenly realized what had happened. Major Gerrit had been given a choice – face the acrimony and shame of a court martial and probably a firing squad, or take the honourable way out. He'd chosen the latter, placing a revolver against his temple and pulling the trigger.

Solemnly X placed his hat upon his head and gathered up his attaché case and coat. 'Sergeant Fitzpatrick, you will assist these military policemen in clearing up the mess, after which you'll be reassigned.

Brigadier Devlin is now in charge of all matters relating to Holland, and Major Gerrit's files will be transferred to Mulberry House this afternoon.'

Marieke cursed under her breath. No way would she have the chance to examine Gerrit's files now. 'Sir,' I piped up. 'We were wondering if Marieke could join us at Mulberry.'

'Out of the question, Finn,' X snapped. 'Miss Maartens has a job to do and will be leaving Dovecote very soon. The situation is grave and we face a race against time.' He gazed coldly at each of us in turn. 'It seems that you are all acquainted. In that case I suggest that you use this opportunity to say your farewells. If all goes to plan, you three will not cross paths with Miss Maartens again – at least not until the war is over.'

The pronouncement sounded so sudden, so final, so *unfair*, I opened my mouth to protest but his glare cut me short.

'Brigadier, a final word in your ear. Outside, please.' X marched out to his waiting car; the brigadier followed hard on his heels, his cane tapping a frantic rhythm on the woodblock floor as he scurried along in an attempt to keep up.

'We leave in ten minutes,' Walker announced.

Desperate to get out of the house, we hurried into the garden and down to the river. Freya and Loki said their goodbyes and wished Marieke luck, and then carried on along the riverbank, leaving just the two of us. 'You could refuse to go back to Holland,' I said. 'Everything's such a mess it may simply be too dangerous.'

Focusing on the far side of the river, Marieke shook her head. 'I have to go. Surely you understand that, Finn. Bram and the others are my friends, fellow Dutchmen.'

I did understand, not that it made it any easier to swallow. Marieke would be heading into dangerous waters. The Germans were all over us and her chances of survival were slim. 'I guess there won't be time for you to visit your grandparents in Oxford before you go.' I knew from past conversations she wanted to see them. 'Pity, it might have been good to get away from all this for a day or two.'

Marieke shook her head. 'No, I doubt there'll be time, Finn. X sounded as if my return to Holland is imminent. *A race against time*, he said.'

'Yes. I wonder what he meant by that?'

'God knows.' She turned to face me and her eyes searched mine. 'We will meet again one day, won't we, Finn? Tell me we will. *Promise me.*'

'Of course we will,' I said, looking away. 'I'm certain of it. I promise.'

But we both knew that such promises were made on a wing and a prayer, with fingers crossed, while clutching a fistful of lucky charms. In truth, such promises could not be made.

'Time to leave,' Walker bellowed from the terrace.

'Goodbye, Finn.' Marieke kissed me and ran off.

Chapter Six
Being Kool

On our return to Mulberry House we witnessed Jan Keppel being driven away. Our cars passed on the drive, and as I turned to look, I saw Jan's face peering out through the rear window. He waved.

'Where's he going?' Freya asked.

Walker flexed his grip on the steering wheel. 'Home.'

'*What?* They're sending him back to Holland?' Loki leaned forward. 'That's madness. Unlike us, he hasn't been trained.'

'Undoubtedly.' Walker sniffed disapprovingly. 'Couldn't agree more. However, needs must and all that.'

We gathered in the lounge to await a briefing from the brigadier.

'I'm sorry you had to witness all that this morning. Terrible business – the worst, in fact. But now you can see why Jan was brought to Mulberry and kept away from Major Gerrit.' Burdened by events, the brigadier sank wearily into an armchair.

I raised a hand. 'Walker said that Jan's returning to Holland. Is that true?'

'Yes, Finn. Jan occasionally helped his brother out over there, ferrying messages to and fro, that sort of thing. He thinks he knows where the airmen were hiding out. He can't remember the address but reckons he could find the place again. It's a long shot, but it's all we've got to go on. We have no idea whether they're still there or have been moved on, or captured. Marieke will find out. Don't worry, Finn, she'll look after Jan. In truth, I expect she'll appreciate the extra pair of hands. Jan's lived in The Hague most of his life and so he knows his way around. Anyway, it's vital we find the airmen. It overrides all other considerations.'

'So,' said Freya, thinking aloud, 'suppose they are still there. What then?'

'We get them out. That's where you're involved.'

We all began talking at once and our meeting quickly descended into a shambles.

'Enough!' snapped the brigadier, slamming his cane down hard on a tabletop. 'Pipe down. If you'd all be kind enough to sit down and pin your ears back, I'll explain everything.

'I intend to keep Fritz happy by letting him think he's one step ahead of us. We'll behave as if Asparagus is still operational. If we get requests for supply drops, we shall oblige. Meanwhile we'll build a new circuit of agents, completely independent of Asparagus. Crucially, because the enemy may know all about our organiz-ation and methods, we'll do everything differently.'

'You mean it's a case of double or quits,' Loki responded. 'And we don't quit!'

'Correct, Mr Larson. If we can convince the enemy that it is business as usual for us and Asparagus, the last thing they'd expect is the creation of a second circuit.'

Freya folded her arms defensively and shook her

head. 'This is crazy,' she muttered. 'We don't even speak Dutch.'

'We've thought that through,' Walker piped up, 'and we believe we've come up with a satisfactory solution, which I'll come to in a moment. Once Marieke has returned to Holland, you three will follow. You'll be dropped by parachute and then must make your way to the farm owned by Loki's aunt near Scheveningen. There you'll hole up until word reaches you concerning the airmen. If they're all right, Marieke will pass them over to you and you'll arrange their escape.'

What I knew about Holland could be written on one side of a postcard. In fact, all I did know was that it now shared some unenviable things with our homeland, Norway. When war broke out, both countries reckoned they could remain happily neutral, only to discover that Herr Hitler had other ideas.

'Now, I spent most of last night questioning Mr Larson about his aunt, Saskia Pol,' Brigadier Devlin began. He signalled to Walker, who proceeded to tape a large-scale map of southern Holland to the wall. 'She lives at a farm a few miles outside Scheveningen. It's located here.' The brigadier reached up from his chair and slapped the tip of his cane against the spot. 'You'll have the chance to study maps of the area before you depart and I strongly suggest you commit as much as possible to memory. Mr Larson assures me that his aunt can be relied upon.'

I looked at Loki in astonishment. 'You've only visited her once, and that was years ago. And I thought you told me that she fell out with your parents big-time, that they've not spoken since. How can you be so sure she's trustworthy?'

'She was born a Larson, Finn. Of course she can be trusted. When you meet her, you'll see I'm right. I got on really well with her son, Willem, too.' He sat back in his chair, folded his arms and looked smug.

'But what about her husband, Gottfried?' I muttered under my breath, much to Loki's annoyance. I now remembered why they'd all fallen out. Gottfried had got mixed up in politics, joining the communists, and Loki's father hated him for it. I began to explain but Loki angrily cut me short.

'Saskia's *family*, Finn. Anyway, blood's thicker than water *or* politics. We'll be fine. Honestly.'

'I know there are risks but they're worth taking,' Walker interrupted. 'As you pointed out, we had to overcome the fact that you don't speak Dutch. There'd be little point in us giving you forged Dutch identities because they'd be rendered useless the first time you were stopped for questioning. Fritz would twig something was wrong the moment you opened your mouths. However, as Loki's aunt is Norwegian by birth, we have the opportunity for the perfect cover. Basically, your story is that you were holidaying with her when Norway was invaded and so couldn't return home. You stayed and worked on the farm to earn your keep. We'll be giving you the appropriate identity papers and will have all the necessary travel, residency and work permits prepared to show that you have permission to reside on Dutch soil.'

I realized the decision had been made – we were going in. 'OK,' I said. 'Supposing all this proves possible, how do we get the airmen out?'

Walker studied the map closely and ordered us to gather round. Pressing a thumb against the coast, he said, 'The small town of Scheveningen's wedged between the sea and the city of The Hague. Virtually the entire coastline has been mined and booby-trapped, although there is one exception. Here on the main seafront boulevard there's a rather swanky building called the Palace Hotel. The German Navy, the *Kriegsmarine*, have commandeered it for their regional coastal security HQ. It's next door to an equally splendid building called the Kurhaus, a hotel and concert hall all rolled into one. It's immediately opposite the pier. Anyway, the point is that a small section of beach behind the Palace Hotel has been cleared of dangers so that the officers stationed there can have the occasional swim.'

'You've got to be joking,' I interrupted in astonishment. 'Right under their noses!'

'That's right, Finn. Using high-powered motor gunboats – MGBs – our evacuation teams can cross the North Sea in under five hours. As they approach the coast they'll cut two of their engines, relying on the third to get them closer to the beach. The engine's tuned to run almost silently but can still make about eight knots, wind and tide permitting. A hundred yards from the beach they'll launch inflatable dinghies and paddle ashore to pick you all up.'

Loki was scratching his head. 'But what about guard

patrols? What about the surf? What happens if they miss the exact rendezvous point? What if some SS storm troopers decide to go for a midnight dip?'

The muscles in Walker's face tightened. 'All I can say is that we'd better make it work!'

'And that's how we're supposed to get the airmen out?' I was incredulous.

'Yes, Finn, and yourselves as well. If all goes to plan, when the moment comes, Marieke will get the airmen to you and you will then escort them to the beach. Marieke will not be involved in that part of the operation as she will be staying behind. There is much more work for her to do building a new network. And the less she knows about the escape route, the less she could divulge if captured. If it works, we'll want to use it again.'

Freya shivered and rubbed away the goose pimples that had made the hairs on her arms stand to attention. 'I don't like it. We'll be sitting ducks. If Marieke is arrested or followed, she'll lead the enemy straight to us.'

The brigadier shook his head. 'No, Freya. We've learned lessons from past mistakes. Marieke won't know your exact whereabouts. Likewise, you'll know nothing about hers.'

I recalled X had said that, all being well, we'd not meet again, but it left me confused. 'How on earth will she be able to hand the airmen over to us? Surely we'll need to work closely together if this is going to succeed.' My outburst was more in hope than anything else.

'It'll work like this,' Walker began. 'There's a flower

shop in Scheveningen called Margo's. When the time comes, Marieke will place an advertisement in the shop window to alert you. It will be written on either red or blue card and will simply request information concerning a missing dog called Puk. Every day or two you must wander past this shop and look to see if the advertisement's been posted. The advert itself is meaningless. The important thing is the colour of the card. Blue means she has the airmen and they are ready to escape. It will also indicate that a message containing detailed instructions has been deposited for you to collect from a safe address. Marieke will suss out the address once she arrives and will let us know by coded message before you leave. You will then contact us by radio and we'll agree a date and time for the pick-up.'

'And if the advert's on red card?' Loki asked.

'It'll mean that it is either too dangerous or impossible for the escape to proceed. Or that something's gone terribly wrong. There may still be a message for you to pick up from the safe address, so you should go there anyway. Then contact us and we'll make urgent preparations for you to leave Holland. So you see, you and Marieke never actually have to meet. Much safer all round. In fact, that's why you said your goodbyes this morning. Henceforth there must be no direct contact between you. That way it's impossible for you to share information: if one of you is captured, the others will remain safe.'

'No approach is foolproof,' I muttered. 'Why not just relay all information by radio?'

'We could and will if necessary,' the brigadier replied. 'But we'd prefer to keep the amount of radio traffic to a minimum. *Others* may be listening!'

My mind drifted to what Marieke had said about the stranded airmen and I decided now was as good a time as any to raise the matter. 'Is there anything special about the pilots and navigators that we're supposed to help? I only ask because Marieke told me that when Bram signalled to say contact had been established, Major Gerrit and X were hauled up to see Mr Churchill and their telephones didn't stop ringing.'

Walker shot a glance towards the brigadier, who thought for a moment and then, appearing to choose his words with great care, replied, 'All you need to know is that it is of the greatest importance that they return home safely. It would be unwise for me to say any more than that. Except, perhaps, to tell you that the matter has become one of extreme urgency.'

Freya still looked troubled. 'If Bram and the others have talked under interrogation, surely the enemy will know about the possible escape route.'

'Last time we got the airmen out by plane. Using the beach is new.' Walker tried his best to sound like it was going to be easy.

'Now, one last thing,' the brigadier concluded. 'The mission will be called Double Dutch. Marieke, aided by Jan Keppel, will be working under the codename *Aardappel* – that's "potato", by the way – and you three will be *Kool*, which means "cabbage". These should be used in all forms of communication from now on.'

As our briefing broke up, I found myself chewing my nails as the enormity of our task sank in. Much of the success of Double Dutch would depend on Marieke. How I wished we could be working closely together as one team. Instead Marieke would be operating more or less alone. Would Jan be a help or a burden? Loki was right – he'd not been trained like we had. And it was so easy to make a deadly mistake.

Training for Double Dutch began in earnest. Clothes-fitting sessions fixed us up with convincing Dutch peasant attire, our corduroy trousers suitably worn, and jacket collars and cuffs deliberately frayed at the edges. Faded Dutch labels were sewn into the seams and we were provided with heavy boots, the leather uppers scuffed and cracked, the heels hollowed out to form small hidden compartments for storing key items. Within days our forged papers and permits were ready. Everything seemed such a rush. We rehearsed our cover stories over and over until they became second nature. Luckily we were using our own names and much of our pre-war history was unaltered, making it easy to recall should we be interrogated. This was highly irregular: agents normally received a completely new identity. But there wasn't time to fabricate three totally convincing fictional cover stories and so we'd make do. I was relieved. Having to learn hundreds of new 'facts' was a nightmare, especially when you knew your life depended on instant and accurate recall. In the end, only the parts about visiting Loki's aunt and our subsequent stay were entirely made up.

A stern fellow – he reminded me of my old geometry teacher at school, who relished subjecting us to endless repetition – introduced himself as Perry van Cleef and set about teaching us some rudimentary Dutch each evening. Although we could never hope to pass for natives, we might need to understand and speak a few common phrases. As usual, Freya picked it up annoyingly fast – she was a natural when it came to foreign languages – while Loki and I stammered and stumbled over strange words that I reckoned could only be pronounced properly if you stuffed one of Mrs Saunders's suet dumplings into your mouth.

Freya brushed up on her Morse and coding skills as she'd be acting as our wireless operator. She also had to get used to a new radio set, having lost her last one on our previous mission into France. She'd been captured and given a pretty rough time under interrogation by the Gestapo. Loki and I had managed to rescue her in the nick of time but the trauma had left its mark – she often suffered nightmares and would wake screaming in the middle of the night. Her replacement suitcase transmitter offered us an unexpected opportunity to let off steam.

'I can't carry that around with me,' Freya complained, staring at the case with her hands on her hips. 'What would a farm girl be doing with a brand-new suitcase? I'll stick out like a sore thumb.'

Although the shiny brown leather suitcase was small, the radio set inside was heavy, the whole thing weighing in at about thirty-two pounds. Carefully we extracted the precision equipment and then immersed the leather case in a bath of water for a couple of hours. Then we played football with it, belting it up and down the hallway at Mulberry, stamping on it, kicking and scuffing it, and finally throwing it repeatedly out of an upstairs window. Then it was just a case of rubbing some dirt into all the scratches and grazes, sandpapering the brass corners to remove the shine, before cleaning it up a bit. By the time we were done it was splendidly 'distressed', and Freya was convinced it looked at least twenty years old. 'Perfect,' she declared.

'Are you OK about all this?' I asked her as we carefully packed the radio set back into the case. 'If you'd prefer, I could ask the brigadier if I can work the radio instead.'

'Thanks, Finn, but I'd better do it. My Morse is the best out of all of us. I'll just have to be doubly careful this time and make sure I always have one of you as lookout while transmitting. If the Germans *do* locate us, they won't take us without a fight.'

Loki glanced up from what he was doing with a *too bloody right they won't* scowl.

'There, it's all neatly back in its case.' Freya snapped the catches shut and wiped some perspiration from her brow using the sleeve of her pullover. 'There is one thing worrying me though, Finn. What if Saskia doesn't want us on her farm? What if she's not willing to take the risk? After all, if we're caught there she'll face prison or a firing squad too, as will the rest of her family.'

'She'll be fine,' Loki responded while checking the barrel of his pistol.

'But what if she *isn't*?' Freya persisted. 'What do we do then? Where's our back-up plan?'

Chapter Seven
An Unsettling Incident

The following morning I awoke to the din of angry shouting downstairs. My room at Mulberry House, sparsely furnished with an iron bed, thin mattress, itchy blankets and little else other than a small wardrobe, was located down the far end of the landing, and my door was shut. For voices to reach me they had to be raised to fever pitch. Dressing quickly, I emerged from my room to see both Loki and Freya had done likewise: Loki was hanging over the banister and eavesdropping on the conversation below. He turned to look at me and announced, half in astonishment and half in delight, 'We've been burgled!'

Hurtling down the stairs, we spotted a bemused Mrs Saunders in the hallway, wiping her flour-covered hands on her floral apron, a puzzled Walker scratching his ginger head, and an irate, purple-faced brigadier firing off expletives like the rat-a-tat-tat of a Bren machine gun in full song. The front door was open and Smithy's face appeared. 'Buggers jemmied the dining-room window, sir. One of the sentries spotted the damage.'

We all trooped outside to inspect the manner used to gain entry. 'There! You can see where the sill and frame have been damaged,' Smithy pointed out.

None of us had heard a thing during the night: nothing had disturbed us.

The brigadier suppressed his anger and issued orders. 'Check everything. See what's been taken. And double-check the inventory of weapons, ammunition and explosives. I want to know what's been nicked, down to the last paperclip. Understood?'

If you could get past the guards on the gates and avoid the perimeter patrols, it wasn't hard to break into houses like Mulberry. They were old and poorly maintained. Warped windows sat in ill-fitting frames, the latches feeble, and the door locks were simple Yale types that could be picked in a matter of seconds. Nevertheless I doubted that it had been local crooks chancing their arm to grab the silverware from a large country house. It would take someone a bit special to get past the guards. It got me thinking, and if I had to bet my life on choosing the most likely culprit I'd not hesitate to suggest that it was an inside job. Who better equipped than someone in Special Ops? We'd all been trained in evasion and housebreaking, and occasionally students were tasked with a night-time 'raid' on another group's headquarters. There were a dozen houses like Mulberry, and as many teams of eager trainees. It could have been any of them.

My theory was supported by the fact that nothing appeared to be missing. I helped check out the dining room – we'd converted it into our operations centre for Double Dutch. The walls were plastered with maps and aerial photographs of Holland, especially the area around Scheveningen, and trestle tables were piled high with supplies that we'd be taking with us. Everything was there; nothing looked disturbed.

A hole was shot in my thinking, however, when the brigadier emerged from his office and announced that he'd telephoned every section commander and they'd all vehemently denied any involvement. The incident appeared to defy explanation and it cast unease over Mulberry for the rest of the day. It was only late in the afternoon when I picked up the book on flight navigation I'd been reading that the mystery took a new twist.

An envelope fell from between the pages. My name was on it. Inside was a single sheet of paper, neatly folded. The page was blank, but in the fold rested a small pressed flower. *Marieke?* I stared at it, trying to figure out its meaning. Moving to the window to get some better light, I tilted the page at various angles and quickly realized that maybe the page wasn't totally blank after all.

I ran upstairs to my room and closed the door. Climbing onto my bed, I reached up and removed the dusty shade from the ceiling light, jumped back down and flicked the switch. I waited for the bulb to heat up and then, standing on my mattress again, gently moved the sheet back and forth a fraction of an inch from the blazing heat. Ever so slowly words began to appear, written by hand using extravagant loops. In minutes the words were as clear as day. They'd been written using one of Witherspoon's finest concoctions.

In emergency contact 'Otto' at No. 17 Nieuwe Siegelstraat, The Hague. It's a tailor's shop. He will assist you. Say the following to him:

'Wij gaan in het weekend naar een bruiloft. Het zijn deftige mensen en we zullen zecker nieuwe kleren nodig hebben.' (It means: We're going to a wedding at the weekend. They're smart people and we shall definitely need new clothes.)

Expect the following reply: 'Je hebt in jaren geen pak gedragen.' (It means: You haven't worn a suit in years.)

Take great care, Finn – those airmen are special – Very Special Indeed!

Good luck, and may we meet again one day.

Love,

Aardappel

I sat down on my bed and digested the contents of the note. Why had Marieke broken into Mulberry to give me this? Why go to such lengths? The questions kept pouring into my head. I took a deep breath and tried to fathom it out. Of course, Marieke couldn't just cycle up to the entrance to Mulberry and tell me, or drop off a letter for me. Such contact was forbidden. Breaking in and delivering it personally was drastic, but presumably she felt it was important enough to take the risk. In doing so she'd committed a cardinal sin; now there was information, and a man named Otto, linking us. It was all information that, if spilled under interrogation, could smash a fledgling new network of Resistance fighters. But she must've known that, and so why?

I supposed Marieke feared for our safety, although she hadn't indicated why and, irritatingly, I couldn't exactly ask her. And there was definitely something special about these airmen. What had she found out? Damn, why hadn't she elaborated? And what now?

I knew the right thing to do would be to take her message straight to the brigadier and let him figure out what the consequences should be. She'd be in hot water, and maybe the whole operation would be postponed – a disaster. No. I decided to say nothing for now – except, of course, to Loki and Freya. I folded up the note and put it in my pocket. Carefully, I placed the pressed flower between the pages of my book on navigation for safe-keeping.

'Didn't I say she was quite a girl,' Loki remarked, handing the message back to me.

We'd gathered on the bench beneath the mulberry tree, out of earshot of anyone else.

'So what shall we do now? Tell the brigadier?' I felt tons better sharing the problem *and* the responsibility.

Loki shrugged. 'Do nothing. No point.'

Freya rested her head on his shoulder and studied the note. It dawned on me that she was committing the contents to memory too. 'That contact could be useful,' she concluded. 'It may be our Plan B if everything else goes wrong.' Then she frowned.

'What?'

'I was just thinking, Finn. What if Marieke took a look around? She broke in via the dining room. She must have seen all the photographs and maps?'

'Hell!' If she'd shone her torch about the walls, Marieke would have observed all the arrows and annotations on the maps. With even a cursory glance she'd know the precise location of our drop, and of Loki's aunt's farm – all information with which to betray us if she fell into the hands of the Gestapo.

'Or maybe she didn't bother,' Loki added. 'She wouldn't have hung around any longer than she needed to. After all, her intention was simply to drop her message off, Finn.'

Was it? I wondered. Or had she risked X's wrath and jeopardized the secrecy of our mission in order to give *herself* a back-up plan – to know where we were; to be able to contact *us* in an emergency?

With just twenty-four hours to go before our departure, Mrs Saunders set about preparing a special celebratory dinner for us – a Special Ops ritual before a mission got underway. Rationing meant that she had to improvise and be creative, and we'd grown tired of her weird culinary experiments in which almost every usual recipe ingredient was substituted by another, often with disastrous results. For special occasions, however, it was Smithy who played a vital role. Somehow he always knew of stuff that had fallen off the back of a lorry. 'All right, lads,' he'd say to us as he entered the kitchen clutching rabbits, pheasant, venison, salmon, butter, sugar, real coffee, Swiss chocolate . . . the list was endless. He may have been as ugly as sin, as Walker always liked to jibe, but whenever Mrs Saunders saw him bearing gifts she eyed him as though deeply in love.

Nils Jacobsen arrived that afternoon and asked to see me. I found him wandering the gardens looking somewhat preoccupied and nervously wringing his cap in his hands. As soon as he spotted me, he hurried over. 'Ah, Finn. Good. How are you?'

'As well as can be expected the night before—'

'Yes, yes, of course. As usual, they've not told me much, but I understand you're going in to sort out a right old mess.'

I nodded. 'Are you flying us in?'

'Yes. Listen, I wanted to speak to you alone. Before you go . . .' He paused awkwardly and looked up at the sky. 'About your father . . .'

'What about him?'

'After our last chat I got hold of the official report of that particular sortie over the North Sea again – the one in which he was shot down – and re-read it. Then I spoke to as many of the pilots who flew alongside us that day as I could track down.'

I sensed his unease. '*And?*'

'Well, two Spits bought it on that mission. It was quite a dogfight. Everything happened so fast. Planes everywhere, coming in all directions, split-second decisions, barely time to think.'

'What are you saying?'

He took a deep, fortifying breath. 'We're friends, you and I, just like I was with your father. And I value our friendship. Its bedrock lies in total honesty, however difficult, however painful. Truth is, Finn, I have a confession to make. I don't know which Spit I saw dropping into the sea. The various accounts of the other pilots all differ and give a confused picture. All I do know is that your father didn't return home. He must've been shot down, but—'

I interrupted, 'But you don't know if he baled out or not.' I scarcely hid my delight. 'So he might still be alive!'

Nils reached out to me. 'I'm not saying he did or he didn't. Just that I can't be sure.'

I fizzed with excitement. 'He's alive. I just *know* he is.'

Nils shook me. 'Listen to me, Finn. *Listen!* I've checked the lists of prisoners of war and information sent by the Red Cross, and his name isn't mentioned. If he *had* been captured we should have heard by now. So don't get your hopes up. *Please!*'

My brain was one step ahead. 'I understand. There are now only two possibilities, aren't there? One, he's dead just like we thought, or he made it ashore and is being hidden by the Resistance.'

'It's a million-to-one shot, Finn. You must understand that. But I'll keep making enquiries. One other thing: let's keep this little chat between ourselves, all right? I'm not sure your brigadier will appreciate me stirring things up. You've a mission to focus on. He won't appreciate you being distracted. OK? Now, I must dash. I've got work to do on tomorrow night's flight plans. Remember, Finn, not a word to anyone.'

For the rest of that afternoon I was the happiest fellow alive. It was just the thought, the possibility, that faintest glimmer of hope, that sent the blood whizzing through my veins and filled my head with pictures of our reunion – father and son together again, maybe one day flying sorties side by side, the wingtips of our Spitfires almost touching, our eyes watchful for bandits on each other's tail. I willed it to be true with every fibre of my being.

Chapter Eight
Photographs Never Lie

Having been converted into a classroom for much of our time at Mulberry House, the dining room was restored to its former glory for our celebratory meal. Dinner was served at eight o'clock on the dot. As a rather flustered Mrs Saunders ladled carrot soup into Mulberry's best set of bone china bowls, X had a few choice words to say regarding our mission. He rose from his chair and tapped his spoon against his glass to gain our attention.

'You should know that I had serious reservations about sending you three to Holland. It is not a country that you know particularly well, nor are you proficient in its language. You will have to muddle through as best you can and rely on the excellent training men like Walker, Killer and Smithy have imparted to you. The actions of Major Gerrit have come perilously close to finishing our organization off once and for all, and not just because we've lost many of our agents. As you know, the Secret Intelligence Services like MI6 don't rate us as much more than a bunch of bloody amateurs. They're looking for the slightest excuse to persuade Mr Churchill to close us down. We have egg on our faces and need to redeem ourselves. So, desperate times call for desperate measures. The dangers you face are almost incalculable. I do not hide such truths from you. Do not underestimate the importance of your mission. Success is vital. Let's show them, eh!' He formed a fist and punched the air.

'We'll do our best,' said Freya. 'But much will depend on Marieke – I mean, Aardappel – succeeding.'

'If she gets the airmen to us, we'll get them out, don't you worry,' Loki added bullishly. 'Provided, of course, you send us those MGBs to pick us up.'

'They'll be sent all right, even if we have to commandeer and sail the bloody boats ourselves,' Walker chipped in.

X reached for his glass. 'All three of you have proven yourselves courageous and quick-witted, both in escaping your homeland of Norway and on subsequent missions as members of Special Ops. Your work goes on in such secrecy that you receive no gratitude or praise from the outside world, and that's because officially you do not exist. Let's keep it that way. I salute you and wish you every success.'

'Here, here,' Smithy bellowed, joining Killer, Walker and the brigadier in draining the contents of their glasses in one go.

'Well, that's about it. I have little else to say other than to wish you luck and a safe return.'

X sat back down, and soon Mrs Saunders was serving us a splendid roast rack of lamb, the carcass having arrived at Mulberry draped over Smithy's shoulder – he claimed it had been run over and that he'd merely found it lying in the road. What he conveniently forgot to mention was that it was he who'd run the poor beast over in the first place: we'd seen the dried blood and tell-tale tufts of wool ensnared in the front bumper of his truck. As we tucked in, our knives and forks clattering noisily, Loki ventured, 'Anything new from Aardappel?'

'No,' Walker responded abruptly. He paused and wiped gravy from his chin with his napkin. 'Except that they arrived safely.'

X added, 'And that Miss Maartens has chosen a café called the Rembrandt as her so-called "dead letterbox" for leaving messages for you to collect. It's in The Hague. You'll get details of its location during your final briefing tomorrow morning.'

'There's something I don't understand,' Freya declared, putting down her fork as if she wasn't going to eat anything else until she did. 'These airmen . . . I realize we're short of pilots and navigators and need to do everything we can to get them out – but surely the members of Asparagus are equally important. They might still be alive. Shouldn't it be our priority to rescue *them*? It's like saying the airmen are worth more than our people.'

Her question led to a jarring silence in the room.

'I understand what you're saying, but that's simply how it must be,' X replied unhelpfully. 'Rest assured, if Aardappel sees an opportunity to get members of Asparagus out of the clutches of whoever has their grubby hands on them, then no doubt an attempt will be made . . . *eventually*. We must leave it at that.'

Unsatisfied, Freya tried to go on: 'But—'

'Drop the subject, Miss Haukelid. That's an order. Have I made myself clear?'

Dutifully she nodded.

Marieke was right, I realized. There was definitely far more to all this than met the eye. I decided to support Freya's misgivings. 'Not good enough, sir,' I said, desperately trying to conceal my trepidation. X was not the sort of man to be messed with. 'Clearly there's something special about these airmen. And, well, if we are going to place our lives on the line, then we don't want any nasty surprises.'

The brigadier's cheeks turned the colour of the claret in his replenished glass and he looked as if he might explode at my impertinence. X sat back and offered an explanation of sorts. 'You have not been told the identity of the airmen for your own safety and, equally importantly, for theirs. It has become a matter of some urgency and importance to the war effort that these airmen are returned safely. So Freya's quite right in thinking that they're receiving our priority. Although that might seem unfair, a betrayal of our own people even, you must also consider this . . . If members of Asparagus are still alive and being held prisoner, and a rescue attempt is made, the enemy could realize that we're on to them. And that would jeopardize our renewed efforts to establish a new network. It's very much one step at a time.'

'So, assuming they're alive, we let them rot in prison?' Loki threw down his knife in disgust.

'That's enough, Mr Larson.' X glared across the table at him in a manner that told everyone the subject was dead. He picked up his fork and resumed eating.

In the ensuing uneasy silence the ticking of the hall clock sounded unnaturally loud. Smithy finally broke the tension by speaking up about the dubious origins of our meal: apparently he'd nearly ended up in a ditch as he swerved to make sure he ran over the sheep. Killer and Walker both howled with laughter and asked whether he'd had to reverse just to make sure. I wasn't really listening. My curiosity was burning a hole in my head, partly fuelled by X's coolness when I'd challenged him. *Very Special Indeed!* Marieke had said in her note. *Just how special?* I wondered. Was she hinting to me? Maybe she wanted me to find out more. But those sitting at the table weren't going spill the beans. That left only one equally unattractive option – the files transferred from Dovecote. They were securely locked away in cabinets in the brigadier's office. It suddenly struck me as obvious – of course, that's what Marieke wanted me to do. She hadn't written it explicitly in case her message was intercepted by the brigadier or Walker. But I had so little time. Tomorrow we were heading for Holland. That just left tonight. Mrs Saunders cleared the plates and served up apple pie and cream.

The hall clock chimed. Ten o'clock. As conversation murmured across the table, cigars were lit and glasses of blood-red port were quaffed, I put the finishing touches to my plan. Catching Loki's eye, I nodded towards the door, made my excuses, got up from the table and left the room. Loki followed hard on my heels. We headed outside, where I explained my intentions.

'They'll skin you alive if you get caught, Finn.'

'That's why I need your help. To keep watch.'

He wavered a moment, repeatedly glancing back towards the dining room, where the brigadier appeared to have launched into one of his harrowing stories of life in the trenches during the Great War: gut-wrenching descriptions of endless fields of gloopy mud littered with rotting corpses and the incessant pounding of shells, some containing the infamous mustard gas. 'OK, Finn. But we'd better make it quick.'

The door to the brigadier's office was open but I knew his filing cabinets remained locked at all times. I ran and collected the necessary tools from a storeroom. Loki loitered in the hall while I crept inside. I left the door open just an inch so I could hear him raise the alarm. To one side of the brigadier's table lay the grey metal filing cabinets: three sets, each five feet tall and each with four drawers. I shone my pen torch onto the small square labels revealing their contents. Most were vague. MISSION BRIEFINGS – I decided that was probably my best bet.

Wedging the torch between my teeth, I removed the lock picks we'd used in training from my pocket. Attached to a key ring were a dozen needle-like instruments, each a different thickness and each with a slightly differently shaped hook on the end. Nervously, all fingers and thumbs, I tried each in turn, shoving them into the small drawer lock. The first two wouldn't even penetrate the mechanism. The third did but wouldn't turn. The fourth was more promising, so I persevered, gently twisting it one way and then the other, trying to feel the point at which the hook would engage the internal workings and – hey presto! – suddenly the pick turned sweetly and I detected a slight click as the mechanism yielded. I glanced towards the door: all clear. I yanked the drawer open and began riffling through dozens of hanging files. There were names of operations that meant nothing. In frustration I slid these forward and grabbed a fistful right at the back of the cabinet. I set them down and examined each in turn, my sense of urgency redoubling as each proved useless. Then, at last! The final one bore the label I was seeking – DOUBLE DUTCH. The manila folder was weighty. I moved it to one side and flicked it open.

'Get a move on,' Loki whispered anxiously from the hallway. 'I think they're finishing up in there.'

'OK, keep your hair on.' The file bulged with memoranda between X, Gerrit and Whitehall, with requisition slips and approvals for the equipment we were taking with us. I paused and steadied my torch on a list of names under the heading 'Asparagus', spotting Bram Keppel's name, and then moved on, flicking over page after page of thin tissue-like paper. There was a section on Aardappel, with notes on Marieke's cover story, copies of her forged identity papers, a whole section containing copies of Asparagus's decoded radio messages, and a section dedicated to us in Kool. Towards the back there was a divider marked

AWAITING REPATRIATION, and beyond, single pages to which small photographs had been attached. *Bingo!* These had to be the men we were going to rescue. I moved my torch a little closer. The first was a Group Captain Wilfred Collins. The handwritten notes were all in Dutch and hard to decipher – Major Gerrit's jottings, I suspected. The only words I could make out with certainty – because they were in English – were *Wolf Squadron*. I turned the page. The second detailed a Pilot Officer Jenkins. Again, the only words I could make out were a reference to Wolf Squadron. More indecipherable scribble lay beneath this photograph. Despite my rush, it struck me that these men looked more like villains than flyers. I turned the pages. The third, fourth and fifth had blank spaces where there were supposed to be photographs; two didn't even bear names – just further spidery scribbles in black ink, in Dutch, and more than a smattering of question and exclamation marks.

I reached the last page and gasped. Anything headed MOST SECRET: LEVEL NINE CLEARANCE REQUIRED was certainly going to grab my attention. My heart quickened and my palms grew sweaty. I steadied my torch on the tiny photograph. Staring up at me was a high-ranking German officer in full dress uniform. Beneath was a name: *Major Klaus Kiefer, codename Falcon*. My pulse raced. The sixth 'airman' was either a German spying for us, or was a British agent pretending to be a German.

'Loki,' I whispered. 'Come and look at this.'

'There's no time, Finn. You've got to get out of there. They're coming out. For God's sake hurry!'

I could hear voices too, much louder than before. I guessed it meant that the door to the dining room had been opened. I had just seconds. Hurriedly switching off my torch, I heard the brigadier say, 'Mr Larson, what are you doing there?'

Holding my breath, I closed the folder, gathered it up with the others and prepared to return them to the cabinet. As I did so, something fell onto the floor.

'Oh, just wanted to say goodbye to X,' Loki replied, raising his voice to make sure I'd hear him. 'And to ask him whether there was any chance he could organize some pilot training when we get back from Holland. He knows Finn and I want to get our official wings.'

Groping around on my hands and knees, I felt about for what I'd dropped. My fingertips ran over a card-like object and I seized it. A photograph. Briefly catching sight of it in the light creeping in from the hallway, I felt as if I'd been struck by a sledgehammer.

'We'll discuss that when you return, Mr Larson. Now, I think you left your attaché case in my office, sir,' the brigadier said. 'Walker, fetch it for X, if you please.'

'I'll get it,' Loki offered – rather too enthusiastically, I thought.

I stood up and blinked. I felt really strange, as if I'd just seen a ghost. Approaching footsteps snapped me out of my daze. Was it Loki or Walker? Hell. Hastily I slipped the photograph into the last of the folders, returned them all to the drawer and eased it shut. Then I flung myself down behind the brigadier's desk. The door swung open and the light came on. I sensed someone approach the other side of the desk. Walker! I pressed my eyes shut and held my breath. I should have been praying that I wouldn't be rumbled, but instead my head was filled with something else – that photograph. It was of Father. What was it doing inside the brigadier's files? Which folder did it fall out of? Something clicked inside my head. Photographs were missing from several of the pages I'd inspected – was Father's picture one of them? If it was . . . that meant . . . he was alive! He was one of the airmen. I felt giddy. Maybe that was what Marieke had meant by *Very Special Indeed!*

I heard the sound of X's attaché case sliding across the desk. More footsteps. The flick of the light switch. Darkness. The sound of the door being closed. Muffled voices outside. The door opened again.

'Quick, Finn. They're outside. Out of there now. It's your only chance. What are you waiting for? Get a move on!'

Chapter Nine
The Drop

Our Whitley roared into the night, thundering east-wards across the coast and over the North Sea. We were already hours behind schedule. Our parachutes were strapped to our backs and our hearts were lodged firmly in our mouths. The inside of the fuselage was dark and cold, and stank of kerosene. The fumes made me feel light-headed. Freya sat next to Loki, opposite Smithy and me, her head resting on Loki's shoulder for comfort, her suitcase radio set beside her and clipped to her belt by a short leather strap. To our side lay two cylindrical metal 'C'-type containers, each almost six feet long and fifteen inches in diameter, containing our gear. Their parachutes were integrated into one end, the static lines operating in the same way as ours. That was Smithy's job – to make sure we were all hooked up properly and exited through the small hatchway in a quick and orderly manner once we reached the DZ, the drop zone.

Beneath our camouflaged striptease suits we wore our Dutch clothes; our forged papers were in our pockets, along with silk maps and tiny compasses. A parting gift from the brigadier, a selection of pills, had also been carefully tucked away in the hollow heels of our boots. There were four types. The Benzedrine tablets would help us stay awake when we were exhausted but needed to remain alert. Our L-pills, the 'L' standing for *lethal*, would enable us to exit this life quickly should we be captured and feel unable to continue. They contained potassium cyanide and reputedly led to a painless death within seconds of being bitten open inside our mouths. There were also pills that induced sleep and pills that made you temporarily very sick and would convince any doctor.

'Wish I was going with you,' Smithy shouted over the din of the engines. I frowned at him. He pointed towards the ground. 'Got old scores to settle. Maybe I'll get my chance one day.'

'You can have my parachute if you want,' Loki yelled. 'I hate heights. Much rather stay in here.'

Smithy laughed. 'Next time maybe.'

I got up and signalled to Smithy that I was going forward to the cockpit. There was something I wanted to ask Nils – had he ever heard of the Wolf Squadron?

'Jesus, Finn, where on earth did you hear about them?'

Nils' co-pilot was equally surprised. 'Wolfie Collins's mob! They're a bunch of lunatics.'

'So you've heard of them?'

'They're legendary, Finn. His elite squadron handles the really tricky stuff, transporting agents deep into enemy territory, sometimes even close to Berlin. Makes our flights seem like little pleasure trips.' He frowned. 'Your turn. Why the question? Who told you about . . .'

He paused. 'Don't tell me they've come a cropper. And you're going in to help get them out?'

I nodded.

Nils' co-pilot whistled. 'Now there's a story for the officers' mess.'

'No!' I said. 'You're not supposed to know. It's top secret – even I'm not meant to know about it.'

'It's all right, Finn. Your secret's safe.' Nils reached out and patted my shoulder.

I'd intended to share with Nils my other discovery, Father's photograph, but decided against it as he suddenly had flak to deal with and needed to concentrate on flying the plane. Instead I returned to the others, sank my head back against a rib of the fuselage and stared blankly ahead. I supposed that the Wolf Squadron had flown in to pick up the spy Kiefer, and something had then gone terribly wrong. And it was up to us to put it right. I wondered why this Kiefer was so important. Waves of tiredness suddenly lapped over me. The previous night I'd not been able to sleep. I'd been running on pure adrenaline and now felt shattered. The enormity of it all was beginning to sink in. Yes, I was on a mission to rescue this Wolfie Collins and Kiefer, but I was also going to rescue Father. That's all I really cared about.

Freya was studying me through the gloom. Our eyes met briefly and she looked away. After escaping the brigadier's office I'd told her and Loki of my discoveries. They were shocked to learn that one of the 'airmen' we were rescuing was a German officer, an agent of some sort, maybe even one of ours inserted into the enemy's lair, but that surprise and astonishment paled into insignificance when I told them about the photo. All that was missing was a fanfare of trumpets.

I'd expected them both to jump for joy, but they didn't. In fact, they simply didn't believe me. 'You must be mistaken.' Loki was adamant. 'It was dark in that office. The light from the hallway couldn't possibly have been enough for you to see it clearly. Let's face it, what you actually saw was a man in flying uniform – at best a man vaguely resembling your father. Hell, there must be thousands of pictures of pilots who look like that. Wishful thinking got the better of you, Finn. You don't even know which file the photo fell out of.'

Of course, I was deaf to his reasoning. I refused to believe any of it. Instead, despite my promise, I let slip what Nils had told me about the confusion during Father's last sortie. I thought it would convince Loki, but it didn't. Freya suggested we confront the brigadier to sort the matter out once and for all but I resisted. To do so, I'd have to admit to breaking into his files, and that might jeopardize the mission: the brigadier would realize we knew about the Wolf Squadron and an agent codenamed Falcon – Level Nine Security stuff! Way above our heads. X might pull us off the mission, and I wasn't going to do anything that might endanger my chance to rescue Father.

Our headphones crackled and hissed into life and Nils's voice announced, 'Five minutes to the DZ.'

The red light came on. Smithy quietly set about

hooking up the static lines for the two supply canisters. One by one we got to our feet and formed a nervous line.

'I'll go first,' said Loki, swallowing hard.

Smithy hooked our static lines up too and checked that they hadn't tangled or interfered with one another. Then, getting down on his knees, he opened the hatch in the belly of the plane to reveal the howling darkness below. He took hold of the first supply canister in readiness. Both canisters would be dispatched ahead of us. I felt strangely numb, woozy, as if I weren't really there, as if it were all part of a dream. I fixed my unblinking gaze on the lamp. The glow of the red bulb seemed impossibly intense, like the flare of a car's brake light. My pulse quickened and I sensed the muscles in my arms and legs tremble. I felt sick too. I took long, anxious, shaky breaths. My mouth was so dry I couldn't swallow properly. We were at the point of no return. This was it. Next stop enemy territory. If we got caught, torture and a firing squad would be our reward. The red lamp went out and the green one came on. For a few seconds I could still see red before my eyes. I blinked frantically. Both supply canisters had disappeared. Loki stepped forward, sat down and dangled his legs through the hole. 'I hate this bit,' he cursed. 'Jumping's just not natural.'

With a helpful shove from Smithy, Loki vanished. Moments later Freya had disappeared too. Then it was my turn.

'*Action stations! Go, go, go!*' Smithy shouted. He waved

me forward. I sank onto my hands and knees and scrambled over to the edge of the hatch. I slipped my legs out, sat on the edge and glanced up at Smithy. 'Good luck, Finn. Stay safe. *Go, go, go!*'

Chapter Ten
Holland

Filling with air, my chute halted my rapid descent with a jarring snap, as if the hand of God had reached down and grabbed me by the scruff of the neck. With the drone of the Whitley's engines fading in my ears, I peered down. I couldn't see much. Where was the ground? Five hundred feet beneath me? Less? I needed to know. I didn't want two broken legs.

I could just make out the canopies of Loki and Freya's chutes – two giant jellyfish floating down gracefully, silently. They were to my right. I adjusted my descent by tugging on the lines. I felt none of the euphoria and delight I'd experienced during our many practice jumps – there was simply too much going on in my head. Eventually the mantra of our training kicked in – *Feet and knees together, head down, and don't forget your Japanese roll.* I scanned the gloom looking for landmarks. The ground seemed featureless, flat, unhelpful. In the distance a river twisted through the landscape like the slimy trail of a confused, drunken snail. That was both good and bad news. It was good as it provided a reference point. It was bad because if my recollection of the maps was right, we were on the wrong side of it. Our DZ had been carefully chosen: about five miles from the coast and a similar distance from Loki's aunt's farm, it was an area of fields and ditches, with pockets of trees to offer cover. We were off target by quite some way, but as far as I could tell the terrain was similar. I saw Loki's chute collapse and turn in on itself. He'd made it. Freya was next, and then, bracing myself, it was my turn. My boots struck soft, tilled earth, my legs absorbing the shock, and I tumbled into my Japanese roll. Then I was up on my knees and frantically pulling in my chute, all the while fearfully listening out for signs of the enemy. Luckily the night air stayed calm. Clutching my chute to my chest, I ran to where I'd seen the others land.

'Finn, is that you?'

'Yes, Loki. Are you both all right?'

'Fine, but do you realize we're the wrong side of the river?'

'I figured as much, Freya.'

We unfastened the two-way zips, and in seconds we were out of our striptease suits. Then Loki and I retrieved the two supply canisters, lugging them through the dark to the far corner of the field, where Freya remained crouched on her haunches, keeping lookout. There, huddled around our handkerchief-sized silk map lit by a pen torch clutched in an unsteady hand, the three of us held a whispered conference. It was three in the morning, early summer, and dawn would arrive far earlier than we would have liked – sometime between half four and five. That didn't give us long.

'I reckon we're here,' said Loki, pointing to a place on

the map that was a good mile from where we'd intended to land.

'Agreed.' Freya nodded. 'Let's bury our supplies here and retrieve them another time. We'll travel light and make for that bridge.'

'What if it's guarded?'

'Then we'll have to get our feet wet, Finn.'

It took us twenty minutes to dig holes large enough to conceal the canisters, choosing a spot amid some trees and dense bushes. The small shovels we'd been provided with made it hard going even though the soil was sandy and loose. To save time and to avoid burying them separately, we placed our chutes and jumpsuits in one canister, having first removed some essential equipment: three revolvers, silencers and spare ammo. These were easy to discard in an emergency. We'd also brought Sten guns, grenades and many other items, but for now these could remain hidden. I grabbed a waterproof rucksack into which we put Freya's small but heavy suitcase transmitter as it had to be kept dry when crossing the river.

We set off across the flat fields, guided by our compass. It took forty minutes to reach the river, twice as long as we'd anticipated. Our progress was frequently interrupted by fences and what the Dutch call *slootjes* – narrow drainage ditches. Approaching the bridge, we spotted guards with dogs strolling back and forth across its span. We counted two but there could well be others nearby. Lying flat on our bellies, we surveyed the scene.

'I estimate the river to be twenty yards wide and it

looks slow flowing,' Loki whispered. 'We should be able to cross safely.'

We made for the shelter of some trees close to the bank. 'Here's no good.' Freya pointed. 'See the way the moonlight's playing on the surface? It's too bright. They'll spot any disturbance in the water. We should wait for cloud cover or try elsewhere.'

I had an idea. 'We could try under the bridge.' At that moment one of the solders stopped, leaned out over the railings and shone a powerful torch down onto the criss-cross network of girders and support struts and piles. 'Maybe not!'

A detour was needed. Cautiously, in single file, we moved upriver to just beyond the first bend. There, one by one, we slipped down the earthy bank, squelched unsteadily through the mud and waded into the water. There was a patch of dense reeds on the far side and we headed for it. Loki swam with Freya's wireless set but struggled to keep it close to the surface. Dripping, our chests heaving, we eventually crawled out amid the slender reeds and forged a path towards the bank. We emerged on all fours and took a moment to wring the worst of the wet from our jackets and sweaters, then prepared to press on as silently as ghosts, our eyes and ears sharpened to detect even the slightest sound or movement.

A dog barked. It came from the direction of the bridge. It barked again. Another dog joined in. There were shouts too. In German!

We scrambled beneath some bushes. 'Hell, the dogs

have either heard us or picked up a scent. What now? Do we shoot them if they come?' Loki reached for his gun.

'No.' Freya sank back deeper into the mass of prickly branches. 'We sit tight. You two move closer to the edge. Closer to the path.'

'What for? If they reveal where we're hiding, we're done for. We should shoot them if they come near, and then shoot the soldiers too.'

The barking grew louder. It sounded as though the dogs had been unleashed. Soldiers were following. I thought I could hear their boots stomping along on the path.

'No!' Freya replied firmly but calmly. 'Shooting anything will just land us in trouble. My father taught me a better way. Once in the mountains back home a pack of wolves showed too keen an interest in us. Father got us both to pee. So, you two have to pee. Right now, by the edge of the bushes. Go on, do it. There's little time.'

'*Pee!* Are you mad?'

'Your scent will make them pee too, and then they'll be all confused. Too many smells. If we lie still they'll ignore us. It worked before. Hurry up!'

Frantically we did as instructed, but my anxiety meant I couldn't go. Kneeling by the path, I swore under my breath. *Come on. Come on.* With the yelps, snarls and barking drawing ever closer, I willed myself to pee. It was no use. *Hallelujah!* I heard a trickling and splashing beside me. Loki had managed it. 'Get a move on,' Freya whispered, so we scrambled back into the undergrowth and lay perfectly still beside her. Moments later the dogs arrived. They were almost on top of us, scampering, lunging back and forth, twisting and turning, sniffing, scratching, searching us out along the edge of the bushes. They were large and strong. I felt inside my pocket for my revolver, just in case. One dog sank onto her haunches and urinated. Almost immediately the other cocked his leg and pissed against a tree. Seconds later they were rushing around in circles, to and fro, noses to the ground, hoovering up a wonderfully confused jumble of scents. The beam of a powerful torch illuminated them. They stopped and looked up at their master, their tails beating excitedly.

'*Was ist los, Heinrich?*' came a call from someone in the distance.

'*Nichts! Füchse oder Kaninchen. Komm da weg! Komm da weg!*' came a reply far too close for comfort. I realized the soldier thought it was just foxes or rabbits that had drawn the dogs away, and he was calling them back.

We lay still for a good five minutes after the dogs charged out of sight, hearts pounding.

Loki rolled over onto his back. 'Quick thinking, Freya. I didn't believe it would work, but it did.' He let out a sigh of relief that made his lips flutter.

As we pressed on, our fear of setting foot on enemy territory slowly waned and our confidence grew. The land seemed empty, flat and featureless, not a building to be seen. We heard no traffic and saw no lights. It was as if we'd arrived after everyone else had abandoned the place. Our only company was a lively pre-dawn chorus slowly waking from hedgerows and fields, the frantic chirps and twittering rising above our heads as birds took flight from their night-time roosts. As time ticked hurriedly by, my anxiety returned. Once dawn broke we'd stick out like sore thumbs, with few opportunities for cover, and would undoubtedly attract the attention of enemy patrols. There was much to be said for being in a crowded place where you could blend in, becoming just one among a sea of faces.

Back at Mulberry, our briefings on the current situation in Holland painted a picture of relative calm and normality. There weren't many restrictions, especially outside the major towns and cities, and to the uninformed eye it might look as if life was unaffected by the occupation. It could lull you into a false sense of security.

When the first glimmers of daylight appeared in the east, our pace quickened. We needed to reach the farm before Holland awoke to a new summer's day. Mist rose from the fields and hung in the air like layers of lint. Dew on the grass sparkled and glistened like scattered diamonds. Our soaked clothes clung to our skin. Cattle in a nearby field watched us creep by with little more than a passing interest. Reaching the umpteenth hedgerow, we stumbled across a lane. Loki stopped, knelt and pointed, declaring he recognized where we were. 'The farm's not far. Half a mile at the most. We'll be there in time for an early breakfast. Come on.'

'Wait!' Freya grabbed Loki's arm and dragged him

back to his knees. 'I can hear something.'

The slow, gentle clopping of horseshoes on tarmac drifted in the air. We scrambled down into a deep ditch and waited, eyes glued to the road – a road that fifty yards ahead of us faded into a blank grey canvas. I removed my revolver from my pocket, broke it, checked it was fully loaded, snapped it shut again, and reached into my other pocket for the silencer.

'Probably just a farm cart,' said Loki hopefully. 'Out to collect milk or something. Who else would be around at this early hour?'

A large horse pulling an open cart emerged from the mist, moving at a funereal pace. Two hunched figures sat eerily still on top. It was like an apparition struggling to take on earthly form. The cart's axle creaked as it turned, and the rhythm of hoof against road remained solemn, constant, like the drumbeat accompanying a man to the gallows. I had a bad feeling. Something about it wasn't quite right.

Our ditch was filled with stagnant water and it smelled awful, especially once our boots had stirred up the stinking mud in the bottom. Pressing myself up against the side and risking a glance over the top, I realized what it was about the cart that had set me on edge, and I dipped down sharply in a moment of panic. The two men – two dark grey smudges in a world of grey – the grey of uniforms, *the grey of the Wehrmacht*. '*Soldiers!* Keep down,' I whispered, the words catching like sharp fish bones in my throat.

Loki and Freya whipped out their revolvers and,

fumbling about in their pockets, hastily set about attaching silencers. The soldiers would surely see us as they trundled slowly past. Our cover was simply not good enough, given their lofty position. Worse, if we made a run for it, they'd spot us at once. There was nothing for it. We were going to have to shoot them. We had no choice. And their disappearance, their failure to return to barracks, would lead to search parties, to every farmhouse in the area being ransacked, to dozens of arrests. We'd have nowhere to hide. Remaining perfectly still, we waited for the inevitable.

Cowering, we listened to the relentless *clop-clop* of hooves; my grip on the handle of my revolver had tightened so much my hand began to throb. I prayed our weapons hadn't suffered in crossing the river. If we rose from the ditch like jack-in-the-boxes only to find they'd jammed, we'd be dead in seconds. The soldiers probably possessed standard issue MP40 submachine guns. Outgunned, we'd have to maximize what little element of surprise we could garner . . . and make damn sure we didn't miss. There'd be no second chances. Thanks to Smithy we'd been drilled in close-quarter combat. *Instinctive firing*, he called it. Point and shoot. Don't waste precious time taking careful aim. Speed was of the essence; it was the only advantage we possessed. A minute ticked slowly by. Oddly, the enemy didn't sound as if he was getting any nearer. Loki risked sneaking a look. He slumped back down and let out an elongated sigh of relief. 'They turned off. Twenty yards up the road. To the left. Just as well too because there were two more soldiers in the back.' His look of relief turned to one of alarm. 'Hell – that road leads to my aunt's farm.'

'And where else?' Freya asked.

Loki shook his head. 'Nowhere else. Just the farm.'

Chapter Eleven
Early Morning Call

'What do they want there? Why aren't they on motor-cycles or in an army truck? A horse and cart? At this ungodly hour? It simply doesn't make any sense.' Perplexed, Loki scratched his head.

The early hour led me to suspect that their visit wasn't official; rather a bit of moonlighting or an illegal raid on the part of the uniformed thugs. We decided there was nothing for it but to follow the cart, keeping a safe distance.

The outline of buildings emerged like a sketch drawn with the softest grey pencil lead, so strangely vague that I found myself squinting to make it out. The sun was waking and its first rays cut sharply across the horizontal land, causing the mist to glow brightly with a pearl-like lustre in an unnatural and unfamiliar world. The farm-house and outbuildings were arranged in a square, partially enclosing a large cobbled yard. Back at Mulberry, Loki had drawn a plan from memory. There was a large brick barn with a substantial hayloft, a single-storey washhouse, disused pigsty, milking parlour and dairy, stables, and various other smaller outhouses in which tools were kept. Surrounded by a sea of slender fields as flat as pancakes and criss-crossed by ditches and fences, the farm sat alone in an exposed position. Just a few trees bordering the west and northern sides offered some protection from the prevailing winds.

The tarmac road petered out into a heavily rutted track, a ditch and hedge to one side. The cart rattled its way towards the cluster of buildings and stopped outside the farmhouse, which reeked of neglect, areas of plaster having crumbled away to reveal the clay and lime marl beneath. Ornate gables fringed the steeply pitched tiled roof out of which protruded the dormer windows of attic rooms. Remaining hidden, we watched as the two soldiers who'd ridden on the back of the cart clambered down, along with one of the soldiers up front. The fourth, reins in hand, remained slouched where he was. I figured he was in charge because he began calling out, '*Hallo! Frau Pol. Hallo!*' There was no reply from the farmhouse. The other three moved cautiously towards the yard, machine guns poised. Had they come to make arrests?

An upstairs window swung open and a woman's head appeared. 'That's my aunt, Saskia Pol,' Loki whispered.

An extremely large, robust, middle-aged woman with rosy cheeks and a shock of curly brown hair leaned out. '*Oprotten!*' she shouted, and then for good measure she spat at them.

Freya let out a little gasp and raised a hand to cover her mouth. 'I don't believe it. I think she's just told them to piss off!'

The soldier clutching the reins pointed to the barn on the far side of the yard. Shouting in German, he informed her that he'd come to take whatever surplus food they had. Loki's aunt yelled something else in Dutch, briefly withdrew from the window, and then reappeared clutching a bucket. She flung the vile contents out of the window with venom – a mix of rotten food and what I suspected was excrement splattered on the ground a few feet from the cart. The soldier holding the reins didn't even flinch. He merely laughed and, clambering down from the cart, ordered his men to take *everything*.

Freya tapped me on the shoulder and pointed. A young man had emerged from the tall wooden doors of the barn clutching a hay fork. Dressed in worn denim dungarees, he was built like an ox and stood firm, sleeves rolled up, ready to defend his property.

'That's the son, Willem, Finn. He's a big bugger. If he's not careful he'll get himself killed.'

'Shall we intervene?' I readied myself for a full frontal assault.

'Let's wait.' Freya grabbed my sleeve. 'See what happens.'

Spreading out, the three soldiers moved slowly across the yard, carefully avoiding the flies swarming about a steaming dunghill, their weapons trained on the upright, statuesque figure of Willem. Barring their way into the barn, he refused to yield. I could see his eyes flash at each brute in turn while nervously adjusting his grip on the hay fork. This was serious. If he made the wrong move, if he failed to submit, he'd be a dead man.

The fourth soldier, the one in charge, called out coarsely, '*Mach Platz, Willem Pol. Schnell!*'

He was ordering the young man to step aside. Bad though the situation already was, the Nazi thug's words added to my trepidation; he knew their names, and that meant they'd had dealings before, they had *history*, and that didn't bode well for the future. What use was a remote farm for hiding out in if the Germans dropped by and were on first-name terms with the owners?

Geese appeared, a dozen of them, and waddled in single file across the yard, right between the young man and the enemy. It was a bizarre sight and halted the soldiers' advance. The fourth soldier yelled something in German but I didn't catch it, although its meaning was soon made plain enough. One of the soldiers steadied his machine gun at waist height and opened fire in a wide arc. The loud burst was met by squawks, a flurry of feathers and much blood. A dozen geese lay slaughtered. Snarling with anger, Willem Pol took a step forward, raising his pitchfork, intent on revenge, but at the last moment he hesitated. I think he suddenly understood the pointlessness of resisting. This wasn't the right time or place. His shoulders sagged in resignation and he flung down the fork. A soldier strode up to him and belted him with the butt of his gun. Willem took the blow full on the side of his face: blood spurted from his mouth as he reeled. For a second I thought he'd remain on his feet, but as he swayed forward he sank to his knees. A second blow had him flat on the ground. Freya turned away and let out a small cry of disgust. There followed a vicious kicking frenzy accompanied by laughter and cruel name-calling. Loki had seen enough.

'He's family, Finn. I can't just remain here and watch. We've got to act.'

'No.' Freya restrained him. 'They'll spot us. It's too far. We've no element of surprise and they outgun us. It would be suicide.'

'I hate to say it but she's right,' I found myself agreeing. I was torn in two. To do nothing seemed cowardly. I began to waver, especially when I saw the look on Loki's face. It was the sort of look that said, *What if it was you or me getting the thumping?* And yet there was a bigger picture – our mission. Willem's cries reached us. I lowered my head and pressed it hard against the earth. I prayed that his drubbing would end soon; that he'd still be alive.

By the time the soldiers were finished Willem lay curled in a foetal position, his face bloodied and bruised by the steel caps of the Nazi jackboots. The barn was emptied of sacks of grain and various produce, all being piled high on the back of the cart along with the slaughtered geese. There was no sign of Saskia Pol. She remained in the farmhouse. The soldier on the cart called out to her again, his tone sharp, uncompromising, full of hate. He said that she should consider herself lucky that they'd only come to take her food, and that next time they might arrest them and take them both away too. Gruffly he bellowed orders for his men to climb back onto the cart. Crawling into the cover of some birch trees, we watched the cart trundle past, turn onto the road and *clop-clop* towards its next victims. I wondered how long it would be before they came back for more: next week, next month, after the summer harvest? We'd have to be watchful *and* prepared.

Saskia Pol emerged from hiding, ran and knelt beside Willem. She cradled his bloodied head as we arrived on the scene. 'Aunt, it's me, Loki. We saw what happened,' Loki called out in our native Norwegian.

She looked up, her mouth opened and she let out a gull-like cry before fainting.

We half dragged and half carried an unconscious Willem into the farmhouse and laid him in the recovery position on the flagstone floor. Freya hunted out some cloths and a ceramic bowl, into which she poured water from a jug. Moistening the cloths, she began wiping the blood from Willem's face.

Saskia soon came round but grew distraught the moment reality kicked in. We sat her down and Loki gave her a hug and quickly explained who Freya and I were and that we'd come to stay for a while, to help on the farm, that it was best that she didn't ask questions, and that she just had to trust him.

She began to shake her head violently. 'No. You can't stay here. It's too dangerous.'

Willem groaned. Beneath the blood his left eye had already swollen to the point where he couldn't open it, and a deep gash on his neck refused to stop haemorrhaging. Freya pressed a cloth against it and applied pressure. He tried to speak but all he managed to do was groan. 'We'll have to see whether anything is broken,' Freya declared. 'How far away is the nearest doctor?'

'Scheveningen,' Saskia Pol replied. 'But we can't afford treatment.'

There was plenty of cash in our supply containers. We'd been told that in the field it was often necessary to bribe reluctant locals, as not everyone we encountered would be willing to back up their fine words about the fight for freedom with personal sacrifices – not when a thriving black market ensured that a handsome profit was to be had elsewhere. Loki explained that money would not prove a problem. Willem struggled to speak. '*Dokter van Alblas halen, moeder. Dokter van Alblas.*'

I think he was insisting she fetch a Dr van Alblas, but Saskia balked at his suggestion. Only when Willem drifted out of consciousness did she capitulate.

'All right. Dr van Alblas it is.' She looked up at the ceiling and cursed. 'They took our horses last time they came. So our cart's useless. And we haven't a telephone. There's one at the Kramers' farm. I'll have to cycle there. Across the fields. I just hope those bastards haven't paid her a visit too.'

'I suspected they'd been here before,' I said. 'That soldier on the cart knew your name.'

She nodded. 'Food's still scarce. It was a hard winter. Hardest in years. The soldiers come and take what they want, whenever they like, and they do not care about us. We are like vermin to them, to be beaten, kicked aside, made to disappear should we prove troublesome. But they have it in for Willem, especially that big man. Grüber's his name. Sets out to make Willem's life hell. Like I said, you can't stay here. I'm sorry.'

I realized it had been a while since she'd spoken Norwegian and her Dutch accent made our language sound odd. She had to concentrate to understand us too. Her ear needed re-tuning, and now and then she paused to search for the right words. She got up and reached for a shawl before going outside to fetch her bicycle. At the door she paused, turned and frowned. 'Why are you all soaked to the skin?'

'We'll talk later,' said Loki firmly. 'Go and make that call. We'll get Willem as comfortable as we can and dry ourselves off. Where's Uncle Gottfried?'

'They seized him and a hundred others three months ago. Rounded them up in the street. Completely at random. They've taken him to Germany. To work in their factories as slave labour.' Suppressing her emotions, she added, 'What's happened to the world?'

'Infected by evil.' Loki gritted his teeth and added, 'And we're part of the cure!'

Chapter Twelve
The Paltrok

We watched Saskia Pol cycle off across the fields, her bike's loose chain slipping, the rusting frame unsteady under her immense weight and poor balance.

I began pacing the room, rubbing the back of my neck anxiously. Things weren't exactly going to plan. 'She's right, you know, Loki. Maybe it *is* too dangerous to stay here.'

'It's just her initial shock, Finn. I'll talk her round, don't you worry.'

'Maybe we should seek out Marieke's contact, Otto, and get him to find us somewhere else.'

'No, Finn. It'll be all right, I tell you.'

Freya intervened. 'Let's not be hasty. We'll wait until she gets back, talk it over, and then decide.'

Willem came to again; he struck me as being more lucid this time round. He recognized Loki and studied Freya and me through his one functioning eye. His first question was the obvious one – what were we doing there? He quickly realized we were going to give nothing away and so gave up, save to impress upon us that Dr Wiardi van Alblas was a *goed Hollander*. 'Wiardi is a leader with the Resistance. You can trust him, Loki. That's why I asked for him.' I was relieved to hear that his Norwegian was fluent.

'Your mother didn't seem too keen.'

'They don't see eye to eye, Loki. My mother refuses to have anything to do with his group. Says I'm crazy to get involved. That I'll end up getting killed.' He managed a pained laugh. 'I also reckon she's worried that if I get into trouble they'll make life even worse for Father, wherever he is.'

'She might be right,' I said.

When Saskia returned she brewed us some *ersatz* coffee made from acorns and a little roasted, ground chicory root. Real coffee was a scarce luxury few could afford. Her chubby hands were still shaking as she reached for some cups. Meanwhile we kept a close eye on a groggy Willem until the sound of an engine drew us all to the window. A large black car was negotiating the potholed track. Dr Wiardi van Alblas had arrived. Catching a glimpse of the tall, wiry, moustached van Alblas as he clambered out from behind the steering wheel, I thought it best to make ourselves scarce, despite what Willem had said. We headed for the barn. In our briefing sessions back at Mulberry House no mention had been made of van Alblas in connection with the local Resistance. Therefore to trust him without question would be to rely entirely on Willem's opinion of the doctor. It was an unacceptable risk.

An hour later the doctor returned to his car. He paused and peered across at the barn. Leaving his leather bag on the passenger seat, he wandered across the yard.

'Hell, he's coming this way,' I said nervously. 'Willem must've let something slip.'

Alarmed, Loki drew his revolver and pressed himself against the wall behind the large barn doors. 'Best not take any chances, Finn.'

Freya and I moved to one side and hid behind some straw bales.

Van Alblas appeared at the entrance. '*Hallo?*' He stepped inside and raised his hands as if in surrender. '*Hallo?*'

Freya moved out into the open. Loki swung the door shut. We had the doctor surrounded. He touched the peak of his hat, as if wishing us a good day. Shafts of sunlight from cracks in the timber walls caught his face and I noticed his expression was relaxed. 'Willem mentioned visitors,' he said in English. 'I am—'

'We know who you are,' Loki interrupted. 'Are you armed?'

The doctor shook his head.

'Finn, give him the once over. I'll cover you.'

I did so and found the doctor was indeed unarmed. I stepped backwards and the doctor lowered his hands.

'Who sent you?' he began, his eyes flashing back and forth between Freya and me. 'Only, we weren't expecting you.'

'We? Who's *we*?' Loki moved forward and pressed the barrel of his revolver into the doctor's back.

The doctor remained calm. 'We call ourselves the *Begrafenisondernemers* – the Undertakers.'

'*What?* Are you trying to be funny?' Loki cocked his revolver.

Van Alblas suddenly grew nervous, as if he'd made a

big miscalculation. 'I'm on your side,' he pleaded, and then suffered a fit of coughing. 'From what Willem said, I . . . I . . . I assumed you'd been sent from England to help us.'

'How do we know we can trust you? We only have Willem's word,' Loki replied bluntly.

The doctor appeared at a loss. He opened his mouth as if about to say something but stopped, instead offering a shrug. Loki's question was a good one but I realized it was virtually impossible for van Alblas to provide a satisfactory answer. Words alone weren't enough, especially from the lips of a stranger. And I could see van Alblas knew it only too well. Trust was born out of actions, built up over time. And we were preciously short of time. The doctor stood motionless, waiting for us to decide.

Freya was first to make up her mind. 'Put the gun down, Loki,' she said, bringing the awkward moment to an end. She stepped towards van Alblas and held out a hand. He reached out and shook it. 'I guess we have little choice other than to trust you. Willem's word will have to do.'

The doctor visibly relaxed. 'Thank you. I understand you witnessed Willem's beating this morning. The Germans didn't catch sight of you, did they?'

'No,' I replied.

'Good. It's not the first time they've come here and I very much doubt it'll be the last. Each time they come they take more and more food. Usually they just shove Willem about a bit, threaten him – Saskia as well. This time was different. Willem made a big mistake trying to stand up to them. In future he must make himself scarce. Leave them to loot the place. Otherwise he'll end up with a bullet in his back.'

'Do you think they'll return soon?' I asked.

'Who knows?' The doctor sighed. 'Probably not until the harvest's in.'

'Well, I hope you're right,' said Freya. 'Please understand we can't say anything about why we're here. At least, not for now. But it would be good if we were able to contact you should the need arise.'

Loki still refused to lower his gun. Freya went over to him and took his arm. 'Think about it, Loki. If he was a Nazi collaborator or informant he would simply have driven off and raised the alarm.'

Eventually Loki reluctantly pointed his revolver to the ground.

Van Alblas smiled with relief. 'Quite so.' Suffering a further fit of coughing, he whipped a handkerchief from his pocket and held it to his mouth.

'Are you all right?' Freya asked. 'You look pretty sick.'

Van Alblas nodded. 'I'll be fine. I am easy enough to find. My house is located in Scheveningen. Willem knows the address. Best avoid mornings as I hold a surgery then. Too many people about. It's a pity you can't confide in me about why you're here. I might be able to assist you.'

Over van Alblas's shoulder, Loki shook his head at us. I agreed that was going a step too far.

The doctor looked disappointed. 'Unwise in my

view, but so be it. Perhaps I can at least offer you some advice. If you have to venture into town, avoid the main roads. Cut across the fields, follow the canal and take the coast road. We're not sure why but the Germans are on alert, so you need to be extremely careful. It's dangerous out there, day and night. Whatever you do, make sure your papers are in order and don't go wandering about armed unless you absolutely have to. There are frequent stop and searches.'

'Thank you,' said Freya.

Van Alblas smiled warmly at each of us and then turned to go. 'Oh, one final piece of advice. Take my word for it – Willem can be trusted. He's been of great help to my group. So, if you do need assistance or to confide in someone, then Willem's a safe bet. He's not lacking in courage and can be relied upon to keep his mouth shut. However, it is best if you tell Saskia Pol nothing. Understand? Nothing.'

'What do you mean?' Loki responded, clearly angered by what the doctor was implying.

Van Alblas thought carefully for a moment. 'Don't get me wrong, young man. I'm not saying Saskia would betray you willingly. It's more straightforward than that. She's scared of what might happen to Gottfried, her husband, should she get caught up in any trouble. Even my coming here today has made her fearful – in case I'm being followed by the Gestapo or the Abwehr.' The doctor's expression darkened and he shook his head. 'I fear Gottfried's fate is sealed. Tell her nothing. It's for the best. Now I'll bid you good day.' Coughing alarmingly, he hurried back to his car, jumped in and drove off.

Loki exploded. 'What did he mean by all that? Making out my aunt can't be trusted. She'd never say a word to anyone.'

Freya put her arm round him. 'I know. But it does no harm to heed his warning. Just in case. Until we make up our own minds.'

Re-entering the farmhouse, we found Willem lying on a sofa, covered with blankets. His wounds had been dressed, the gashes stitched, and Saskia said that she had to keep a close watch on him for the next few days. Van Alblas suspected a detached retina, so Willem was to keep as still as a corpse and lie in the dark. Any sudden movement might lead to blindness.

Events finally caught up with Saskia and she sank onto a stool in the kitchen and wept. 'What am I to do?' she wailed. 'Willem's all I have. How am I going to keep the farm going?'

Loki seized the moment. 'We can help – work on the farm to earn our keep. All you need to do, Auntie, is show us how. We'll make sure the cows get milked and the chickens fed. We're your knights in shining armour arriving to save the day.'

She wiped her eyes, blew her nose and took Loki's hand. 'I know you mean well but the situation here is difficult. The Germans have stepped up their searches for *onderduikers*.'

'Who or what are *onderduikers*?' I asked.

'People in hiding. All over Holland men, women and

children fearing arrest, deportation or other trouble are seeking refuge.'

'Like the Jews?' Freya added.

She nodded. 'And there are others – people who've dared to speak out or cause trouble. If the Germans find you, they'll arrest you and transport you to the camps. Willem and me too. We'd never survive that. I hear such awful things about—'

Loki shook his head. 'Not us, Auntie. They won't think we're *onderduikers*.' He showed her our forged papers, which she scrutinized with the aid of spectacles while muttering and making strange sucking noises through her teeth. He also explained our cover story: that we'd been stranded after Norway was invaded.

'These look real. I mean, I can't tell that they're forged,' she admitted. Handing them back, she nevertheless remained stubbornly unconvinced. 'I'm sorry but I can't help you.'

'It won't be for long, Auntie. Just until it's time for us to act, and then we'll be gone for good. A few weeks at the most.'

Saskia held her hankie over her nose and mouth and shook her head. I could see she was determined to deny us refuge, while Loki was equally dogged in his insistence that we had to stay. Their conversation led nowhere. Eventually frustration got the better of me. 'We're wasting our time discussing it,' I said coldly. 'Maybe we should find somewhere else.'

'Shut up, Finn. Go outside and get some fresh air. Leave me to talk to my aunt alone.'

'Happy to. Good luck!' I stomped out into the yard and decided to explore the outbuildings properly. I did not think much of Saskia Pol, I decided. In my book you don't turn your own flesh and blood from your doorstep, not when they need your help. Of course there were risks, but my father always said that family came first. And Loki was her family. Climbing a ladder to inspect the hayloft in the barn, I couldn't help being puzzled by something else. Not once since our arrival had Saskia asked why we'd turned up on her doorstep unannounced. Willem and Van Alblas were quick to enquire. It was the obvious question. It was as if she either didn't want to know, didn't care, or simply wanted to be rid of us. She was strangely deaf to Loki's pleas.

'Finn?' Freya had come looking for me. Blowing out her cheeks, she cast her eyes to the heavens. 'What a nightmare! I expect all that trouble with those Nazi thugs has made her especially fearful.'

'Perhaps.' I climbed back down the ladder and brushed off pieces of straw that had clung to my coat. 'We could simply insist. Take the place over,' I said, thinking out loud.

'That's a really bad idea.'

I sat down on the dusty floor. 'Yes, you're right. A rubbish idea. So, should we move on and look for somewhere in town?'

'Might be best.'

'Maybe the doctor could help us find somewhere.'

Whistling cheerfully, hands in pockets, Loki arrived. 'All sorted.'

I gaped at him incredulously. 'What do you mean, all sorted?'

'We can stay. At least for a week or two. Until Willem's better.'

Freya mouthed, *How?*

'What have you told her?' I asked accusingly.

'Not much. That we've come to rescue some airmen, that's all.'

'*That's all!* You idiot – the last thing we need is for others to know our purpose here. And what did van Alblas just say to us? For God's sake, I hope you said nothing about Aardappel or the agent codenamed Falcon?'

'Of course not. I'm not stupid, Finn.' Loki gave me the evil eye for daring to suggest such a thing. 'She won't breathe a word about us being here. After all, if the enemy found out, she'd be in hot water too.'

Freya was confused. 'And *that* was enough to persuade your aunt?'

'Not entirely,' he confessed. 'There are loads of jobs on the farm that need doing. Without Gottfried she relies on Willem and, well, given the state he's in he's not going to be of much use around here for a while. Basically, like it or not, she needs us. After some persuading she realized she hasn't got an alternative. Anyway, I don't see any harm in working for our keep. I think it's a fair deal.'

'I'm not so sure,' Freya said hesitantly. 'We were thinking that maybe we ought to find somewhere else.'

'No need.' Loki looked at us questioningly. 'What's the problem?'

'It's like this,' I said bluntly. 'If I was in her position and one of my family arrived on my doorstep, I'd welcome them in and offer all the help I could give. And I'd not ask for anything in return.' I made no attempt to hide the fact that in my book Saskia Pol was verging on the loathsome.

'Yeah, well, she's been through a lot. I figured one good turn deserves another. Anyway, she said she'd walk us round the farm. Show us what needs to be done. Come on, you two. Cheer up. Everything's fine.'

The farm extended to about a hundred and fifty acres, divided into lush strips of pasture, interspersed with the occasional narrow field of corn that swayed in the breeze like a sea of molten gold. Another area was set aside for root vegetables. Overwhelmingly the vista was one of far-reaching views across land so flat that it was as if a giant spirit level had been used to iron out even the slightest bump. The sky seemed unbelievably big and overwhelming in comparison. The farm was located on the edge of what the locals called the *Groene Hart*, the 'green heart' − a large, sparsely populated farming area with a man-made landscape of elongated fields, some little more than tiny parcels of land, surrounded by waterways, peat lakes and marshland.

Saskia led us round, listing the hundred and one tasks that needed doing: repairs to fences, clearing of waterways clogged by weed, and the digging of ditches that had partially collapsed. Loki responded to each pointing of her finger by declaring that the task would be no problem, that we'd make a start the very next morning. He was bending over backwards to please her, and if she was at all grateful she didn't let on. She was sour-faced and struck me as burdened by a great weight on her shoulders. As we walked, I realized not all was well on the Pols' farm. Many cattle had been lost over the previous winter due to a lack of feed and sickness, and of the dozen or so that remained, most had scours, their backsides darkened by diarrhoea, magnets to swarms of flies. Saskia barely gave them a glance but grumbled that at least her husband, Gottfried, wasn't around to see them in that pitiful state. It would break his heart to see them suffer like that, she told us.

On the northern edge of the farm lay the Pols' windmill. It dominated the landscape and stood proud, reaching up more than eighty feet, piercing the sky. Fifty yards from it we stopped to admire its splendour. I'd never seen anything quite like it.

'We use windmills for many tasks in Holland,' Saskia explained, hands resting on her ample hips. She sounded just like a schoolteacher taking us on a field trip. 'One thing we're not short of is wind. Of course, some are used to grind corn. There are many such *stander* mills in this area. Others pump water. Ours is bigger, though, but not as tall as the mills that produce dyes, oil and paper.' She lifted a hand to shield her eyes, and then swept away the beads of perspiration on her brow. 'Ours is rather special. It's a *paltrok*. It was built over two hundred years ago. It's a saw mill.'

We took a closer look. The four long sails were

stationary and bare of their cloth covers, revealing a skeleton of square wooden lattices, broken in places. The small windows were so dusty they'd become opaque and reflected the sky like mirrors. The external wooden weatherboarding had once been painted white, but now there were large areas where it was peeling away. Elsewhere, exposed wood had been ravaged by the seasons and bleached by the sun to a mellow silvery grey. The entire mill was mounted on a rectangular wooden floor reaching out a considerable distance to either side of the main structure; although lacking walls, this was protected by a gently pitched roof, forming an extended porch. Saskia explained that this space housed the saws and benches, and the cranes used for lifting the mighty tree trunks arriving by barge on the canal running past the back of the mill. What I found astonishing, however, was that the whole building, including the cutting floor, was mounted on a circular track: when working, the complete structure would turn to face the prevailing wind. Short flights of wooden steps led up to the cutting floor and door to the mill's inner workings; a door on which had been nailed a notice – ACHTUNG! EINTRITT VERBOTEN.

'After the occupation they closed us down,' Saskia informed us bitterly. 'All materials were seized and became the property of the Reich. Most of the timber goes straight to Germany now. Those logs are all we have left.' A shoulder-high stack lay ten yards from the mill.

The cutting floor bore signs of the hard,

sinew-stretching graft undertaken by Gottfried and Willem before the occupation. A piece of oak remained on the cutting bench, the vicious teeth of the saw emerging from its flesh. It must have been there for months. To one side of the cutting floor a few panels of neatly cut wood rested against a beam. They struck me as odd-looking. Saskia saw me staring at them. 'They're for making *doodkisten*. Coffins.'

'Coffins!' A spark flew through my brain. Van Alblas had mentioned his group were called the Undertakers and now I was looking at coffins. There had to be a link.

Saskia went on, 'Gottfried had a contract with one of the funeral parlours in The Hague. It brought in welcome extra cash.' Her tone dripped with irony. 'Pity really, there's been a lot of demand recently! Loki, you said you wanted to see inside.' Reaching into a deep pocket at the front of her ankle-length skirt, she withdrew a massive iron key and inserted it into the lock. It proved difficult to turn, the mechanism in need of a shot of lubricating oil. She grunted and cursed but eventually the lock yielded.

Inside we were confronted by huge shafts and cogged wheels, their teeth worn but sturdy enough to last another two hundred years. Heavy-duty drive belts linked the mechanism to the bench saw outside through gaps in the wall. The place smelled of wood shavings and mildew; it was covered with a thick layer of dust, and a thousand cobwebs decorated the ceiling and every nook and cranny. We got to work examining everything: the wooden walls, the timber planking on the floor, the interesting little spaces between and beneath machinery. We weren't looking at the mill as a marvel of Dutch ingenuity, or a feat of engineering and construction, but rather as a place with infinite possibilities for concealing our supplies and Freya's transmitter.

'Seen enough yet?' an impatient Saskia shouted from outside.

Ignoring her, we climbed creaky curved steps to one of the upper levels, inspecting the bowed tread boards to see if any were loose and could be readily lifted to stow a stash of grenades or explosives. 'Perfect,' Freya whispered when we reached the top floor. She forced open the window and peered out. 'I'll transmit from here. We can drape the aerial out along one of the sails. There are a dozen places for hiding my transmitter too. We'll just have to be careful not to leave traces of our presence. There's so much dust on the floor, we'll leave footprints. When we come back later this evening, we should sweep it. Remember to bring a broom, Finn. And make sure we see where Saskia keeps the key. I don't fancy trying to pick that lock.'

On our way back to the farm Freya questioned Saskia Pol about comings and goings at the farm. If Loki's aunt was to be believed, visitors were rare and mainly comprised her neighbours.

'Can they be trusted?' Freya asked.

'As much as anyone you've known for almost thirty years,' Saskia replied dryly. 'Mrs Kramer's daughter, Laura, comes most often. She and Willem have been going out together for a couple of years. You may spot her on the farm as she often takes a short cut on her bicycle. She wears a blue headscarf, rain or shine. I'll discuss with Willem what we should say to her about your sudden arrival.'

Dropping back, I let the others wander on. I stopped and took in the panorama, the unrelenting flatness. I could just make out another farmhouse in the distance – probably the Kramers' – and realized that when working out in the fields we'd be visible from the road. We'd have to be careful.

As night fell, Saskia retired to bed, climbing up the narrow stairs a little unsteadily and with the smell of gin on her breath. Maybe that was why Dr van Alblas thought it best we tell Saskia as little as possible – alcohol had a nasty habit of loosening tongues. We removed the heavy iron key from a drawer, seized our heavy suitcase and a broom, slipped out the back way, and headed for the mill.

With a pen torch wedged between my teeth, I set about sweeping the floor in the millhouse while Loki leaned out of the upstairs window and draped the long aerial over one of the barren sails. Freya readied herself, opening the suitcase on the floor, hooking up the battery, headphones and Morse key, and then checked that the set was operating properly and hadn't been damaged during the parachute drop.

Our wireless schedule, or sked, had been agreed with the brigadier before we left: to report in within forty-eight hours of arriving and then be ready to receive incoming traffic between eleven o'clock and midnight each evening. Any messages we sent were to be kept brief and were best avoided unless essential. Our initial message would be especially short – a single word. GOLD would indicate we'd arrived safely. It would take just a minute to transmit, even with several repetitions. Any German detector vans in the vicinity would have no chance of pinning down our location in such a short time. We were ready and it was time. Freya donned her headphones, switched to transmit and began tapping by torchlight.

MESSAGE FROM KOOL STOP GOLD STOP REPEAT GOLD STOP END

She reached forward and flicked the switch from transmit to receive. Her earphones came alive with a flurry of dahs and dits. Hurriedly she scribbled the letters down. Within seconds of HQ signing off, she had completed the decoding based on a poem she'd learned by heart.

SPLENDID NEWS KOOL STOP NOT HEARD FROM AARDAPPEL STOP CHECK OUT MARGOS ASAP THEN SIT TIGHT STOP END

That night I lay in an unfamiliar bed in a small attic room gazing at the night sky through a dormer window I'd thrown wide open to let in some cool air. The Pols' farmhouse was as warm as an oven and oppressively claustrophobic – the rooms were small and the Pols lived amid tons of clutter. Blue and white Delft china filled the kitchen, and the parlour shelves were jammed with tatty old books. My attic room, reached via an extremely steep and narrow enclosed staircase, contained a single bed surrounded by boxes of broken toys, old newspapers neatly bundled and tied with string, and battered suitcases with bust handles and catches. Barely an inch of the frayed rug covering the floor could be seen. Being in the eaves also meant there was hardly room to stand up. Worst of all, there was a hidden danger. If the house was raided I'd have little chance of escape. I made a mental note to hunt out a length of rope, one long enough to tie to the bed, dangle through the window, and use to climb down the outside wall.

Although I was exhausted, my sore eyes and heavy lids refused to settle. I gazed up at the rafters. In truth I was worried. If Grüber and his men decided on another round of bear-baiting for their sick amusement, something would have to be done. I pictured dealing with them permanently.

My thoughts turned to my family and the old life back home in Norway. My longing made me restless. I tossed and turned beneath my coarse blanket. Homesickness was like a bellyache: you could feel it coming on, you knew you'd have to ride out the pain for an hour or two, and then it would pass. I'd grown used to it. I'd even tried to put a positive spin on it. The mountains and fjords where I'd grown up always made me feel thankful to be alive. The air was as fresh and clear as if it had just been made. It was good to recall such wonders in these dark times. Holland wasn't like Norway at all. It was flat, dull, uninspiring. *And* my cramped room stank of mothballs. *Get a grip, Finn*, I told myself. *This isn't any ordinary mission you're on. This one's special. This one's personal.* I willed myself to sleep. I needed to rest. In the morning we were heading into town. It was time to do a little reconnaissance, and to look the enemy in the eye.

Chapter Thirteen
Scheveningen

Up at the crack of dawn, Saskia shooed the cows into the milking parlour and proceeded to demonstrate to us how to milk them by hand. We all took turns and soon got the hang of how to squeeze the teats and direct the stream of warm milk into the pail. Loki and I then spent an hour making repairs to a wooden gate before we decided we'd done enough hard labour for one day. At ten o'clock, refreshed by cool water drawn from the Pols' well, we were joined by Freya. We removed three bicycles from the barn and set off for town. Mindful of van Alblas's advice, we headed out across the fields, making for the coast. Our bikes rattled and squeaked, and warm sunshine bathed our faces as we bumped along tracks and embankments, avoiding the roads. I had the feeling the day would turn out to be another scorcher. The heat had been building across Europe for weeks, the air growing thick, heavy and humid, the horizon shrouded in a haze of moisture. It would soon break with storms. You could almost sense them coming. Reaching the coast road, we turned left.

In this part of Holland the North Sea rolled in onto sandy beaches, the land behind protected by a broad area of dunes. We'd studied the maps back at Mulberry, and the vista was much as we expected. What we hadn't anticipated were so many families out picnicking – mothers and babies lying beneath umbrellas, others in swimwear stretched out on towels, their bicycles dumped beside them. They were like petals scattered on a vast golden cloth. Cycling past, the wind in our faces and sand catching in our hair, we found it unreal. I wanted to shout out, *Hey, don't you know there's a bloody war on?* but I couldn't find the right Dutch for it.

Swimming was *verboten* but I couldn't see any soldiers patrolling the shoreline. I presumed the threat of mines and barbed wire proved sufficient deterrent. After a mile or so we stopped and filled our lungs with fresh salty air, sharing in this unexpected display of normality. I wiped beads of perspiration from my brow. Loki had packed a small rucksack with some bottles of water and we each took a refreshing swig. 'You know, it might be better to arrange the pick-up here rather than in Scheveningen,' he declared, shielding his eyes. 'There are hardly any buildings and the road is as straight as an arrow. We'd see and hear the enemy coming. It would be easy to get the airmen onto the beach. And we could clear a path through any defences.'

Straddling her bike, Freya leaned across, tapped him on the shoulder and pointed. On the other side of the road, hidden amid further dunes tinged green by clumps of spiky marram and couch grasses, prickly buckthorn and sea holly, lay pillboxes and gun emplacements every fifty yards or so. Most were extremely well camouflaged. If you looked hard enough, though, you could just make out the grey of helmets and barrels of machine guns.

We hurried on. The road led us into Scheveningen. Cycling along the boulevard next to the beach, we caught sight of the pier jutting out into the sea. It was made entirely of wood and had a round building at the end of it. It looked deserted. We slowed as we approached the awesome splendour of the Palace Hotel and adjacent Kurhaus. Barriers and barbed wire forced us off the boulevard and away from the beach. We stopped opposite the front of the Kurhaus on a sweeping, curved section of road from which other main thoroughfares radiated like the spokes of a wheel. Gazing back towards the Palace Hotel, I whistled under my breath.

Its name was apt. The hotel did indeed look like a place fit for kings. It was huge. Its imposing stone façade, along with that of the Kurhaus, dominated the whole seafront and oozed the kind of power and permanence the Nazis liked. No wonder they'd commandeered the hotel. It probably reminded them of the Reichstag in Berlin. Swastikas hung from flagpoles above the main entrance. Soldiers were everywhere. The area buzzed with the business of occupation. 'So, this is the regional HQ of the Nazis' Coastal Command, is it? Impressive,' I commented.

'It's more than impressive, Finn. And that area of beach behind the hotel is supposedly our way home.' He gulped. 'One thing's for sure: this ain't going to be easy. Maybe we should try to blow the whole place up first.'

Freya laughed. 'Trust you, Loki, to come up with that crazy idea. Let's get to work.'

Our training kicked in and we set about memorizing the positions of guard huts and barriers; we noticed that access routes to the beach were limited; that there were machine-gun positions on the roof of the Palace Hotel amid various tall aerial masts; that any number of buildings on the roads opposite the hotel and Kurhaus afforded an excellent panoramic view from their upstairs windows; that one or two of them looked like residential apartments that were unoccupied. They had TE HUUR signs in the windows – 'for rent'.

'We should look into renting one of those,' I said, committing the telephone numbers to memory. 'If we bring the airmen here it's just a short walk to the rendezvous on the beach.'

We drank in the scene, observing the many and varied other hotels and guest houses in the immediate vicinity, the nearby station, the cafés, the general bustle of the place. The road directly opposite the Kurhaus was broad and struck inland as straight as an arrow. It was signposted to The Hague. It was busy too, with trams, cars, cyclists and soldiers on horseback. The area around us felt very open – possibly too open for a group of escapees. There was little useful cover. A detailed mental picture of the place was forming, something that could prove vital during our planned escape.

'That's Dr van Alblas's car, isn't it?' Freya suddenly announced. She'd cast her eyes back in the direction we'd come from. A large black car resembling the one we'd observed at the farm was parked up some distance away.

'Could be,' I said. 'He did say he was based here in town.'

'I think he's been following us,' Freya added.

'Don't be daft. Your imagination's running riot, that's all.' Loki looked at me and then cast his eyes to the heavens. 'Want to check it out?'

Freya shook her head.

'Thank God for that.' Loki grinned. 'I reckon we've seen enough for now. Let's go and locate Margo's.'

We cycled deeper into town, away from the beach and into streets where life appeared to be going on much as usual. The address we'd memorized – number twenty-four Wagenaar Straat – was wedged tightly between a *groenteboer* and a *bakkerij*. A long, sweaty, irritable queue stretched out from the door of the bakery and snaked along the pavement. Other shoppers sifted through the rather pathetic assortment of vegetables left in boxes outside the greengrocer. We ground to a halt on the opposite side of the street. The *bloemenwinkel* called Margo's was tiny, easily missed if it hadn't been for the colourful bunches of blooms in buckets of water in the recessed doorway. In the window I noticed various small notices and advertisements taped to the glass. I scanned them from a distance.

'Hell!' Alarmed, I swung across the road to take a closer look. I'd spotted a small red card. I felt the blood drain from my face. It was in Dutch but I could understand the gist: *Missing dog – answers to the name of Puk*. Loki and Freya appeared beside me. 'Aardappel's in trouble!'

We kicked off, pedalled hard for fifty yards along the street and dipped into a deserted alleyway. Freya hurriedly unbuttoned the left cuff of her blouse, twisted it inside out and used her nails to grip the tiny corner of silk. She tugged at it to reveal the handkerchief-sized map. 'It's called the Rembrandt,' I said breathlessly. 'That's where any messages will have been left for us to collect.'

'Yes. Yes. Just give me a second, Finn. I know where it is. I just want to check that I've memorized the route correctly.' She held the silk map close to her face and studied the tiny print. 'Right, there's the Rembrandt and we're here.' She pressed a thumb against our location. 'OK, as we agreed back at Mulberry House, the best route is definitely to head into the centre of The Hague to get our bearings and then it should be easy to locate.' She traced the route with the tip of a finger.

'Agreed.'

Our training had taught us the importance of memorizing a route, the street names and major land-marks. The one thing agents needed to avoid was repeated stops to inspect maps or study road signs. It was a real give-away. We had to move about with confidence, like people who'd lived here all our lives. But Freya was right to pause a second in our moment of panic. Learning a route from a map is one thing, but seeing it for real can often disorientate you. Things can suddenly seem different, the change in scale from map to reality can catch you out, and if you're careless, one wrong turn can get you instantly lost.

The road to The Hague led us out of Scheveningen and through parkland. We cycled as quickly as we dared. Freya, ever watchful, noted that the black car she'd spotted earlier still seemed to be following us, albeit at a distance. Her observation did nothing to soothe our frayed nerves. Like Loki, I doubted it was Dr van Alblas behind the steering wheel. After all, why would he be tailing us? I couldn't make out the occupants of the vehicle as the sun's reflection from the windscreen was blinding. If the car *was* tracking our movements, in all likelihood it was the enemy – intelligence officers from the Abwehr or Gestapo. I reckoned we'd been pretty careful not to look suspicious, and I couldn't think of anything we'd done to draw attention to ourselves.

It wasn't long before the grand ornate palaces and mansions of The Hague towered about us majestically. Moving through busy traffic, we slowed when we caught sight of a large pond. It was the Hofvijver, and a nearby gateway led into the Binnenhof, a vast courtyard which housed the old chapel-like building known as the Ridderzaal. We knew our exact location and headed off.

Away from the imposing grandeur of the town's centre the streets took on a more faded splendour, all shabby browns and dusty greys. The traffic thinned and it seemed as though cyclists ruled the streets and pavements. I'd never seen so many in one place. They paid scant regard to the rules of the road. Just as when a blazing sun suddenly gets masked by cloud, the light seemed to fade and the hairs on my arms rose like the fur of a cat sensing danger. Maybe it was the faces of people here that made me feel uneasy, or the way the tall buildings seemed to be leaning over us threateningly. Shops had been boarded up, ACHTUNG JUDEN! scrawled in thick paint across their windows and doors. There were other signs too – JOODSCHE WIJK and JUDEN VIERTEL – reminding everyone that this was a Jewish district. It was not a good place to be. In this part of town people walked the pavements with their heads down, eyes averted, scurrying like animals who avoided staying out in the open a second longer than was absolutely necessary – especially those with the yellow Stars of David stitched to their coats. You could almost smell and taste the fear.

We'd seen such sights in Norway too. It was no secret that the Nazis despised the Jews. They set about exerting their will over them like a chronic, creeping, debilitating sickness. One by one, week by week, month by month, decrees tightened the screw of oppression: Jews can no longer hold public office; Jews are forbidden to walk in the parks; Jews cannot go to the cinema, or to concerts, or to public school, or swim in public baths, or use the trams, or shop anywhere other than Jewish shops, and must be off the streets by eight o'clock, *or else*!

Swinging round a corner, I caught sight of a sign that said we'd entered Nieuwe Siegelstraat, the street where Marieke's contact 'Otto' resided. I kept an eye out for number seventeen and spotted it opposite a funeral parlour and wedged between a hardware shop and a second-hand furniture store. The tailor's shop was called Brueghels, the two windows on either side of the central door displaying mannequins clad in very expensive-looking clothes – the sort aristocrats might wear to dinner parties at one of the palaces or mansions: long dark jackets with tails, starched shirts and top hats.

Freya had spotted it too. 'Want to stop and check it out?' she asked hesitantly.

'Unwise,' I replied, and she looked relieved. 'At least we know where it is.'

Half a mile further on we entered the street in which the café-bar Rembrandt was situated. The pavements were broad, the houses tall and narrow with large windows, and some bore decorative cornices while others boasted ornate gables shaped like bells or shells. Loki saw it first. 'There it is. Eyes left. The place with the tables and chairs outside.'

Two German motorcycles suddenly appeared from a side street. They were followed by an open-top Mercedes SS staff car and a truck carrying soldiers. The motorcycles swerved across our path and stopped, blocking the road. Braking hard, I almost slid into the back of Loki's bike but just managed to avoid him. Freya wasn't so lucky. She clipped my rear wheel, cartwheeled over her handlebars and ended up on her back in the middle of the road, the bicycle clattering down on top of her. She cried out in pain. Loki dumped his bike with its wheels still spinning in the air, and hurried to her aid, helping her to her feet. I remained where I was, straddling my bike, inches in front of one of the motor-cyclists, inches from the face of the enemy, so close I could almost smell his breath.

Beneath his grey helmet the rider wore goggles. Even so, I could still see his cold grey eyes gazing at me, or rather *through* me. It was as if I wasn't there, didn't exist. His helmet's chin strap framed a face that was square and utterly expressionless. Ever so slowly I backed away, turned and made for a rubbish-filled alley to one side of the Rembrandt. Dismounting, I leaned my bike against the wall and shrank back into the shadows.

The Mercedes and truck had drawn to a halt behind the motorcycles. The car's driver hurriedly clambered out and rushed to open the rear door, snapping to attention and saluting. A senior SS officer climbed out. He was probably in his early forties, immaculately turned out, his uniform pressed, the sun catching the polished buttons and glinting off the edges of the Iron Cross pinned to his tunic. Looking up towards the sun, he yawned and stretched, placing his hands against the base of his spine, and then glanced around as if looking for something. Then he glared at Loki so coldly I felt myself turn to ice. What was happening? Why were they here?

Swift movement caught my eye. A young woman sped past, dragging a child behind her. Everyone was scattering in a growing panic, many dipping inside the nearest shop or open door. Loki, meanwhile, was frantically trying to replace Freya's oily bike chain, which had slipped off when she fell. Looking dazed, Freya sat on the kerb. In seconds the whole street had emptied apart from us and the enemy.

The SS officer spent a moment peering up and down

the street, at the upstairs windows of the tall, narrow buildings, and at various shop signs, his eyes eventually returning to the Rembrandt. The handful of pavement tables outside its dusty, nicotine-stained windows lay deserted where seconds before many had been occupied. Half-finished drinks stood abandoned. The pages of an open newspaper fluttered in the light breeze. One chair lay on its back, another on its side. The officer seemed satisfied: his thin lips broadened into the faintest of smiles. He barked the order for his men to climb out of their truck. Obediently they formed two orderly rows.

Loki managed to fix the chain and help Freya back onto her saddle. They moved closer to me. 'Let's head off slowly,' he whispered. 'I don't think it's us they're interested in.'

I had a nasty suspicion that the Rembrandt was the target of the raid. This was a disaster. The message from Aardappel lay somewhere inside. Maybe Marieke was there, hiding out, waiting for us. Loki began cycling away. He'd gone barely ten yards when the officer bellowed at him in German, '*Halt!* Where do you think you're going?'

As Loki squealed to a stop, my legs turned to jelly. He had no option but to comply.

'You will wait until I give you permission to go,' the officer snapped. He then turned his attention back to the café, ordering the front row of soldiers, numbering about fifteen, to enter the premises.

Shouts and screams came from inside. Soldiers yelled,

''Raus! 'Raus!' A dozen civilians emerged, one by one, each roughly manhandled or encouraged by prods of gun barrels. There were elderly men and women, young couples, a few businessmen and a boy of about fifteen wearing an apron.

Shoved, kicked and slapped, the customers were made to stand shoulder to shoulder on the pavement close to the empty tables. Some glanced around frantically as if contemplating a bid for freedom, calculating how far they'd get before lumps of lead felled them. One or two, mainly the older women, cursed at the soldiers lining up before them as if in a violent stand-off between two rival gangs.

I had a sinking feeling in my belly. This raid was surely no coincidence. The officer removed a piece of paper from his tunic breast pocket, unfolded it and cleared his throat.

'Oh God,' Freya whispered. 'I don't want to be here, not now, not if I'm right . . .'

Chapter Fourteen
The Big Sweat

From my vantage point in the alley I could witness events unfold without being seen. The SS officer began his speech in German. 'My name is Major Steiff. Somewhere in this town a group of British airmen are being hidden from us by members of the Dutch Resistance. By order of the German High Command they must be handed over to us immediately. Non-cooperation with the glorious Third Reich will not be tolerated. Such acts will be met with swift reprisals.' After each sentence he paused so that his driver could repeat it in Dutch, just so there were no misunderstandings. 'We want to know who is involved. Names and addresses. They will be given a fair trial. I give you my word.'

'Yeah, if you believe that you'll believe anything!' Loki muttered under his breath.

Steiff carefully folded up the piece of paper and put it back in his tunic pocket. 'We shall remain here until one of you speaks.' He drew his pistol from its holster and began walking slowly along the line, his finger caressing the trigger, his gaze dwelling on each frightened face in turn.

'Any ideas?' said Freya without moving her lips.

Loki shook his head and then threw me a glance. Lost for ideas, I shrugged.

They were both unable to move, unable to do anything. The sun beat down remorselessly, and ten minutes ticked by painfully slowly, followed by twenty more. The tension in the air was so thick I found it stifling and hard to breathe. Steiff's patience wore thin too, and he took to shouting at the line of terrified souls that they should speak now; that it would be for the best; that if they didn't they'd regret it. Still nobody spoke.

The Rembrandt was a rather ordinary café-bar where locals met day in, day out – a place unlikely to be frequented by soldiers. Its shabby stonework, the brown window frames and the grubby glass behind which hung even filthier net curtains made it look perfect for clandestine business – whispers over beer and coffee, messages dropped and collected with little more than a nod and a wink. Marieke had chosen it too. Perhaps someone had recommended it to her. Maybe one of the people now standing in line.

The sun was directly overhead and there was no shade to be found in the entire street. I was lucky. I was in the shadows of the alley. Taking stock of the situation, I decided there was only one thing for it. I edged backwards and made for the rear of the building. There I found a small yard filled with barrels, crates and rubbish, and a door wedged open with a brick. I slipped inside and listened.

The place was deserted. The soldiers had cleared it out. Cautiously I made for the bar, passing through a hall and past a staircase to the upper floors. The bar was a gloomy room with a scattering of tables and chairs, and cheap oil paintings of windmills and dykes and Dutch barges plying the canals. It smelled of stale beer. I set about searching behind the bar, looking for anything that might be for us – a folded piece of paper, an envelope, a small package. There was nothing. I gently eased the till open and removed the tray. Nothing there either. I ran my fingers through my hair in exasperation and scanned the room. *Nothing!*

I headed upstairs and searched every room. A cat stretched out lazily on a quilt raised its head, looked at me, yawned and then closed its eyes, oblivious to the horrors unfolding in the street below. Empty-handed, I returned to the bar, approached one of the windows and peered out through the net curtains. I watched and waited. An hour ticked by. The relentless, burning heat began to take its toll, especially on the elderly captives. There was barely a breath of wind to take the edge off it. I could see glistening faces and sweat trickling down temples. One woman started to sway and her eyelids fluttered as if she were about to faint. I willed her to remain on her feet, defiant. Somehow, she did. The soldiers simmered away beneath their helmets too; they were sweltering in their uniforms, their faces dripping with perspiration and their arms tiring from holding their weapons. This was a battle of wills and I knew the enemy would not back down.

Steiff continued pacing the line-up, back and forth, back and forth. It was hypnotic, like gazing at a pocket watch being swung on the end of a gold chain, or watching those demented polar bears you see padding restlessly from one end of their cages to the other at the local zoo. The street remained deserted; anyone approaching unawares beat a hasty retreat. Looking up, I could see faces at windows on the upper floors of the tall, narrow houses on the opposite side of the street; mostly furtive glances, mouths in motion as the fearful relayed events to others simply too scared to look. I reckoned the enemy was happy for them to watch, to observe, to witness the spectacle. It would all serve to reinforce the message: that resistance was futile and would be met with overwhelming force; that one person's act of defiance would mean tragedy for others, mostly the innocent.

Suddenly Steiff's patience ran out. Midway along the line, he stopped and turned. '*Sie!*' he snapped at a smartly dressed elderly businessman. 'Step forward.'

Hesitantly, his lips trembling, the man took one small tentative pace out of the line. He did so with such reluctance I thought it must've felt like stepping off a precipice into the terrifying unknown.

'*Namen,*' Steiff bellowed into his face. 'Give me names. Speak now. It's your last chance.'

The man cowered like a dog that knows it's just about to be kicked, and pressed his eyes tightly shut.

'*Spreken!*' the major yelled.

The man couldn't bring himself to speak, even to say that he knew nothing. Steiff took a step back and raised his pistol, straightening his arm. The end of the barrel lay just inches from his victim's forehead. For a few seconds nothing happened. Then, stiffening up, the old man threw back his shoulders, just like an old soldier from the Great War standing to attention on Armistice Day. He had his back to me, and suddenly I saw his head jerk. Steiff swore and wiped the man's gob from his cheeks.

Without a flicker of emotion Steiff pulled the trigger. I flinched as the blast echoed. At point-blank range, the force of the bullet flung the man backwards, lifting him slightly off his feet. Bits of his brain struck the window. Instinctively I ducked. One woman shrieked like a strangled cat; another's knees gave way and she had to be supported by the man next to her. Spread-eagled on the pavement, the old man lay still, the circular hole in his forehead clearly visible above open, lifeless eyes. A tiny trickle of blood forged a path of least resistance towards the gutter.

My teeth ground from the intense desire to rush outside and rip Steiff to shreds. But I remained where I was. Something had to be done, and fast.

Steiff selected the next man in the row and dragged him forward. Lowering his gun, he announced that they had one hour to spill the beans, otherwise he would shoot him too. If that didn't persuade them, then he'd shoot another individual on the hour, every hour. Just for good measure, he added that it did not matter to him whether he had to shoot all twelve of them: it was no trouble to round up a further dozen. His driver continued translating each sentence into Dutch with a relish I found sickening.

It was the oldest trick in the book but no less

effective for that. I understood the Nazi psychology. Until then, all twelve had stood shoulder to shoulder as equals, each having a one-in-twelve chance of being picked out. Any Resistance fighters among them might have been thinking about sacrificing themselves for the cause, a selfless act in the name of *vrijheid* – freedom. Now, though, the callousness of the enemy was clear. The next person in line for a bullet was plain for all to see. A man in his late twenties – surely too young to die. The remaining ten people knew that if they didn't talk, they'd be responsible for his death. Did they have the right to remain silent? Could they make that choice?

I found myself repeatedly peering at my watch. The major, meanwhile, stepped over the body as if it were nothing more irksome than a napping dog and wandered across to one of the tables. Removing his cap, he swept a chair with it and sat down. He reached for his handkerchief and mopped his brow. Then he set about fanning his face with his cap.

How on earth was this going to end? If nobody talked, I feared Loki and Freya would become victims too. *Think, Finn, think!* My inner voice was so panicky, so frantic, it made me feel dizzy. Although Steiff was resting on a chair, there was still no shade for him there. And he was particularly fair-skinned too. I could see that being out in the sun was as much a torture for him as it was for everyone else, maybe more so. A scheme began brewing in my frazzled brain. Its chances of working were about as slender as a blade of grass but I couldn't come up with anything better: I simply had to give it a go.

Back out in the alley, I waved to attract Loki's attention. I gestured to him, pretending to drink out of an imaginary glass. He frowned as if I was mad but I persisted. He eventually got the message and reached for a bottle from his rucksack. I gave him the thumbs-up and returned to the bar. Through the window I watched first him then Freya drink from the bottle. Again and again they took turns downing refreshing sips. 'Come on,' I muttered. 'Surely it's making you thirsty too.' I noticed Steiff staring at them both. 'Good. That's it. You'd like a drink too, wouldn't you, Herr Major. You must be dying of thirst.'

Eventually it worked. I'd sown the seed of desire. '*Sie*,' Steiff barked, pointing at the boy in the apron. 'Fetch me a beer. At once!'

I ran behind the bar and grabbed a bottle of beer and a glass. The boy hurried inside. He saw me and stopped in his tracks. He looked startled. I raised a finger to my lips and then beckoned him to come close. He did so, but kept flashing an eye towards the rear, towards the back door, towards his escape route. That was the last thing I wanted him to do. 'Do you speak English?' I whispered.

Now he looked shocked. 'A little.'

'Good. I want you to take this beer out to Herr Steiff.' I smacked the rim of the bottle against the edge of the bar to flip off the metal cap.

He pointed to the rear door. 'But I . . . I get away. I go.'

'No. Wait!' I leaned across the bar and grabbed his arm. 'Wait!'

I reached down and yanked off my left boot. Twisting the heel revealed the hidden recess in which we stored our emergency tablets. The boy gasped. I took out the small blister containing my L-pill but then thought better of it. The cyanide would work in seconds and it would be obvious that the drink had been tampered with. Instead, I removed another blister, the one containing the pill that would temporarily incapacitate, bringing on an acute, debilitating sickness. For good measure I grabbed the one that induced sleep too. I didn't know how long they needed to take effect but it was my best bet. As the astonished boy looked on I popped the blisters, placed the tablets onto the counter and used the bottom of another empty glass to crush them. Sweeping the powder into the glass, I then poured the beer. Steiff yelled for the boy to hurry up. The sound of his voice made us both flinch. I gave the drink a quick stir and then handed the glass to the boy. 'Go on. Take it. It'll be all right.'

The boy backed away and shook his head. 'No. I go. You take.'

'*No!*' I stared hard at him and then pointed towards the street. 'Take it and you all live. Run away and they all die.'

He understood. Wiping his hands nervously on his apron, he nodded and took the glass from me. He was shaking. 'Don't spill it!' I shooed him towards the door.

As Steiff drank, I saw envy on the faces of his men. It

was tormenting them, and I had the feeling that at that moment they hated their superior about as much as we did. Steiff drank quickly too – all the better for my plan. For twenty minutes nothing happened. Then I noticed Steiff belch. Five minutes later he was rubbing his belly, clearly in considerable discomfort. He rose from his chair and began walking about, but not like before. Now he was sweating profusely and yet his face looked deathly grey, bloated and doughy. He seemed a little unsteady on his feet, resting a hand against the back of a chair for support. I heard a sudden groan, then he bent over and was violently sick. When done, he straightened and momentarily appeared recovered – an observation that made my heart sink. But it was a false reprieve. Soon he was bent double again, heaving up his guts, his whole body jerking in spasms. His driver rushed to his assistance but was angrily ordered to get back into position. Steiff turned round, leaned his back heavily against the window of the Rembrandt, closed his eyes and then, ever so slowly, slid down. I reckoned he was unconscious by the time his backside hit the ground.

Confusion reigned. While most of the soldiers looked at one another, bemused, a few ran and tried to get Steiff to his feet. Without their superior officer they were suddenly rudderless. No one was in command, and it seemed no one wanted to take responsibility. I ran to the alley and grabbed hold of my bike. Loki caught my eye and mouthed, *What was that all about?* I pointed to my heel. His look of bemusement turned into one of delight.

As a sick Major Steiff was helped to his car, I knew the most dangerous moment of all had arrived – our escape. The soldiers were in disarray and we had to make the most of it. I slipped out of the cover of the alley. 'The show's over. Let's try and get out of here,' I said. 'Nice and slow.'

We pushed off and headed up the street, not daring to look behind us. We dreaded hearing the order to stop, to turn round. But it didn't come. After a hundred yards we turned right into a side street.

We'd done it. We'd got away. Loki slapped me on my back. 'Inspired, Finn.'

'Did you find any messages,' asked Freya.

I shook my head. 'I looked everywhere.'

'Should've used your L-pill on that bastard, Finn. That's what he deserved.'

'Too obvious. They'd realize—'

I was interrupted by the nightmarish stutter of machine-gun fire. Not one weapon but several, a chorus of deadly chatter and shattering glass, of bullets ricocheting, of screams.

'Oh, no!' Freya cried out. 'Surely they haven't . . .'

Loki slowly cycled back to the corner, just far enough to see the café. His eyes widened with horror and he lost his balance, his feet slipping off the pedals. 'They've shot them. All of them. They're just lying there.'

We set off, hammering the pedals with all our might, hurtling through the streets, everything a blur, our bikes swerving in and out of traffic, our bells ringing to warn others to get out of our way. We didn't slow or contemplate stopping until we'd left The Hague and Scheveningen well behind and were once again on the long, straight coast road amid the dunes.

They were two different worlds. The beach was still littered with bathers, bicycles, colourful towels and vivid umbrellas, the same scattering of petals on the same vast golden cloth. Vibrant cries and shouts drifted on the air – of children playing games, a boy sobbing because another had stolen his ball, a girl screaming hysterically because she'd got separated from her mother. Amid it all I slammed on my brakes and skidded to a halt. I was breathing really hard. Angrily I yelled at them in Norwegian, 'How could you? Don't you know there's a bloody war on! How dare you . . .' My voice trailed off and my vision grew misty. I blinked and wiped away the tears.

'Come on, Finn,' Freya said to me. 'You did your best.'

I wasn't really angry at the bathers. My tears were for that boy. All I could see was his face. I'd persuaded him to take out the glass. Me and no one else. I was to blame. I could have taken it out myself. But I didn't. He'd had his chance to escape, to live, and I'd denied him. Now he was dead. They were all dead.

Chapter Fifteen
A Gathering Storm

On our return we stopped by the Pols' windmill, and Loki and I dumped our bikes in the long grass, brambles and nettles. Freya carried on to the farmhouse, returning with the key. There was no time to waste. An urgent message had to be sent without delay. I kept watch outside as Freya tapped frantically on her Morse key in the little room at the top of the paltrok, alerting HQ that Aardappel had placed a red card in the window of Margo's, but that we couldn't retrieve their message as the Rembrandt had been raided. We requested our immediate return to England. HQ told us to sit tight and await further instructions.

Angry, frustrated, and hot and bothered, we needed to cool off. Stripping to our underwear, we plunged into the cool waters of the canal behind the windmill. It was good to wash the day away. Loki complained that the back of his burned neck felt like it was on fire, and the first time he dipped his head under the water he cried out in agony.

The canal stretched in both directions as far as the eye could see. We swam for ages. Then, chests heaving from the exertion, we dragged ourselves out, lay on our backs and gazed up at the sky. Way off in the distance I could hear thunder, and the horizon to the east was smudged grey with storm clouds. For the first time in hours I felt safe. I also felt a complete failure. I hadn't come this far to give up so easily. 'We should make contact with Otto,' I announced. 'Try to find out what's going on. I want to know if Marieke's safe. And we need to find out what's happened to those airmen and to Asparagus.'

'No point, Finn. Operation Double Dutch has to be abandoned. End of story.' Loki rolled over onto his side. 'We had a pretty close shave. Something must've gone terribly wrong. After today's disaster I can't wait to get the hell out of here. I'm not going back into town.'

I turned onto my belly and began tugging out tufts of grass in front of my face. I tore up a dozen clumps and laid them side by side. 'I still think we ought to contact Otto,' I persisted. 'Maybe there's still a chance we can succeed. After all, if the SS are searching for the airmen, it can mean only one thing – that they haven't been captured yet. Otto might have contacts. And, anyway, I'm not leaving without trying to rescue Father.'

Loki sank his head into the grass and groaned. 'How many times do I have to tell you, Finn? He isn't here. You're deluded. Bloody hell, what'll it take to get it into that thick skull of yours?'

Freya reached out and placed a comforting hand on my arm. I snatched it away and scrambled to my knees. 'No, you're wrong. I just know it!'

'So you three made it out of The Hague alive, then.' Startled, we turned round to see the tall slender figure of Dr van Alblas standing on the towpath beside the canal. He was clutching a pistol.

Panicking, Loki sprang to his feet.

'Stay perfectly calm,' van Alblas said. He looked up and down the path and, satisfied no one was approaching, returned his gun to his coat pocket.

'You were following us earlier, weren't you?' said Freya. 'I saw your car – you might have blown our cover.'

The doctor studied us a while, his gaunt, moustached face hidden in the shadow created by the broad brim of his hat. His expression revealed nothing. 'Why were you making for the Rembrandt?' he asked finally.

'What's the Rembrandt?' Loki responded unhelpfully.

'We don't have time to play silly games. Why there?'

We remained stubbornly silent.

Removing his jacket, the doctor sat down on the ground next to us and sighed. 'I'm sorry I couldn't help you earlier. Willem's girlfriend, Laura Kramer, telephoned me this morning and said you were heading into town. Knowing you were on unfamiliar territory, I thought I'd keep tabs on you. Unfortunately I got stopped in The Hague, just a few streets away from the café. By the time my papers had been checked I'd lost sight of you. I drove around a bit and saw there were problems in the Nieuwe Siegelstraat. I figured Major Steiff had decided to raid the Rembrandt again. It's the third time in as many months. We stopped using it after the first raid. That's the trouble with those thugs:

no imagination. They believe we're as stupid as they are.'

'Who *exactly* is this "we"?' Freya interrupted.

He raised a hand to the brim of his hat, removed it theatrically and held it against his chest. 'As I mentioned yesterday, we call ourselves "the Undertakers",' he announced solemnly. Then he laughed but it quickly turned into a coughing fit. Recovering, he added, 'A bit morbid, I know, but it wasn't my idea. We're a mixed bunch but with one common aim – to kick those goose-stepping oafs all the way back to Berlin.'

'Your English is even better than ours,' Loki observed.

'Went to medical school at Cambridge,' he replied. 'Now *there* was a hotbed of subversion if ever I saw one. Place was crawling with communists, anarchists, and no doubt one or two fascists too. Stacked to the rafters with them.'

'Are you one?' I asked. 'A communist, I mean.'

'Good Lord, no. Perish the thought.' The doctor put his hat back on his head. 'There are plenty over here though. What about you three?'

I shook my head.

'Glad to hear it. Such people are not to be trusted.'

'The Undertakers is a weird choice of name,' Loki commented.

Van Alblas laughed again. 'Yes. It's based on our preferred method of transporting weapons and explosives.' He twisted round and pointed towards the windmill.

It took a moment for me to understand what he

meant. 'Ha! I get it. You move stuff around in coffins. *Perfect!*'

Proudly he informed us that 'Scheveningen cemetery currently contains over one hundred rifles just waiting to be dug up and put to good use. Bit short of ammo though.'

Unable to see his car, Loki asked, 'How did you get here? We didn't hear you approach.'

'I'm not surprised. My car's parked up by the road. You three were talking so loudly an entire Panzer Division could have crept up on you. And you were talking in Norwegian. I'd call it sloppy. I suppose I ought to blame your superiors.' He divided his stare between us. 'Well, I'm assuming whoever sent you are the same lot that sent Asparagus. I'm right, aren't I?'

The questions flew from my lips. 'You know members of Asparagus? Do you know what's happened to them? Where are they? Are they still alive?'

Van Alblas replied in the gravest tone he could muster. 'It pains me to say it, but I fear we have a traitor in our midst. Asparagus were rounded up weeks ago. It all happened so fast we had no chance to warn anyone. I can't answer your question fully, but I believe most were taken to Scheveningen prison. There were several of our lot among them. A few, however, were taken to that big building on the boulevard.'

'The Nazi HQ? The Palace Hotel?'

'Yes. And that's highly unusual. As far as I'm aware they're still being held there. I've not figured out why yet.'

While we hurriedly dressed, Freya had a thought. 'I

suppose they must have installed some seriously powerful radio equipment there. At that hotel, I mean.'

'There were aerial masts on the roof,' I recalled from our reconnaissance. I understood what she was getting at. 'You think Bram and the others are being forced to transmit from there, don't you?'

'Do you mean Bram Keppel?' Van Alblas interrupted.

'Yes. They're playing a deadly game,' Loki explained. 'They don't just have our agents, but their code books too. They've been forcing Bram and his fellow wireless operators to transmit messages as if nothing's happened. As a result we've been sending in more agents and supplies and the Germans have been waiting for them.'

'Dear God.' Van Alblas clenched his fists and looked towards the heavens. 'If I ever find out who's betrayed us, I'll bury them alive.'

'There was a problem our end,' I told him. 'A rotten egg in our basket. It's been dealt with.' I thought it best not to mention names or the fact that Major Gerrit had chosen to blow his own brains out.

We explained that Bram's brother had escaped to England and alerted us, and van Alblas was cheered to learn that Jan was alive. He'd presumed the boy had been caught too. We said nothing about Jan having returned, or about Aardappel.

'I assume your job is to rectify the situation. To rescue Bram and the others.' Van Alblas was on his feet now and pacing back and forth, a hand caressing his chin as possibilities flew through his head. 'We can help you. Did you bring any explosives?'

'Yes, but we had to bury our supplies when we parachuted in. They're several miles from here,' I said.

'I'll get help. After I've looked in on Willem I'll go to the Kramers'. Laura can round up some volunteers. We'll fetch your supplies tonight and bring them all here.'

Freya looked hesitant. I knew what she was thinking. How on earth could we tell van Alblas that our mission wasn't to free Bram and the others in Asparagus, and that for the time being a rescue attempt was out of the question? I had to focus on our priorities. 'Dr van Alblas, have you ever heard of the Wolf Squadron or someone known as Falcon? Are you aware of any stranded airmen in this area?'

'No.'

I was disappointed. Although he'd come across Asparagus, they clearly weren't collaborating as far as the airmen were concerned. Just for a second I'd hoped he might have known their whereabouts.

'So what do you think? Shall we go tonight?' van Alblas asked.

Having just sent a message requesting our urgent return home, I supposed our supplies were redundant – why not let van Alblas's lot make good use of them? I took Loki and Freya aside and we discussed it. 'All right,' I told the doctor. 'It would be good to have some help bringing the gear here. There are some Sten machine guns you can have too. As the stuff's buried on the other side of the river, you'll probably have to make quite a detour to avoid that bridge. Loki will take you there.'

'Excellent! We'll use the river and canals to our advantage. Leave it to me.' Van Alblas could barely conceal his glee. He picked up his jacket and slung it over his shoulder. 'We'll assemble at the Kramers' farm at ten thirty tonight.' He strolled off down the path, raising a hand to wave as he continued, 'I'll inform Willem. I'll need his help when we return. He's the only one who knows how to operate the saw mill.' He jabbed a finger skywards. 'Looks like the weather's breaking. Wind's picking up nicely. Perfect!' He coughed hard and slammed a fist against his chest. And we heard him coughing all the way back to his car.

Rain dashed against the windows and thunder rumbled above the farm. It was joined by the hammering of a stick on the floor of Willem's bedroom. 'Is there no peace for the wicked?' Saskia remarked, flinging down her paper and tearing off her spectacles.

Loki had already left for the Kramers' farm, and Freya waited just seconds before slipping out too, making for the windmill. We were hoping to receive instructions from HQ. It was almost a quarter to eleven. I'd gathered up my things and was intending to catch up with Freya so I could keep watch outside. Willem thumped the stick on the floor again and repeated his call for some water. Saskia hollered something back, sharply and irritably. From her manner I suspected Willem was in for a long wait. As if suddenly remembering something, she eased herself up out of her chair and padded softly across the parlour to a bookcase. 'I've got something I've been meaning to show you, Finn.'

'I'm just off out. Can I see later?' I hovered by the door.

'It won't take a second. Now, I have a feeling I put it somewhere in here,' she continued, pulling what looked like a photograph album from a shelf. Thumbing through a few leaves, she stopped and declared, 'Yes, thought so.' She handed me the album, keeping the pages from turning by pressing a thumb near the spine. 'Recognize anyone?'

I peered half-heartedly at the old photograph, quietly cursing Saskia's bad timing. My village near Trondheim! Loki's house! I gasped. Smiling faces peered into the camera lens.

'That's Gottfried standing behind me,' she said, pointing over my shoulder. 'Doesn't he look a handsome fellow?'

I wasn't looking at them. My eyes were fixed on a much younger Mother and Father standing to the left, little Anna in between, me cradled in Mother's arms. And Loki and his parents were there too.

'That was the last time we visited,' she said wistfully. 'So long ago. I really must go again when all this horror is over. To tell you the truth, I miss the old country.'

I raised the album to within inches of my face. Everyone looked so young, so different. Father was quite skinny and Mother so much prettier than I'd remembered. I stared at the picture for ages. 'Are there any others?' I began turning the pages.

'Not that would interest you.'

'I'd heard that your side of the family fell out with Loki's. Is that right?' I asked.

'A long time ago. All water under the bridge.' She waved a hand in the air to demonstrate. 'Gottfried and Loki's father never saw eye to eye on anything. Seems so silly now. Tell me, Finn, how are your family? You must miss them.'

I looked up to see her studying me intensely. 'Yes. Of course. Mother and Anna were arrested. They hadn't done anything wrong, so I hope they'll be released eventually.'

Saskia snorted derisorily. So many innocent people had been arrested. 'What about your father? He went to England, didn't he?' she added.

I nodded. 'How did you know that? To be honest I didn't know that you knew any of my family.'

She returned to her chair, slumping down heavily, the cushions farting under her weight. 'Can't say I know them well, but Loki's mother has written to me now and then over the years with all her news. Mentioned you all once or twice. Of course, the letters stopped coming after the occupation.' She gazed at me inquisitively.

'Father was shot down. He was flying a Spitfire. That's what I want to do . . . eventually.'

Saskia directed her stare towards the floor. She looked as sad as I often felt.

'He's missing,' I added. 'Maybe he was picked up.' I did my best to sound optimistic, upbeat about it all.

'What about Gottfried? Have you had news about where the Germans took him?'

She shook her head vehemently. 'Not a word. Just that they were shipped to Germany to work in the factories. That's all anyone can find out.' She glanced up towards me and I saw she was close to tears.

I peered at the clock. Hell! Freya would be wondering where on earth I'd got to.

'It was brave of your father to take off like that – at the outbreak of war, I mean, Finn. I doubt many rushed off to England to join the RAF.' Sighing wearily, she switched tack. 'So, you've come to rescue some fellow airmen. Loki told me.'

I nodded, reaching into my jacket pocket to check I had my torch and revolver. I edged into the hall.

'Things must be going badly for the British if they've resorted to sending children behind enemy lines.' She laughed, but in a forced manner. Raising her voice as if calling after me, she added, 'Of course, you must be part of something much bigger. I realize that. It's obvious. I suppose there must be others working with you both here and back in Britain.'

'I really must go, Mrs Pol. Freya will be worried.'

She ignored me. Leaning so far forward in her chair that she almost fell off it, she shouted, 'That Grüber's a pig! A *pig*, I tell you.' She mumbled something else in Dutch and then continued, 'But the SS . . . Now they're vile creatures, Finn. Monsters!'

Willem banged his stick on the floor again and called out. I saw my opportunity to get away. 'You stay there,

Mrs Pol. I'll take the water up to Willem.'

I hurried to the kitchen and grabbed a glass. Saskia continued talking. 'Willem will be better soon. I want you gone from here. Do you understand? You're not welcome. The price is simply too high.'

I took the glass of water upstairs. 'How are you feeling, Willem?'

'Much better. Thanks, Finn. Just so damn annoying having to lie here day and night in the dark. Dr van Alblas says I might have stay like this for a fortnight. There's so much to be done. Still, when he visited earlier he said something about needing my help later. Down at the mill.'

I guided the glass through the darkness and into his hand. 'Yes, he said something about that to us too. What will he need you for?'

'Getting the mill going. We have to make more coffins. For all your supplies. That's the way we get them into town.' He listened out and grinned. 'Sounds like the wind's picking up nicely.'

'Seems risky to me. Your eye, I mean. Can't someone else do it? Your mother perhaps? Can't she help out just this once?'

'No. I have to do it, Finn. Anyway, she doesn't know how to operate the bench saws. Father and I always did that bit. You have to know what you're doing. One slip and you'll either wreck the machinery or someone will lose an arm.'

'Listen, Willem, I can't hang around. Freya's waiting for me at the windmill. We're expecting updated orders.

We'll be going home sooner than we thought. Still, at least your mother will be glad. Did you hear her just now? Still insisting that we're gone from here.'

Willem reached out and seized my arm. 'Don't be too hard on her, Finn. It's not been easy for her. After they arrested my father they took him to the local police headquarters with all the others they rounded up. As soon as the news reached Mother she went there and caused merry hell. So much trouble, in fact, that she was arrested too. She was given a rough time by the SS. *A really bad time, Finn*. She was lucky to get out of prison alive.'

'I won't breathe a word.'

'Thank you, Finn.'

'I suppose she must be scared witless every time Grüber and his band of thugs turn up.'

Willem nodded. 'Yes. Still, we can always grow more food and beg, steal or borrow from our neighbours if we run short. Mother rants and raves and spits at men like Grüber but doesn't cause any real trouble. She thinks she has to tread carefully or else my father will suffer, that they'll make life unbearable for him. I've tried telling her that Father's one of tens of thousands of slave labourers, just a number, just a face, hundreds of miles away. The Germans know he's a communist and they hate them almost as much as the Jews. Mother's actions won't make any difference. But naturally she fears for my safety too. So far they've contented themselves with dishing out a beating or two, but if she doesn't do as she's told she thinks . . . Anyway, to tell you the truth,

Finn, I've had enough. Next time Grüber shows his ugly face round here I intend to put a bullet in his head.'

Heading quickly back downstairs, I rushed past the door to the parlour. Saskia was still sitting in her chair, staring at the photograph album. Luckily she seemed lost in her thoughts and didn't call out to me. After what Willem had confided in me I saw her in a different light. Her life must be a living hell, I supposed. Not only having to run the farm without Gottfried, and worry about his plight, but live with the constant fear of what they might do to her and Willem if she put a foot wrong. It had to be eating away at her, grinding her down, sapping all her energy and hope. I almost felt glad we'd soon be leaving – for her sake. It would be one less worry for her. But if Willem carried out his threat, I knew it would probably sound the death knell for both of them. I checked my revolver, wedged it into my belt, and wished I could help them both in some way.

Driven by a howling wind, the rain pelted hard into my face as soon as I opened the door. It stung like gravel. I raised the hood of my jacket and set off along the path. The darkness was complete. It was after eleven and so I hurried. I ran, splashing through puddles, my torch barely able to light the way. Lightning circled the farm and a violent crack of thunder sounded like wood being split along the grain. The violence of the storm unnerved me.

Nearing the paltrok, I could just make out its silhouette towering into the sky. I slid and skidded over to the steps, climbed onto the cutting floor, ran to the door and grabbed the handle, throwing my weight against it, expecting it to open easily. I was mistaken. The door was locked. Confused, I took a step back and glanced around. 'Freya . . . Freya! Where are you?' My words were snatched and smothered by the wind. I tried the door again. I hammered a fist against it. No reply. What the hell was happening?

I ran round to the front of the mill and looked up. I wanted to see if the small window was open and the aerial dangling out. Maybe with her headphones on and the noise of the storm Freya would be unable to hear me. I figured she'd probably locked the door behind her for safety.

The rain stung my eyes and I blinked frantically to clear the blur. My pen torch was too feeble to reach the top window. I simply couldn't make anything out. Then a flash of lightning lit everything. It lasted a fraction of a second but it was enough. The white weatherboarding shone for an instant, making the mill look like an apparition, its barren sails the flailing arms of a giant skeleton. The window *was* open. The aerial *was* hanging out. Freya *was* inside. But there was something else. It nearly made my heart stop. Someone dressed in black was using the sail as a ladder, climbing towards the open window.

Chapter Sixteen
The Coffin Makers

Cupping my hands about my mouth, I yelled out a warning. My voice didn't carry. Another bolt of lightning lit the figure. It looked like a man but it was hard to tell. He was too high up – at least forty feet. I snatched my revolver from my belt. I had a tough decision to make. Should I shoot? And if I did, should it just be a warning shot? What if there was a German patrol in the vicinity? Would they hear it too? All I knew was that Freya, concentrating hard on her wireless work, probably wouldn't hear the man until he was already climbing through the window. By then it would be too late. I raised my gun, took aim, and decided a warning round was best. I pulled the trigger and a shot rang out. I shouted as loud as I could and then fired again. I couldn't work out whether I'd achieved anything until lightning revealed that the figure was climbing more hurriedly now. Blinking frantically, the rain thrashing down on me, I steadied my aim and fired twice more, intent on stopping whoever it was – permanently.

I waited for the body to fall to earth but it didn't. Another dizzying, zigzagging bolt of lightning forked across the land and lit him. He was still up there, rock still, hanging precariously. But I had to be sure. I couldn't take the risk he'd feigned death. Wedging my gun back into my belt, I clambered onto the cutting floor, then onto a wooden handrail. I steadied myself for a moment and calculated what it would take to bridge the gap. Stretching my hands out as far as they'd go, I said a quick prayer and leaped.

The sail's frame creaked horribly as I grabbed hold. I swung like a trapeze artist and then began hauling myself up. At first the spaces between the wooden lattices were large, wet and slippery. Scaling them was awkward but it meant I gained height quickly. All the while the sail flexed under my weight. It was like climbing the rigging of a tall ship amid a howling tempest. The pelting rain and battering wind were intense, as if they were trying to defeat me. Amid it all I could hear what sounded like sobbing. Gasping, my muscles burning, I climbed, not daring to look down. The sail was old and in poor repair. Several struts were broken, others so fragile, so eaten by rot, that they snapped in my hand. But I was gaining on the stationary figure. I could see him clearly about ten feet above me. He was still alive. I could hear his cries. I reached up for the next hand grip. My left foot slipped. My right followed and I felt myself sliding. Frantically I reached out and grabbed a horizontal lattice. It held me. I searched out a foothold and tentatively transferred my weight to it. That held me too. Pressing flat against the sail as it twisted from side to side, I ascended a couple of feet more. Deciding I was near enough, I reached for my gun and pointed towards the figure. Time to make sure!

'No. No shoot. Please no shoot. It is I. Jan. Jan Keppel.'

My astonishment nearly caused me to fall. 'Jan? What on earth are you doing here?'

His breathless reply was bursting with anxiety. 'Brought message from Marieke. Urgent. I see Freya go in. But she lock the door. Help, Finn. I cannot move.'

'Hang on. I'll come up to you.'

Jan was clinging on for grim death. He'd gripped the sail so tightly the wood had cut into his hands, making them bleed. I tried to calm him. His jacket was caught up on a protruding nail. I began shouting instructions. 'Hold tight. I'll help you.'

Freya's head appeared at the window. She looked terrified until she realized it was me. 'I heard shots. What in God's name are you doing, Finn?'

'Rescuing Jan!' I shouted that I was going to climb down a few feet. 'Then put your feet on my shoulders. I'll take your weight for a minute.'

I descended and positioned myself directly under his boots. 'That's it . . . I've got you. Take some deep breaths and then we'll head down . . . That's it . . .' I helped guide his boots back onto the sail. 'One step after another . . . I'm still beneath you in case you slip . . . All right?'

Slowly we lowered ourselves. Just as I thought we were doing fine, Jan froze, let out a fearful cry and whimpered, 'I can't, Finn. I can't.'

'Don't look down,' I shouted between gasps. The last thing I needed was him having a fit of the terrors on me. Despite my encouraging words, I was worried that I'd be unable to break his fall if he slipped. Inch by inch, foot by foot, my muscles burning, my arms feeling as if they'd been wrenched from my shoulder blades, I encouraged him to clamber down, stopping every few seconds so I could guide his boots onto the next precarious foothold.

At last – the bottom of the sail. I let go, landing lightly, rolling in the mud to break my fall, just like when I'd para-chuted. Jan overcame his trepidation and eventually let go too. Scrambling to his feet, he turned and flung his arms around me. 'Thank you, Finn. I think I nearly die.'

Freya arrived in the doorway and we hurried inside. She closed and locked the door behind us. I used our handkerchiefs to bind Jan's bloodied hands. He was hyperventilating, his chest heaving, and I could see from his grimace that his ribs were still a little sore.

'Calm down. You're all right. You're safe now. It's safe here.' Freya's face, however, told a different story and she mouthed something to me that looked like: *What on earth was he doing?*

Jan began talking nineteen to the dozen. 'We hear of Rembrandt. Marieke think you not get message so she send me here.'

'Is Marieke all right?' I asked.

Jan nodded and I felt a surge of elation.

'What's happened? We saw the red card at Margo's.'

'I take Marieke to house. Where Bram take me before. But airmen not there. Neighbour say house raided by Gestapo.'

That was odd, I thought. If Steiff was to be believed, they'd not yet captured the airmen.

'So Marieke put red card in shop. But contact tell her airmen move. *Before* Gestapo come.'

'Does she know where?' Freya asked.

'Yes. But it not safe. Gestapo raid many houses. Search everywhere. She must move them again. She need help.'

'Where are they?'

'Marieke not tell me. Not safe I know.' He pushed up his sleeve and held his watch close to his face. 'Very late. Marieke worry.'

'So what's the message?' I asked.

'Marieke give you contact. For emergency. Yes?'

'Yes.'

'Marieke say you go there tomorrow. Midday. There you get instructions. Marieke say just one go. Understand? Take parcel with cloth. Marieke say pretend you make delivery – for if Germans stop you. She say you understand. Gestapo and Abwehr everywhere. You be careful.'

'Message understood, Jan.'

He seemed relieved – his mission was complete.

'How did you know we were using the windmill?' Freya asked while inspecting Jan's hands.

He shook his head. 'I not know. Marieke say go to farmhouse. I come on path by canal. I see you go in windmill. I try door but locked. I think you all inside. I think you stay all night. See window open and climb up . . . I go now.'

'All right. Tell Marieke I'll be there tomorrow at midday. Will she be there?' I asked hopefully.

Jan shrugged. Freya unlocked the door and he disappeared into the night.

'Anything new from HQ?'

'No, Finn. Not a dicky bird. Still, from what Jan's just said it looks like we might still be on. I'll go and send an update, tell them to await further instructions from us.'

'Keep it short. Loki's going to be disappointed when he finds out. He was hoping we'd be out of here.'

With the message sent and the radio stowed safely away, Freya was locking the door and I was telling her what Willem had confided in me when we heard a noise. We dashed across the open ground and hid behind the stack of logs. The noise grew louder. It sounded like a small diesel engine.

'It's coming from the canal,' Freya whispered. 'Look, a barge is coming this way.'

We watched as the vessel slowed and came to a stop behind the windmill. There were voices and shapes moving in the dark. People came ashore: I counted five. They began unloading stuff. Lamps were lit. Then I heard a voice I recognized. Loki! We emerged and called to him.

Van Alblas strutted about issuing orders like a general between frequent bouts of coughing. Loki introduced us to Laura Kramer. It was hard to tell by lamplight but she looked extremely pretty and about Willem's age. Strong and determined too. She smiled at us and then ran off in the direction of the farmhouse.

We filled Loki in on Jan's appearance. He then

explained to us that, as well as our gear, other members of the group had gathered up their surplus equipment as van Alblas wanted it all brought together. 'He's got a plan, Finn. He wants to bust everyone out of Scheveningen prison.'

'He's mad.'

'No. He has someone on the inside. A guard. Someone who'll help. It could work, Finn. Really. But first he must get all the gear into town.'

The mill suddenly became a hive of activity. Two brothers about our age, Guus and Pieter de Clerk, took the key from Freya and fetched large cloths from inside the mill. Clambering over the sails like monkeys, they set about attaching them. Laura returned, guiding Willem through the night. I ran to help. A cheerful van Alblas approached us. 'Excellent. Willem, you'll be fine as long you don't go straining yourself. Try not to make any sudden movements. Let me know if you start to feel faint or unsteady on your feet.' Water dripped from the brim of his hat but even in the gloom there was no hiding the excitement in the doctor's eyes. He jerked a thumb in the direction of the mill and informed me, 'Willem's the only one who knows how this monstrosity works. Could you lend a hand? We need all those logs moved to the cutting floor.'

When all the preparations were complete, and Willem had checked the settings for the mill's workings and the bench saws, he gave the order for the windmill's braking mechanism to be released. At first nothing happened, but then, slowly, the paltrok groaned and creaked into life – the sails began turning, straining to capture nature's breath. Willem disappeared inside to make some fine adjustments. I was awestruck. The great beast had come alive. She twisted slowly too, first to the left and then to the right, each movement accompanied by a rumbling that shook the ground. She was rotating on her rails, always keeping herself turned into the wind, to face the full force of the gale.

Van Alblas lit several additional oil lamps and set them down close to the cutting benches. Willem threw a switch to set the bands running, optimized the gearing ratios, and then checked each of the bands for the correct tension. Instructing everyone to stand well back, he pulled a lever. The circular blade of the bench saw began spinning ferociously, its hideously sharp teeth quickly becoming a blur. The old log that had been left there from months before was yanked free and the first new one was placed carefully into position on the bench. Spitting into the palms of his hands, Pieter de Clerk then grabbed hold of it and pushed it in the direction of the blade. The teeth made light work of slicing the log, the accompanying noise deafening despite the storm raging above us. Satisfied that the de Clerk boys knew what they were doing, Willem stepped back and looked on through one eye while offering guiding words of encouragement. Sawn pieces of timber were hurried across to another bench. There the rest of us began nailing the pieces together to make the coffins. They weren't fancy, just plain rectangular bone boxes.

'Van Alblas wants us to make as many as we can,' Loki yelled above the din. 'I told him that we could arrange for more supplies to be dropped.' Moving out of earshot of the doctor, he leaned over and whispered to me, 'I know that's Marieke's job – the second Special Ops network and all that – but I can't see any harm in us making the request.'

Looking exhausted, Willem leaned against the rail. Laura ran over and steadied him in her arms. Van Alblas went to check that he was all right, and tried to tell him to return to the house, but he insisted on staying – just in case something went wrong.

An hour later all the wood was used up and Willem cut the power to the bench saw. Then he applied the brake to the sails. They shuddered to a halt. Guus and Pieter quickly set about removing the cloths, folding them and returning them to the millhouse. Van Alblas was delighted with the products of our labour, running his fingers over the coffins. 'Fill half a dozen now and we'll take them with us on the barge. The rest can remain here.'

'There is something we must explain to you,' I said to the doctor as we sheltered under the porch. 'Loki told me about your plan. Any attempt to rescue people from Scheveningen prison is going to have to wait.'

He frowned at me.

'Finn's right,' said Freya. 'Our mission has been given priority over everything. We can't tell you any more – only that it's extremely important.'

'Out of the question. We must do what we can for

them,' van Alblas snapped. 'Whatever it is you're up to, I have *my* people to think about.' He began coughing again, quite violently this time.

'Some of our people are there too,' I said. 'Asparagus is part of our organization. Our orders come from the highest level.'

'I see.' Van Alblas removed his handkerchief from in front of his mouth and briefly inspected the sputum he'd coughed up. 'Very well. I shall hold back for now. Not for long, mind. Maybe my people can assist you – chivvy things along a bit.' He saw me staring at him with a look of concern. 'Don't worry yourself, I'll be fine.'

'Sounds like more than an ordinary cough to me,' said Freya. 'You shouldn't be out in the rain.'

Van Alblas ignored her and returned his attention to me. 'Well?'

'When our plan's finalized, we'll let you know,' I said. I spotted Guus de Clerk loading our supplies into one of the coffins. 'Wait!' I hurried over. 'I need some of this stuff.' I grabbed three Sten machine guns, clips of ammo and a couple of grenades, and handed them to Loki. After a bit more rummaging I chose a sleeve pistol, a handful of tyrebursters, some explosives and detonators and, for good measure, a packet of incendiary cigarettes. 'OK. You can take the rest.'

As van Alblas, Guus and Pieter chugged off into the night, six heavy coffins loaded aboard their barge, the rest of us walked back to the farmhouse. Saskia was sitting at the kitchen table kneading dough. I expected her to ask what we'd been up to but she said nothing. She just seemed glad Willem had returned unharmed. Laura brewed some *ersatz* coffee, and while she was waiting for the water to boil, Willem sought answers to questions that had clearly been on his mind since our arrival.

'I know you're probably not allowed to say much, but can you tell me about your escape from Norway to England? How on earth did you manage it?'

Loki peered across at me questioningly and I shrugged. 'I don't see any reason we can't tell him about that,' I said. Freya agreed. And so began our tale – about how vital maps had fallen into our hands, how the Germans were on to us, and how we escaped by stealing a float plane from the fjord close to our home town of Trondheim.

Willem was all ears. 'And so,' he said, 'after you made it to England – what then? How come you're here?'

'Let's just say we were recruited into an organization set up to cause the Krauts as much trouble as possible,' I replied.

Willem sat back in his chair. 'And they've trained you as Resistance fighters.'

'Yes,' Loki replied. 'We've been taught many things – how to survive on the run, pick locks, set explosives, unarmed combat, propaganda – you name it.'

Clearly impressed, Willem whistled. 'And how do you get to join this organization of yours?'

Laura placed steaming mugs down in front of us

and huffed, 'That's enough, Willem.'

'No, I want to know,' he insisted. 'It sounds good. To have the chance to fight back.'

'Don't be silly. You *are* fighting back,' Laura insisted.

'Yes but not like Loki, Finn and Freya.'

'Joining is by invitation only,' Freya said.

'I guess you need to have proved yourself. That you've got initiative. That sort of thing,' I added.

I expected more questions from Willem but he fell silent; he was as white as a sheet and visibly exhausted. Saskia seemed relieved that particular conversation had come to an end. It was late, and she insisted Willem should go to bed – he'd seen enough action for one day. After putting the dough aside to prove, she followed him up.

'Do you think he'd be up to joining Special Ops?' Loki asked me in Norwegian.

'Reckon so. But it's not up to us, is it?'

Unfortunately I think Laura somehow gained the gist of Loki's question because she suddenly appeared anxious. Clearing away our mugs, she said firmly, 'Willem's place is here. He is needed to run the farm. Saskia couldn't manage without him.'

I caught Freya's eye and could see she was thinking the same as me. What Laura was really saying was that *she* couldn't manage without Willem.

'I must go. It's late.' Laura shook our hands and pulled up the hood of her coat. 'Thank you for the supplies. If you need help, come over to our place, day or night. My parents can be trusted too.'

We all bid her goodnight. After she'd gone, we decided it was time to plan the following day's business. Conversation focused on Marieke's instructions to meet at Otto's. Loki sat back on his kitchen chair and pulled a face. 'I don't like it. I've got a bad feeling. Going back into town's surely too risky, Finn.'

'That's what Marieke wants me to do, so I'm going.'

He grinned. 'Of course you are. And we're coming with you.'

'Marieke said I should go alone.'

'To hell with what she said. We stick together. That's our motto.' He looked to Freya for support. 'I'm right, aren't I?'

Freya agreed. 'We'll keep watch outside Otto's, Finn. While you go inside.'

'And another thing,' Loki added. 'This time we go prepared.'

I examined the residue of our supplies. 'We can only take the stuff we can conceal. That rules out the Sten machine guns.' I picked up my favourite weapon, the sleeve gun. 'I'll take this. And those cigarettes.'

Freya separated out the tyrebursters and grenades. 'It's too risky carrying these in our pockets. They need to be hidden in something . . .'

I glanced around the kitchen, and my eyes lit on the dough proving by the stove. 'That's it – we can hide them in the bread!'

Chapter Seventeen
Otto

We rode into The Hague with quickened pulses, avoiding the numerous roadblocks and checkpoints along the way by cutting across wasteland, and negotiating alleyways and paths. The sun had returned but it felt cool in the stiff easterly breeze. Suspicious characters on street corners did little to quell the butterflies in our bellies as we ventured deeper into town. They weren't in uniform but we knew they were almost certainly German Intelligence, probably Abwehr. Equally suspicious were cars parked beside the kerb at key junctions. The suited men inside were probably Gestapo. The enemy was clearly on high alert, looking out for anything remotely suspicious. The Nieuwe Siegelstraat was bustling as we made our way towards Otto's. A bustle was good as it meant we could go about our business without attracting attention.

If we were stopped, our papers would be in order and we'd be able to explain our reason for being in town and visiting the tailor's shop. The parcel of cloth in my bike basket would add credence to my tale – a delivery, to be made into a suit. I'd found the material in a box in my attic room. I reckoned I'd be pretty convincing. And even if some grumpy servant of the Third Reich decided to subject me to the customary search, their pats and prods of my clothes were unlikely to reveal much. The cigarettes in my pocket would appear unremarkable – the Belgian Vega brand of tobacco was readily available in Holland. However, each slender cigarette contained a small incendiary pellet that, when ignited, would burn with an incredibly hot flame. Any search would also have to be pretty thorough for them to detect my sleeve gun. The single-shot weapon was less than nine inches long and just over an inch in diameter, including its silencer; perfect for close-range combat. When needed, it simply dropped down into your hand and you pressed the muzzle hard up against the enemy. The trigger was activated with your thumb. One of its merits was that it made little noise. After firing it, you slipped it back up your sleeve and walked away; even the empty shell case was retained in the device. Good in a tussle but useless at any distance over about three yards. Loki and Freya had split some of the other items between them. The cloth-wrapped bread smelled delicious, yet each loaf and bun hid something that might just get us out of a tricky situation. The deadly débâcle outside the Rembrandt was not going to be repeated – if there was a raid we'd fight our way to safety.

As I approached the tailor's shop, a distant church bell rang out the hour – midday. We were bang on time. Loki and Freya wished me luck and fell back, stopping to casually window shop. I checked up and down the street. All clear. It was safe to proceed.

I leaned my bike up against the window, pressed my

nose against the glass and peered inside, past the smartly dressed mannequins to the gloom beyond. I couldn't see anyone. All the way into town I'd been repeating the code phrase under my breath, trying to remember what Marieke had written in her note to me at Mulberry House as if rehearsing lines for a school play. It was a really long sentence, hard to remember and even harder to pronounce. I took a deep breath, grabbed the parcel from the bike's basket and pushed open the door. A brass bell above my head tinkled. I stepped inside and closed the door behind me.

Shelves from floor to ceiling were stuffed with fabrics of different colours, weights and textures. There were mirrors too, some fixed to the walls, others freestanding. A long counter ran across the back of the shop, and behind it a doorway was shrouded by a drape. It billowed, and a short, elderly man appeared as if he were the grand finale in some sort of astonishing magic trick, a tape measure draped around his neck. From behind round wire-framed spectacles he studied me expectantly.

'Otto?' I asked hesitantly.

Pursing his thin lips, he returned the faintest of nods.

'*Wij gaan in het weekend naar een bruiloft. Het zijn deftige mensen en we zullen zecker nieuwe kleren nodig hebben,*' I tried my best to say.

'*Je hebt in jaren geen pak gedragen,*' he replied dryly. Then he smiled and switched to English. 'I've been expecting you. Wait a minute.' He hurried round the counter and brushed past me. He set about bolting the door to the shop, top and bottom, and turned over a sign to indicate the place was now closed. Glancing both ways along the street, he then visibly relaxed. 'Your Dutch is accurate but poorly pronounced,' he informed me. 'You must practise. Now, come with me.'

Otto led me towards the rear of the premises, into a long work room with large windows in the roof and lamps suspended from steel beams every few feet. It was a place of great industry: tables were strewn with partially unravelled swatches of material covered in chalk lines and crosses. There were scissors, tape measures, needles and thread everywhere, along with oddly shaped bits of paper, lengths of braid and shiny buttons. The sight of several Nazi uniforms, including one for a high-ranking officer of the SS, sent a shiver through me. Otto saw me gawping at them.

'The Germans pay well for my services. They appreciate quality workmanship and attention to detail. And they often visit in twos and threes. I don't mind listening in on their idle chatter during fitting sessions. One can always learn something useful. I trust no one followed you here.'

'No. I did the usual checks.'

'Good.' He gestured for me to sit down but I preferred to remain standing. I put my parcel on the nearest table. 'As you're here, I take it Marieke's message reached you last night,' he continued.

'That's right. Yesterday was one hell of a day, what with the shootings outside the Rembrandt.'

'Ah, yes, the Rembrandt. Terrible business.'

'Do you mind me asking – are you a member of the Resistance?'

'No. To the outside world, I am not a member of any group apart from the Dutch Guild of Master Tailors,' he responded. 'And I'd like to keep it that way. My involvement in all this is merely to assist my granddaughter, Marieke.'

'So you're Marieke's grandfather!'

'Yes. On her mother's side.'

'Really?' I was surprised. I couldn't see any resemblance, and Marieke hadn't said. For a split second I became suspicious of the man before me. 'What can you tell me about her parents?'

'Drowned in the floods. That was before the war. Then she went to England to live with her other grandparents. Oxford, I believe.' He turned his head and looked at me. 'You're testing me, aren't you?'

'Yes, sorry. But I need to be sure I can trust you.'

'Very wise. She confides in me and seeks my advice now and then. I am not a courageous man. I have no desire to wind up in some dark cell or face a firing squad. A coward, some might say.'

'Hardly,' I replied.

He sighed as if he wished that things were different, that he was different; that he had the stomach for bearing arms, the courage to fight back. Of course, he *was* fighting back in his small way. No Resistance movement could survive or flourish without men like Otto.

'Now, we should get down to business.' He went over to a small writing desk in the corner of the room. From it he removed a rather tatty map. 'Marieke said that you are to meet her at a shop not far from here. At one o'clock.' He glanced at his watch and tutted as if I might have to hurry.

'I've got a bicycle,' I told him, trying to hide my excitement. I would be seeing her again after all.

'Good.' He showed me the location of the shop and told me that it was a *fournituren*, which left me stumped. He pointed to boxes of buttons and zips, so I supposed he meant some sort of haberdashery.

'Has Marieke told you why she's here?'

Otto shook his head. 'I merely listen to what she decides to tell me. I don't pry.'

'I see. Do you know where she's staying? Only, if we fail to rendezvous, it's vital I find her.'

'I rely on her visits to me. I have no idea where she's staying or when she'll next turn up. She was most insistent that I know as little as possible.'

'Then if we fail to meet up for any reason, can I come back here and leave a message for you to give to her?'

He nodded, then led me back out into the front of the shop and unbolted the door. 'Good luck, young man.'

Clambering back onto my bike, I nodded to Loki and Freya and they joined me as I cycled off. 'We have to meet Marieke at a shop. It's not far. Otto's her grandfather.'

'Some soldiers stopped and questioned us while you were in there, Finn,' said Loki.

I looked over my shoulder at them both. 'Papers were in order, then. That's a relief.'

'Yes,' added Freya, 'but for a moment I thought they were going to confiscate our bread. Luckily they got distracted, though I had the impression they were looking out for someone about our age.'

I led the way deeper into town, Otto's directions firmly lodged in my brain. I reckoned we had plenty of time and slowed, not wanting to arrive too early. Having time to kill meant we'd be forced to improvise in unfamiliar surroundings, and that was something I wanted to avoid. Loki suddenly called out, 'Bloody hell, Finn, that's Jan, isn't it?'

Having dashed out of a side street about a hundred yards ahead of us, a boy set off at full tilt in the direction we were heading, dodging and shoving past pedestrians, shouting at them to get out of the way as if his life depended on it. It *was* Jan.

We set off after him, overtook him and swerved to a stop on the pavement. At the last second he recognized us and staggered to a halt. His eyes were wide, scared, his face glistening with perspiration. His horror seemed to double on seeing us. Chest heaving, he leaned a hand on my shoulder and gasped, 'They follow me, Finn.' He looked around fearfully. 'You must go.'

'Who's after you?'

'Abwehr. Two. They try to grab me. I kick one between legs and hit one hard on the nose. I come to meet you and Marieke. But now I lead them away.'

'Uh-oh! There they are.' Loki had spotted Jan's pursuers.

Jan didn't waste a second. He set off like a shot, his arms pumping, his legs a blur as his feet pounded the pavement. I was about to shout to him to wait a second, but then I hesitated and looked the other way, towards the two suited figures, and to my dismay realized they'd spotted Jan too.

Loki spoke fast. 'Finn, you make for the rendezvous with Marieke. Freya and I will try to help Jan get away. Give me your sleeve pistol. I might need it. *Quickly!*'

Hurriedly I slipped the tubular weapon down my sleeve and surreptitiously passed it to him. I turned to see that Jan had disappeared from view. The two Abwehr men flew past us, each clutching a revolver. 'We'll meet up again later, outside Marieke's shop,' Loki said as he and Freya set off in pursuit.

When they'd all disappeared round a corner, an awful thought struck me. Would I ever see them again?

Shaken, I carried on into the old town, aiming for the Groenmarkt and the Grote Kerk, an ancient gothic church, both landmarks Otto had pointed out to me on his map. With every passing second, with every turn of my wheels, my fear for Marieke grew. Had she been pursued too? Was she running for her life? She held the key to everything. She knew where the airmen were. She knew where Father was. I stood up on my pedals and pumped my legs.

The shop chosen for our rendezvous was located near the entrance to a smart upmarket shopping arcade.

I saw it at the same moment I spotted Marieke weaving her way along the pavement, largely against the flow of other pedestrians. Her footsteps were hurried, almost breaking into a trot, and she kept peering over her shoulder. In truth she stuck out like a sore thumb. *Don't keep doing that*, I wanted to shout to her. *It's a real give-away. It looks too suspicious.* We'd been taught lots about evasion. If you wanted to check whether you were being followed without drawing attention to yourself, then it was better to cross the road, giving you the excuse to look both ways. Or you could stop to retie your shoe laces, sneaking a furtive glance back down the street from your crouched pose. Then there were shop windows – or rather, the reflections in them. They could tell you if someone was approaching, or watching you. In a moment of panic, had Marieke forgotten the basics? I doubted it. She was too good an agent for that. The alternative explanation made me shudder. It could mean only one thing: she *knew* she was being followed.

I slowed to a crawl and observed those who were behind her and heading in the same direction. The first promising sign was the absence of soldiers. My gaze took in a young woman pushing a pram, several older ones carrying their shopping, a boy carrying a stack of newspapers, and three men unloading sacks of coal from a cart. I couldn't see anyone suspicious.

Marieke slipped into the shop. Seconds afterwards I arrived. Judging by the contents of the windows, it was indeed a haberdashery. I swung onto the pavement, leaped off my saddle and propped the bike up against

the wall. Following her in, I was confronted by a
labyrinth of tall shelves, most sparsely filled. I weaved
among them and soon spotted her.

'Marieke!' I grabbed hold of her arm.

She turned sharply on her heels. 'Finn!'

A fat old lady clutching a small rat-like dog in her
arms squeezed past, tutting disapprovingly.

'It's so good to see you, Finn.'

'You too. Listen, bad news: Jan's in trouble,' I
whispered into her ear. There were others browsing the
shop and I didn't want them to overhear, especially as I
was speaking in English. 'He's being followed. Freya and
Loki are trying to help him get away.'

'I'm being followed as well. Did you see them? Two
men in a black car. Gestapo.'

'No. Are you sure?'

'Yes. Listen, Finn, we haven't got much time.' Rising
onto her toes in order to see over the shelving, she
glanced towards the door of the shop. She was in quite
a state, as if she'd not slept for several days. She was
twitchy too, her whole being tensed like a coiled spring.
'I'm sorry about the red card at Margo's. Jan took me to
the house he'd visited with Bram but the airmen had
gone. I assumed I was too late and the mission had to be
abandoned.'

'I know, Jan told me. He also told me that afterwards
you learned that the airmen had already moved on.'

'That's right. But the Germans have informers everywhere. One of them must've been keeping an eye on
the house after it was raided. Having seen us turn up,

and with me asking questions about comings and goings, the collaborator must've reported our descriptions to the authorities. I figure that's how they're on to Jan and me. They think we might lead them to the airmen. Everything's happened so quickly I didn't have a chance to remove the card at Margo's or swap it for a blue one. But then I realized I needed your help anyway, so I hoped you'd go to the Rembrandt.'

'We did. You heard about what happened there?' I explained about using my pills, and that despite hunting high and low I'd not found any messages left for us.

'It was verbal, Finn. Too risky to write anything down. I left it with the owner. An old family friend. Now a dead family friend.' On tiptoe she glanced towards the door again. 'It's too dangerous to keep the airmen in town, Finn. They need to hide somewhere else. I've had to keep them on the move, from one safe house to another. I've run out of options, and like I said, the Germans have informants everywhere. It's a nightmare. I was thinking of the farm, or maybe the windmill.'

'That night you broke into Mulberry wasn't just about delivering a message, was it?' I said to her. 'You wanted to find out where we'd be.'

'Yes. As things are turning out, I think it was a wise move. Can I bring the airmen to the Pols' farm? There's no other option. I've exhausted all my local contacts.'

'There's a real problem,' I told her. 'Germans come to the farm to steal food. It'd be too dangerous.'

Marieke looked defeated. Her shoulders dropped. 'Then we're lost.'

'No!' My raised voice attracted a few stares. Marieke pressed a finger against my lips. '*No!*' I repeated softly, thinking of Father. 'If there's no other option, the Pols' farm will have to do. I reckon if we keep them at the windmill they'll probably be safe, provided they steer clear of the farmhouse itself. It would have to be just for a few days, no longer. Others might need to be told as well.' I was thinking of van Alblas and his team.

Marieke hugged and kissed me. 'Thank you, Finn. I prayed you'd agree to it. I was at my wits' end.'

'Well, those airmen are *rather special*, aren't they? I took your advice and had a look at Gerrit's files.'

'Then you understand what's at stake, Finn. Just how unbelievably important this all is?'

'Yes, I do.'

Casting her eyes towards the door again, she whispered. 'I've got to go. Must try and stay one step ahead of the enemy. I'll bring the airmen to the farm. Just as soon as I can. Maybe tonight. If not, then tomorrow. Definitely no later.'

'I'll come with you,' I said without thinking, then remembered Loki had said he and Freya would meet me here at the shop, assuming they succeeded in helping Jan escape. 'Hell, I can't. I must wait for the others.'

'Stay here, Finn. Best you're not seen with me. Listen, in case it all goes horribly wrong, I'll give you the address where the airmen are hiding out. If you don't hear from me in the next forty-eight hours, assume I've been arrested. It'll be up to you to move the airmen. I

187

think I could resist interrogation for that long. You should be able to get them out.'

She whispered the address into my ear and I got her to repeat it just to make sure. I felt odd inside. They were just a few words but it was like hearing someone tell you the location of a hidden hoard of fabulous treasure. She turned to go.

'Wait,' I said. 'You should at least try to change the way you look.' I reached out and grabbed a dark green hat from a stand next to a display of colourful buttons. 'Here, try this on. Put your hair up inside it. And maybe we can find a few other things to help disguise you.'

'There's no time, Finn.' She tried to stop me but I managed to force it onto her head. Our hands got tangled up and somehow we managed to laugh together.

'Then that'll have to do.' I helped tuck her hair beneath the brim. She raised a hand and felt for the scar on her face. 'You look fine. It doesn't show,' I lied. Our eyes met and we held each other's gaze. 'Be careful, Marieke. I'll be waiting for you at the windmill.' We hugged again and I whispered, 'Well, I kept my promise, didn't I? That we'd meet again.'

She forced a smile. 'Yes, and let's hope it's not for the last time. I have to go, Finn.'

Paying for the hat, Marieke left the shop and turned right. I counted to ten and then left as well. I seized my bike, settled onto the saddle and covertly peered around for any sign of Loki or Freya. Nothing. As if that wasn't worrying enough, some fifty yards to my left a car was parked up. Two figures were sitting inside. Marieke was indeed right to be scared. Like us in Special Ops, the enemy were highly trained in surveillance. I suddenly doubted whether Marieke's newly acquired hat would be sufficient disguise and I was quickly proved right – the car edged slowly off, heading my way. They were definitely following her, either intending to apprehend her at an opportune moment, or content to bide their time in case she led them to where the airmen were hiding. Either scenario would prove a total disaster. An idea flashed into my head and I came to a decision. They had to be stopped, and it was down to me to do it.

Chapter Eighteen
A Deliberate Accident

I followed the car as it moved slowly towards a busy crossroads. Removing the packet of cigarettes from my pocket, I shook one out and placed it between my lips.

Marieke was some way ahead. She'd been clever too, befriending the old woman who'd squeezed past us earlier in the shop. Marieke was now walking beside her, chatting and laughing, the woman's ugly little rat of a dog scrambling and tugging at the end of its lead, a lead that now yanked Marieke's hand. She had offered to carry the woman's shawl too, and had thrown it over her own shoulders. With her hair pushed up under her hat she was barely recognizable. But the men in the car hadn't been fooled. They'd seen her emerge from the shop. I feared the worst – Marieke might believe that she'd got the better of them, that she'd given them the slip, that she was safe.

The car drew to a stop at the crossroads and waited as a heavily laden horse and cart trundled across the junction. This was my chance. Striking a match and cupping my hands to shield the tip of the cigarette, I lit up. All the while I kept one eye on the men in the car. Their attention was firmly fixed on Marieke and they were totally unaware of my presence. *Perfect*, I thought as the driver crunched back into gear and began rolling forward. The cart was almost out of his way. Deftly I swung round to the near side of the car. Now came the tough bit. It was all a question of timing. As the car began accelerating I reached out and flicked the cigarette through the open rear window. *Bingo!*

Dropping back, I followed the car at a sensible distance of about twenty yards, placing another cigarette between my lips in case for some reason the first went out and I had to try again. Now it was a waiting game.

I imagined the moment the incendiary flared up and set the back seat alight. They'd have to pull over to extinguish it. Marieke would have a chance to slip away. On we went, but nothing happened. Maybe the cigarette was a dud, I thought, or maybe it had gone out. Or . . . perhaps the incendiary pellet was near the unlit end and needed more time, something we had precious little of.

My plan wasn't given time to reap its rewards because Marieke suddenly glanced over her shoulder, and even I could see from the change in her expression that she'd clocked the men in the car. Realizing the enemy had seen her react, she let go of the dog's lead, flung the old women's shawl to the pavement and began running. Instantly the car pulled away from me, accelerating hard. The game of cat and mouse was over. They were moving in on her, about to pounce.

I rose up on my pedals and gritted my teeth. Racing after them, I willed Marieke to escape. Frantically she barged a path along the street, the little dog scampering along at her heels. It was the hunters versus the hunted – a deadly game. The car was gaining on her. I had to pedal furiously to keep up. The passenger leaned out of his window, pointed his pistol at Marieke and fired. He missed and she kept going, her strides lengthening, her coat trailing in her wake. Her hat fell off and spiralled to the ground. People dodged out of her way, scattering, fearful they might be struck by a wayward bullet. A second shot rang out. People sprawled flat, covering their heads with their hands. Marieke was the only one standing, the only one running. I swerved violently to avoid vegetables that had spilled from hastily dropped shopping bags; they bounced across the road like discarded marbles. The German steadied his arm, taking aim more carefully. He'd surely hit her this time – they were perilously close. I had only a second to think. Marieke was about to die and I couldn't let it happen. I just couldn't. In a rush of blood, in a moment of astonishing clarity, it dawned on me that she was far more to me than just a fellow agent. There was only one thing I could do to save her . . . but it was going to hurt.

With my legs pumping, my muscles burning and my lungs complaining bitterly, I made one final bid to accelerate past the car. There wasn't a moment to lose, no time even for a hasty prayer.

I swung out in front of the car.

The bumper ploughed into my front wheel and catapulted me across the bonnet. I hit it hard and rolled, and rolled again, smacking my head against the windscreen before spinning round and dropping awkwardly onto the road the other side. I landed heavily, winded. I tried to draw breath but it hurt like hell.

Opening my eyes, I found that the world was spinning, and despite the daylight there were millions of stars before me. I heard angry voices, German voices. Doors opened and slammed shut. I tried to blink my dizziness away. My head throbbed. Someone grabbed hold of me by the scruff of my neck and hauled me to my feet. I couldn't stand properly and swayed drunkenly. I was spun round and my back slammed hard up against the car. I groaned feebly. A hand took hold of my chin and held it like a vice. I blinked. A face came into focus, a face inches away from mine.

'*Dummkopf!*' His spit landed on my cheek.

He let go of me and I wiped his gob from my face with the sleeve of my coat. Could I make a run for it? Hell, I could barely stand up. My elbow felt sore, but it was my head that hurt the most. There was a strange metallic taste in my mouth too, and when I spat, a streak of bright red spittle landed on the road by my feet. I raised a hand towards my throbbing left temple and felt the unmistakable sticky ooze of blood.

'*Stehen bleiben!*' the man barked, pointing his pistol at me. He looked so agitated I had the awful feeling he was about to shoot. But he didn't. While I gradually regained my senses the German inspected the front of the car and dragged the remains of my bicycle from beneath the bumper. It was a write-off. The front wheel was misshapen and about half the spokes were broken. The basket was crushed and the front forks bent too. He cast it onto the pavement in disgust and then called out to his partner, who'd leaped from the car and given chase after Marieke on foot. In the midst of it all there was good news – he'd lost sight of her. Marieke was safe!

The driver returned in the foulest mood imaginable. Receiving a hefty cuff about my already sore head, I was ordered to produce my papers, which I gladly did. For once I was happy that they took their time examining them. The longer I kept their attention, the better for Marieke, for the airmen, for *Father*.

'*Ausländer*,' snapped the man scrutinizing my identity card. '*Norweger*.'

They cursed at their misfortune at encountering a reckless, stupid, idiotic foreigner. Then they began questioning me – searching questions – and despite feeling sick and woozy, I had to think quickly and carefully. They got me to explain how I'd been stranded in Holland after the invasion of Norway. I responded to their questions in almost fluent German and merely looked confused when they tried their fragmented Dutch on me. My cover story seemed to be holding up. All the while, however, beneath my relatively calm and innocent – if somewhat battered – exterior, I had a growing sense of alarm. I could smell smoke. And it wasn't just cigarette smoke. The back seat of the car was smouldering. My earlier attempt at a distraction suddenly no longer seemed such a great idea. I had the feeling I'd inadvertently dug a deep hole for myself, maybe my own grave. Doing my best to look shocked, I cried, '*Feuer!*' and pointed.

Sharing my dismay, they set about beating the fire out, one of them ruining a coat in the process. Their bad day had just got worse. Not only had they lost sight of their target but they'd have to explain to their unsympathetic superiors how on earth they'd managed to damage valuable property of the Third Reich. Each angrily accused the other of discarding a lit cigarette butt and each denied it with equal bile. Riled to boiling point, they needed someone to blame. That someone was me. It was simple: it was my fault and I was going to pay dearly for it. I was searched – roughly too – and the contents of my pockets removed.

Amid all my hurt, all my trepidation, I rejoiced at the good fortune that Loki had earlier taken my sleeve pistol from me. Had he not, my cover would have been blown. As it was, I at least had a few things in my favour: my papers appeared in order, I was unarmed, and these thugs couldn't prove I'd done anything wrong. I thought I was going to get away with it.

Then one of them decided to take a closer look at my cigarettes. I couldn't figure out what had made him suspicious – after all, most people smoked. Having a packet on me wasn't incriminating in itself. Had he put two and two together? Had I underestimated him? Maybe it was just a hunch, or perhaps he'd seen such things before. My heart skipped a beat as he removed a cigarette and raised it to his nostrils. He sniffed it . . .

pulled a face . . . sniffed again . . . looked me in the eye
. . . grinned at me . . . and began rubbing it between his
fingers. As it disintegrated, fragments of paper and
tobacco fell from his fingers like confetti. Then he
cupped his other hand and dropped the residue into his
palm – the incendiary pellet. He proudly revealed it to
his partner. I was a dead man.

Chapter Nineteen
Cell Number Four

The thug grabbed my wrist and twisted my arm brutally behind my back. I cried out but to no avail. People in the street looked on. Of course, they could do nothing, and they dared not try. My captors' anger was replaced by great excitement. They knew what they had – at the very least a member of the Resistance; maybe something even more special, a foreign agent. As if to celebrate, they punched me in my kidneys. It made my knees buckle. I was bundled into the back of the car, then one of them followed and slumped down next to me. He grabbed hold of my hair, wrenched my head back and pressed the barrel of his gun hard into my ribs. The other drove at speed. I quickly guessed our destination – the German HQ situated on the boulevard at Scheveningen.

Dragged in through a side entrance of the Palace Hotel amid much fanfare, I was forced to stand upright in front of a desk and ordered to remain silent while my papers were handed over and re-examined by an official. Several SS officers were encouraged by my captors to come and look at the incriminating evidence against me – *those bloody cigarettes*!

The official scribbled down a few key facts, and his paperwork then received several inky stamps of eagles and swastikas. Asked whether I'd been properly searched my captors replied, *'Natürlich.'* Nevertheless, I was ordered to remove my boots, my belt, and my pockets received a second examination – just to make sure.

'Zelle vier,' the official snapped, waving us away.

Cell number four. I was pushed and shoved down a flight of stone steps, then along a basement corridor with whitewashed brick walls. The heavy iron door with the number four painted on it was hauled open and I was thrown inside. The door clanged shut and I heard a heavy bolt slide across. Footsteps faded. Voices and laughter softened to whispers. Silence.

The room stank of unmentionable things, so strongly that the stale air hummed with its sharpness and made me retch. There were no windows. A single naked bulb lit the ten-foot-square space. The only furniture was a wooden bench for a bed – no mattress – and a bucket.

I sat and let the tears stream down my cheeks. They were tears of failure. Furious that they'd got the better of me, I slammed a fist against the wall. It hurt like hell and had me gasping in pain. It served me damn well right. I knew only too well what lay in store. My stay at this 'hotel' was going to be far from comfortable. The horrors of interrogation awaited me. Of course, I wouldn't cooperate, not at first, but they expected that. In fact, if I spilled the beans without a fight they'd think I'd spun them a yarn. So there were the formalities to go through: the yelling of questions to be met by my stubborn, bullish silence; the threats of unspeakable acts to be met by defiantly tight lips; and then the grand finale, the agony of torture, comprising my screams, my eventual confession, my losing consciousness and my death, roughly in that order, maybe drawn out over several excruciating sessions – if I was really unlucky. How long could I resist? Twenty-four hours? Forty-eight? Could I yield slowly, drip-feed them stuff, string it out? That's what we'd been taught. If we couldn't hold out, then our aim had to be to buy others time. Damnation, I thought, if only they'd let me keep my boots. It'd only take a second to grab my L-pill, and only a few more to swallow it. I'd be dead in moments. I'd be beyond their reach. They'd not be able to touch me, to get me to talk. I leaned back against the wall and drew my knees up tightly, wrapped my arms around them and cursed the world.

As I awaited my fate, a new storm of awful thoughts gathered and raced around my head like a destructive whirlwind. The obvious frustration – that by being caught I'd placed everyone in mortal danger with no way of warning them – was quickly replaced by an overwhelming sense of alarm at the realization of a terrible truth. The Gestapo didn't need to break me in order to unravel our operation. They already had everything they needed – my identity papers. They gave the Pols' farm as my address. The enemy would waste little time raiding it. Imagining how events would unfold was like watching a horrendous car accident in slow motion. Unable to find me, Freya and Loki would eventually head back to the farm. And Marieke was risking life and limb to take the airmen, including Father, to the farm too. Everyone I cared about was converging on the one place the Germans were bound to search. And I was utterly helpless. I'd been reckless. By trying to save Marieke I'd jeopardized all. *You bloody idiot, Finn.*

Hour after hour I waited in my cell, my restless anxiety causing me to pace back and forth, periodically stopping to pummel a fist on the door, to shout and curse my captors. Eventually my fury dissipated and was replaced by an overwhelming sense of having been crushed like a fly beneath the sole of a boot – a Nazi jackboot. I slumped down on the edge of the bed and could only imagine the miracle of my escape.

Gradually a strange calm came over me. It was as if I'd accepted my predicament and needed to prepare for what lay ahead. I began noticing things too. The white-washed walls of my cell weren't entirely blank. Words had been scratched out with improvised tools – possibly a tie pin, button or belt buckle. Most were in Dutch, and I suspected some were prayers or verses from the Bible. There were names and dates too, and what looked like messages. I supposed prisoners wrote them in the vain hope that others would read them and pass them on if they survived their ordeal. Elsewhere, vertical lines had been etched in groups of six with slashes through them – the weeks of incarceration remembered. Then my eyes moved on to drawings that were almost child-like in their simplicity. A gallows with a man in German uniform dangling by the neck, a bearded face, and something that at first glance looked extremely rude. It struck me with a jolt. It wasn't rude at all, but a drawing of an asparagus tip. Bram or one of his team had been in this very cell and left a calling card. I recalled van Alblas saying that some members of Asparagus had been brought *here* and not to Scheveningen prison. I wanted to shout out names, hoping I'd be heard, but knew that was foolish. If Bram or others could hear me, then so could the guards. I scanned my cell looking for a ventilation grille: if I could whisper into it, my voice might carry to the neighbouring cell. There was no grille. But there were pipes, and they stretched from one wall to the other, and almost certainly ran the length of the building. They were low down, a foot from the floor. Crouching, I tore a metal button from my coat and began tapping out the Morse for SOS. Then I paused and placed my ear against the pipe. Nothing. I tried again and again. Still nothing. I tried tapping the Morse for 'Asparagus', and after the third repetition I thought I heard a reply. Yes. Someone was tapping a single word over and over: my word – Asparagus.

Is that Bram? I tapped.

No. Bram very sick, came the reply.

Who are you? I tapped.

Theo Drees, came the reply.

I remembered him from our training sessions with the agents from Dovecote: a skinny boy, brilliant at coding but so short-sighted he couldn't hit a bus at point-blank range. *Finn from Mulberry*, I tapped, adding, *Who else is here?*

There was a long pause. Then came, *Not safe . . . Not safe . . . Talk later.*

Bizarrely I found myself considerably cheered by our brief exchange. I suppose it was the thought that others were still alive that gave me strength. Bram was sick, but how sick? I decided to compile a list of questions for later. Who was here? What's wrong with Bram? Any plans for escape? Could any of the guards be bribed?

It was evening when the sound of footsteps snatched me from my thoughts. They ceased outside my cell. I leaped up and turned to face the door. I was shaking. I didn't want to. I wanted to stand tall, head held high, to show them I was prepared for anything. The bolts slid across. Maybe this was it. Was the final chapter in my short life about to begin? *Make it a good one, Finn,* a voice inside told me. *Remember you've been trained for this moment. Tell them nothing. Not for at least forty-eight hours. That might give the others a chance.*

The door swung open and I swallowed hard. Two guards stood in the corridor. A third marched in and grabbed my arm.

Chapter Twenty
A Room with a View

The office on the third floor occupied one corner of the hotel and had far-reaching views of the coast and sea. It was large, light and airy, and furnished with the splendour of a bygone era, all rich velvets, polished wood, gilded ornate mirrors and thick-piled rugs. I entered and saw a figure with his back to me, looking out of one of the tall windows. He had one hand behind him, the other raised close to his face and holding a cigarette. The glare of a glorious sunset streamed in through the window. Though he was little more than a silhouette, I could tell he was a senior SS officer.

'*Bitte setzen Sie sich, Herr Gunnersen,*' he instructed without even bothering to turn round.

The guard roughly manhandled me to a chair in front of a mahogany desk and made me sit down. He then retreated to the door and stood next to it.

'I understand your German is very good,' the officer said in perfect English.

I'm not falling for that old trick, I thought. I said nothing.

He turned to face me and I shuddered – Major Steiff, the utter sadist. My immediate panic was whether he recognized me from the Rembrandt. If he did, he didn't let it show. He also appeared to have recovered from the effects of my pills, although he did look a little pale, as if his stomach still felt dodgy. He approached the desk and sat down, stubbing out his cigarette. Briefly he peered at the dried blood on the side of my face but made no mention of it. Although I'd managed to stem the bleeding, my head still throbbed miserably. *Be calm, Finn. Be careful. Concentrate.* It struck me as unusual that the desk bore no files, no paperwork, no signs of work in progress whatsoever. There were pens in stands and a large, heavy silver inkwell, official stamps and blotting paper, a lamp and an ashtray and a telephone, all set out with an unhealthy precision. Steiff was fastidious: everything had to be *just so*, in its rightful place. The habit gave me an insight into the way his mind worked – methodical, rational and thorough, but lacking in imagination.

He opened a desk drawer, took out my identity papers and placed them on the table. '*Gefälschte Papiere, nicht wahr?*'

He reckoned they were fakes. I just folded my arms and stared at him hatefully.

After peering down into the drawer again, he looked up at me and tutted smugly. He was teasing me, amusing himself with some sort of silly game. He dipped a hand in and produced the packet of cigarettes. Holding out the packet, he offered me one. I shook my head. 'Thought not,' he said. He removed one and placed it carefully down in front of him. Breaking it up with his fingers, he located the incendiary pellet and held it aloft between finger and thumb. He nodded approvingly. '*Sehr gut!*'

I wanted to spit at him.

He raised a finger as if to say, *Wait, there's more — you must see this.* Producing my left boot from beneath his desk, he revealed to me the hollow heel in which my various tablets were kept. He laughed across the table at me. 'I've been a little unwell and I think you know why! I never forget a face, you see. There were three of you on bicycles yesterday outside the Rembrandt when I arrived and I noticed that one of you disappeared no sooner than I'd got out of my car. And that person was you. Definitely *you.*' His face grew sour. 'Your biggest mistake, of course, was not choosing this pill.' He held up my L-pill, and for once I agreed with him. I briefly thought about leaping over the table and ramming it down his throat. But he wasn't going to give me the chance. Sweeping everything back into the drawer, he slammed it shut and sighed as if bored with the game. He continued in English, 'You see, Herr Gunnersen, we know all your little tricks.' Slumping back into his leather chair, he added, 'You're a member of Special Operations, aren't you? We know all about your organization. Tell me, how is Sir Reginald these days?'

Sir Reginald? Who the hell was he? I remained calm and pretended I didn't understand a word.

He suddenly looked apologetic. 'Forgive me, I expect you only know him as X.'

God, it was hard not to show my surprise. Just how much did he know about us?

'And is Major Gerrit still complaining about being transferred to Special Operations?' He studied my face for a reaction. 'I would have thought Dovecote was right up his street. Nice big house and waited on hand and foot by that Sergeant Fitzpatrick. Although I suppose the place must seem very empty these days.' He laughed. 'Major Gerrit and I go back a long way. Before the war he worked for the Dutch embassy in Berlin. We met at many lavish parties. And he has such a beautiful wife. A delightful woman. Very cultured. Loves the opera.' He leaned back in his chair and lit another cigarette, exhaling towards the ceiling and no doubt feeling triumphant.

He thought he was being so clever, but in truth he was telling me far more than he realized. He evidently had no idea that Gerrit had been exposed and had blown his own brains out rather than face the ignominy of a court martial. And that meant our side of the operation was still secure. Steiff had no idea about Aardappel or that we knew all about his little sham.

'As I expect you already know, we have many members of your Asparagus circuit safely locked up.' He shifted back in his chair and crossed his legs. Drawing long and hard on his cigarette, he seemed totally relaxed, totally in control. 'To be honest, we thought we had the lot of you, so I must congratulate you for evading capture for so long.'

That confirms it, I thought. *He reckons I'm a member of Asparagus.*

'What you probably don't know, Herr Gunnersen, is that we've been in almost constant contact with your HQ for months now, asking for more agents, more supplies, all kinds of things. And your superiors have been most accommodating. Several of your team have been most helpful too, providing us with their code books and, indeed, sending these messages themselves.' He expected me to look shocked but I continued to act as though I didn't have a clue what he was on about. Casually examining the thumbnail of his left hand, he began questioning me. 'How long have you been in Holland, Herr Gunnersen? How did you get here? Who are your contacts? What is your real name?'

I stared right through him.

Sighing wearily, he leaned forward. 'You will tell me – *eventually*.'

My silence filled the room.

'Very well. I can see you prefer to do this the hard way. Let me show you something.' Irritated at being stonewalled, he removed a piece of paper from his desk drawer and placed it on the table in front of me. He tapped it with a finger. 'Take a good look. I'm sure you'll recognize a few of these names.'

I leaned forward and scanned the list.

'Some are presently assisting us with our little wireless game.'

There were about a dozen names. Several I recognized, including Bram's and Theo Drees's. Since most agents entered the field with false cover identities, it was quite shocking to see that Steiff knew their real names.

Steiff removed another list from his drawer. This one was longer, much longer, maybe a hundred or so names. My heart sank at spotting the heading *Todeskandidaten*.

It was a list of those condemned to die. He spun it across the table to me. 'Most have already been executed,' he declared. 'Those with crosses beside their names have had their sentences carried out.'

He was trying to frighten me into cooperating. I scanned the list looking for names I recognized. I suppose deep down I feared seeing Loki or Freya's name, or those of Marieke and Jan, even though this was highly improbable. To my relief their names weren't there. I turned the piece of paper over. More names. More crosses. Then one caught my eye – Gottfried Pol. It had a cross against it. Saskia's husband, Willem's father, was dead. Worse, Saskia and Willem had no idea. They presumed he'd been taken to Germany as slave labour to work in the factories. I recalled what Willem had told me: that the Germans knew his father was a communist and that they hated them almost as much as the Jews. That was probably enough to seal Gottfried's fate. An intense anger ignited in my belly. I looked up and stared venomously into Steiff's eyes.

'So you understand the choice facing you,' he said, rummaging in his drawer for a blank piece of paper. Removing a pencil from his tunic pocket, he placed both in front of me. 'I require two things from you, Herr Gunnersen, that's all. Furnish me with them and I'll make sure your life's not made too uncomfortable. Fail to cooperate, however, and you'll regret the very day you were born.

'Firstly, I wish to know the names of everyone still active as part of Asparagus, together with any civilians who have assisted you. Secondly, we are aware that there are presently some British airmen being hidden by the Resistance. Among them is someone we're extremely keen to speak to. It is of great importance. We know that Asparagus was given the job of helping them to escape, and so I want you to write down the address of their safe house.'

Peering at his watch, Steiff seemed surprised at how late it was, and got up from his chair. 'Now, I have important business to attend to but I shall return in one hour. By then I expect you to have written out everything I have asked for. If not, we shall begin again, and you will not like what we'll do to persuade you to talk. Not one little bit. Understand?' Removing the drawer and all its contents, he placed it under his arm and made for the door. He saw me staring at it longingly. 'Well, you didn't really think I was going to leave these here, did you? Don't want you popping your lethal pill. That wouldn't do at all.'

I heard the door close behind me. I turned in my chair and saw that the guard had remained in the room. I tried to stand up but he barked at me to stay seated. I glanced at my watch – ten o'clock. One hour. One hour to think of something.

Chapter Twenty-one
Welcome to Hell on Earth

For fifteen minutes I fiddled with the corners of the sheet of paper, then picked up the pencil and put it down again. I wrote nothing and had no intention of doing so. Instead I desperately tried to recall our very first visit to Scheveningen, when we stopped outside the hotel and memorized the positions of everything. I was on the third floor, corner room, the windows more or less facing north and west. What lay beneath them? Was it a sheer drop or was there a flat roof below that I could safely drop down onto? Yes, there was an extension to the building on the west side, I recalled. But did it extend that far? I couldn't be certain. Even if it did, that still meant a substantial drop. I needed to get a look, to find out if it was possible. Pretending to come over all hot and bothered, I asked the guard if I might open a window to let in a little air. '*Nein!*' he responded sharply. I threw a few more questions at him. Could I go or be escorted to the lavatory? '*Nein!*' Could I have a glass of water? '*Nein!*' Did he know any word other than *nein*? . . . '*Ja!*' It was hopeless.

The second fifteen minutes was consumed with scanning the room with my trained eye, trying to fathom whether anything might be useful to me. Although transformed into an office, the room had once been a luxurious bedroom, I reckoned. Long crimson velvet drapes framed the tall windows and were tied back by heavy cords. If I'd been alone in the room I might have been able to fashion some sort of rope or slide with them. The guard had put paid to that idea. Unless I could overpower him. Just as I'd begun to think it might be possible, the door swung open and Steiff reappeared. He'd returned far sooner than expected and wasn't alone. Two men followed him in, one a gaunt, evil-faced junior SS officer, the other an elderly man in a white coat and carrying a leather case. Steiff glanced at the blank sheet on the desk, sighed wearily and then bellowed the order for me to be tied to the chair.

My hands were bound so tightly behind me I feared the blood flow to my fingers would cease. Satisfied that however much I struggled I wasn't going anywhere, the young officer removed his tunic, rolled up his sleeves, raised a hand, and slapped me hard across my right cheek. It stung like mad but I didn't cry out. He evened it up by striking my left cheek. Steiff repeated his questions and I shook my head defiantly. He gestured for my beating to continue.

More slaps, harder. Gritting my teeth, I continued to shake my head. *This is all right*, I kept telling myself. *Doesn't really hurt that much. Not much at all.* I could keep this up for hours. Back and forth his hands went, slap after slap. My cheeks began to burn and my neck jarred each time my head resisted his swinging palms. Slowly numbness replaced the pain.

There was a pause in proceedings as the man

removed a steel knuckleduster from his trouser pocket. Sliding it over his fingers, he clenched his fist. The instrument fitted his hand perfectly, as if he'd had it specially made. He looked at Steiff, who returned the faintest of nods. With sickening purpose the officer swung his fist and slammed the metal into my jaw. My head reeled and my ears rang. Again and again he struck, one blow dislodging a tooth. I groaned and felt my consciousness slipping away. My head dropped. He grabbed hold of my hair and lifted my head up. I could taste blood. My lip was cut and I had the awful feeling I'd bitten into my tongue.

Steiff raised a hand, came close to me, bent down and peered into my face. Satisfied I was still conscious, he screamed his questions at me again, demanding answers immediately. When I refused, he looked disappointed and turned his back on me. As the metal of the knuckleduster greeted the side of my face once more, the light faded and their voices grew muffled. The next thing I knew a glass of water had been thrown into my face to revive me.

'This is just the beginning, Herr Gunnersen. You do know that, don't you? It is pointless resisting. You will be begging to tell us everything by the time we're finished. So spare yourself any more discomfort.'

I was punch drunk, but although my jaw felt stiff and my speech slurred, I hissed, 'Go to hell.' The broken tooth fell from my mouth.

Steiff laughed. 'We are already there, Herr Gunnersen. We're already there!'

During training we'd experienced interrogation. They tried their best to make it realistic. They had us working for days on end with little sleep and even less food, and when we were utterly exhausted they waited until we fell asleep and then dragged us from our beds. Disorientated and confused, we were confronted by unfamiliar faces – instructors from other Special Ops teams dressed in SS uniforms – and were stripped, roughed up a bit and spent hours undergoing harsh questioning. At the time it had seemed real enough. Now I understood its shortcomings. There'd be no end to this torment other than death. And the pain – nothing can prepare you for it. We'd been told to do our best to hold out for forty-eight hours. Forty-eight hours! *Impossible*.

When I lost consciousness for a third time, I entered a strange dream world. I'd escaped to another place. It felt like heaven. I was home, in my beloved Norway. At least, I think I was. Everything was hazy, bathed in a strange light, and fragmented just like in my usual dreams, all jumbled up and making little sense. I glimpsed the mountains and fjords where I grew up. I heard Mother's voice and saw flashes of my sister, Anna. And then there was Father, repeatedly saying goodbye to me, waving as he clambered into his float plane for his flight to England. He was smiling at me and shouting to me to be strong, that one day soon we'd be reunited. I stood there and watched him take off, the water streaming off the end of the floats as his plane rose from the surface and climbed. Then I was at Mulberry

House. I saw Jan Keppel's face. He was wrapped in blankets and rocking back and forth on the sofa. Loki took hold of me and was shaking me. Freya stopped him and then told me everything was all right. Next I was groping on the floor in the dark. I couldn't fathom where I was. Then somehow I knew – the brigadier's office. I'd picked something up and was trying to make it out. A photograph. A picture of Father. He was talking to me. *Be strong, Finn. Freedom is worth the sacrifice. It's the most precious thing we possess.* He often told me that. He smiled and waved. Then the image faded. I called after him, *Come back. Take me with you*, but all to no avail. With *Be strong, Finn, be strong* . . . echoing somewhere deep inside my head, I gradually came to and realized Steiff was shouting at me, his face inches from mine. I groaned, realizing I was back in Hell on Earth.

Steiff's frustration was written all over his face. *God, my head hurts*, I thought as I watched him stand up and begin pacing the room. He seemed a little blurred. My right eye had swollen up. I felt woozy and weirdly unbalanced. I tried struggling but I remained tightly bound to the chair.

Steiff casually lit up a cigarette and leaned on the corner of his desk. 'You are more determined than most, young man, and I respect that. You've done your bit. You've proved your courage. Your country can ask no more of you. Now let us put an end to this unpleasant business. You must realize that your situation is hopeless. Answer my questions and I will see to it that we make life a little more comfortable for you. I'll even make it easier for you. Let's forget about your fellow agents for now.' He reached into his tunic pocket and removed a photograph. 'Just tell me where this man is.'

It was a picture of Major Kiefer, the German officer I saw in the file back at Mulberry; the spy codenamed Falcon.

'Surely you can do that,' Steiff added. 'He's among those airmen I mentioned. He's a German, Herr Gunnersen. And we want him back. So surely it's no problem for you to tell us where he is. After all, he's your enemy.'

I was groggy. All I wanted to do was curl up and sleep, to make the pain go away. I was weak and vulnerable, but not yet weak and vulnerable enough. I raised my bloodied head and spat at him. He tutted and shook his head as if in pity.

It was now the turn of the man in the white coat. I'd been dreading finding out his part in all this misery. From his leather bag he removed a small roll of material. He set it down on the desk and unravelled it. Inside lay a series of pockets, each containing a scalpel with a different-shaped blade: some were straight, others curved, one or two had hideous-looking hooks to them. He ran his fingers over them but instead chose an implement that looked like a cross between a pair of pliers and giant nail clippers. Despite my writhing, he knelt down and removed my socks. My heart sank into the floor. I was about to lose my toenails, one by one. I swore, spat, tried to wriggle free, tried to kick the man, but it was useless.

As he prepared to do his worst, the oddest feeling came over me. I thought of that old man outside the Rembrandt. He knew his time had come too. And he'd stood tall, shoulders back, and accepted his fate. I stopped struggling in my chair and ceased trying to kick the bastard in the white coat. I sat still, closed my eyes and prayed that it would be over quickly. And I'd come to a decision. What will be will be. There was only one thing left within my control now – whether to yield or stay silent. And I'd made up my mind, once and for all. I would remain silent, no matter what . . . *so help me God*. I'd come to rescue Father; failing in my mission was one thing, but it was quite another to be responsible for his capture. I clenched my teeth and braced myself. I felt an excruciatingly sharp pain and cried out.

Steiff's telephone rang.

'*Ja! . . . Was? . . . Mein Gott!*' Struck with a sudden fury, Steiff listened intensely, shouted something about sending everyone available, and finally declared he'd come immediately. He hung up and gestured for the man in the white coat to stop. 'I'm afraid we must interrupt our little chat, Herr Gunnersen. We must leave you for a while but we shall return.'

He gave the order for me to be untied. I had the impression the telephone call had delivered bad news. I was no longer worthy of occupying Steiff's full attention. Stabbing a finger at the piece of paper on the table, he said, 'Save us all a lot of trouble, Herr Gunnersen. The address of the safe house. That'll suffice.'

Suddenly I was alone in the room with the solitary

soldier guarding the door. Despite my swimming head, I noticed that it was dark outside and my thoughts returned to the possibility of escape. This would undoubtedly be my last chance. I looked towards the window and studied the heavy velvet drapes. Maybe, I thought, just maybe there was a way.

Chapter Twenty-two
A Window of Opportunity

One thing was in my favour. The guard was carrying a standard issue MP40 machine gun slung from his shoulder by the usual leather strap. He wasn't expecting me to cause him much trouble: I was sitting with my back to him, and about twelve feet separated us. He'd rested one hand lazily on top of the gun's muzzle, and I spotted that he'd left the safety catch on.

Despite my pounding head, I began calculating; the most important calculations of my life. I knew that if I sprang up and smashed my way through the window, it would take me about four or five seconds to get out. Too long. If I grabbed a pen or the solid-looking inkwell from the table, then turned and rushed him, it could be done in two to three seconds. The element of surprise might make him fumble, and that would buy me precious fractions of a second too. My palms glistened with sweat. Was it possible? It *had* to be possible. I considered grabbing the lamp instead. It was solid brass and it would be easy to clout the oaf with it. But, no, the flex needed tearing from the wall socket, and that might delay me by half a second. Too long. I'd be dead. *Pen or inkwell? Pen or inkwell?* I couldn't decide which. The alternative was to put everything Kip 'Killer' Keenan had taught me into practice – unarmed combat.

I knew the techniques. We'd spent hours, weeks even, practising them. Even so, I wasn't exactly in the best shape – my right eye was closing up, and my left foot was sticky with blood oozing from where my toenail had once been. Damn! Then again, perhaps there was one move worth trying out together with a makeshift weapon. But which weapon? *Pen or inkwell? Pen or inkwell? Think, Finn, think!* I was in turmoil. My good eye darted back and forth between them. I was running out of time. With every passing second I risked Steiff's return. It was now or never. I reached out and placed a hand about the base of the inkwell. It felt solid, weighty. I lifted a pen from its stand. Although as long and slender as a dagger, it felt very fragile. The inkwell was better. Sliding it nearer, I hunched over the table and feigned writing with the pencil, shielding the piece of paper with my other arm just like I used to do during school exams when I didn't want anyone to see my answers. Slowly I wrapped the fingers of my free hand around the inkwell and eased my legs to one side of the chair. I needed to twist round, ready to spring, all without making it appear obvious. Still scribbling away on the paper, I took a series of long, deep breaths to fortify me, all the while counting down in my head to the moment of no return . . . *three . . . two . . . one . . .*

Spinning up from my chair, I accelerated. Twelve feet proved little more than three strides. Startled, the guard juggled with his machine gun as if it were a boiling hot potato, lifting it awkwardly and reaching blindly for the trigger. Drawing my right arm back, I made as though I intended to bash him with the inkwell. He saw it coming and flinched in anticipation. But my move was a feint. On my third stride I planted my right foot firmly and swung my left as if making a hideously vicious football tackle, pivoting my hips to add power. My left shin ploughed through his legs. He flipped and fell heavily onto his back. As he struck the floor I followed him down, my full weight behind the inkwell. I struck him once. It was enough to render him unconscious.

Up in a flash, I dragged him away from the door, seized the chair I'd been sitting on and wedged it beneath the handle. Then I leaned on it and drew breath. I felt exhausted and every tiny movement sent shooting pains through my head . . . and my foot. Summoning my strength, I slung the strap of the guard's machine gun over my shoulder, removed his pistol from its holster and wedged it into the waist of my trousers. Steiff had left my boots beneath his desk and, although it was agony, I put them on and hurriedly tied the laces. Limping across the room, I threw open the window facing west, leaned out and peered down. I'd been right. The drop was about fifteen feet onto a flat roof. But I spotted there were guards at the front of the building – lots of them – and all it would take was for one of them to look this way. So I checked the other window, the one facing north, overlooking the boulevard and the beach. Beneath lay a flat roof too. *Hallelujah!* For once the gods were smiling on me. The velvet curtains were about ten feet long and attached to a heavy metal rail by a series of brass rings. Taking hold of the curtains I brought my full weight to bear and tore them, complete with rail, from the wall. Gathering both curtains towards the centre of the rail, I tied them into a bunch at the top with one of the rope-like cords. It was time.

Leaning out of the window, I searched below for signs of guards. There was one – a solitary figure on the boulevard, pacing extremely slowly along the length of the building, turning at the end and making his way back. I could also see what looked like a massive concrete bunker at the corner of the adjacent Kurhaus and reckoned it was best avoided. Back and forth the guard went, never stopping to look round or up. I waited until he reached my end, turned and began his way back, before flinging the heavy velvet curtains out, bracing the rail against the window frame – the rail was a good two feet wider than the opening and so served as a decent anchor. Leaping onto the sill, I steadied myself, turned and eased myself out, placing my feet against the wall on either side of the curtains. Then, taking hold of the material, I leaned back. It held me. It was no different to the abseiling we'd done during training. Cautiously I began clambering down. I'd barely descended two feet when I felt the material jerk in my hands. It had torn away from one of the brass ring fastenings. A second went with an audible ping. Then a third. And a fourth. Panicking, I skipped down the wall quickly, knowing that when the material ran out I'd still have about another five or six feet to go. But I was ready, and when the moment came I kicked off the wall, dropped and landed on my toes. I stifled the urge to scream out in pain. On all fours I crawled to the edge of the flat roof, located a cast-iron drainpipe and, checking the guard hadn't yet turned round, shinned down.

I found myself on a wide paved area leading to the boulevard. Knowing I'd never get past the sentries and barriers to the front, I realized that the sand dunes offered my best chance of escape. Crouching in the recess of a doorway, I swung the MP40 from my shoulder, removed the magazine and checked it was full of ammo, replaced it and released the safety catch. There were lights on inside the hotel and I could hear German voices and piano music filtering out from open doors and windows. I dreaded that at any moment several officers might stroll outside for a breath of fresh air. I could be certain of only one thing: it wouldn't be long before my escape was spotted – as soon as anyone looked up they'd see the long velvet curtains flapping in the moonlight. Failing that, Steiff would undoubtedly raise the alarm the moment he realized the door to his office had been barricaded. I had to make a dash for it.

My plan was simple. I'd head away from the hotel, tear along the beach, lose myself in the dunes, discard the machine gun there and rejoin the boulevard at a safe distance. If I made it that far, I'd then have a crucial decision to make. Either head back into The Hague, seek out Otto and hope that he could help me in some way, or make for the farm and pray I'd be in time to warn Loki and Freya and the others.

A wall on the far side of the boulevard separated it from the beach. As best I could tell there was quite a drop the other side: maybe five or six feet to the sand. The beach was broad, the sea some hundred yards away. Moonlight gave the surface a rich satin sheen. I spent a moment studying the silhouette of the pier to my left but couldn't detect any movement on the walkway. The lazy footsteps of the sentry regained my attention. He was heading back my way. He needed to be silenced.

I emerged from the doorway like a tiger setting upon its prey. Keeping low, I crossed the paved area and then the boulevard, approaching the guard from behind. Using the butt of the MP40, I clobbered him with all my might and bundled him over the wall. He vanished and landed with a hefty thud. Leapfrogging the wall, I dropped down the other side, stifled a yelp as I landed and checked him over to make sure he was out for the count.

Sticking close to the wall for cover, I hurried along as far as I dared, at which point I estimated that I still had about two hundred yards to go to reach the dunes. In my battered state it seemed an impossible distance. *Keep as low as you can and don't make a sound*, I told myself. *Run as fast as you can and don't stop, no matter how much it hurts, no matter how exhausted you are.*

Checking the coast was clear, I set off into the night as fast as I could, clutching the MP40 in both hands in front of me. With every hobbling stride I completed without hearing the alarm being raised, I rejoiced, and even dared believe that I might sneak away without anyone being the wiser. But, having covered barely half the distance, I heard shouting to my right. A patrol had spotted me – two soldiers with motorcycles up on the boulevard. They were some way away. I didn't slow or change direction. There wasn't any point. I had to reach the dunes – it was my only hope.

I could feel the blood pumping through me and my head was pounding as if it might explode. My big toe was agony too. The muscles in my calves began to burn, strained by my uneven stride. Running in sand was cripplingly hard at the best of times. It was soft and yielding under my feet, slowing me down and sapping my energy. Hearing the stutter of machine-gun fire, I took to darting first one way and then the other, zig-zagging to make myself a harder target. I kept focused on my goal. The dunes were getting closer. I tried to lengthen my stride. The splutter and roar of motorcycle engines being kick-started filled me with dread. I imagined them in pursuit, squirming and weaving as they struggled to gain a grip, their rear tyres sinking in, spraying clouds of sand behind them. The further I went, the more the dunes appeared to rise before me like the beginnings of a great desert. Their silhouettes in the moonlight were eerie, wild, unnatural.

I made for a gap between two hills of sand. I knew that to try and scale one of the bigger slopes would prove disastrous, the gradient rapidly bringing me to a grinding halt, and my scrambling would get me nowhere. The gentler slopes enabled me to reach one of the lower ridges, held firm against erosion from the wind by large clumps of spiky marram grass. There, I turned and threw myself down. I could hear the roar of the engines closing in. I needed to know exactly what I was up against, so I rolled onto my stomach and peered back over the ridge. Two bright headlamps blinded me. They were heading my way, and fast. No way could I outrun them. I rose onto one knee, steadied my MP40 by pressing the butt into my shoulder, felt for the trigger and took aim with my good eye. I let off a short burst and found the weapon possessed quite a kick. I missed as the barrel arced into the air. *Hold your nerve, Finn. Grip it firmly. Let them get as close as possible. The bigger the target, the better.* I fired another short burst. One rider tumbled from his machine. The other accelerated, rising up off his saddle and leaning forward over his handlebars. I could sense he had just one thought in his head: he was going to run me down, crush me beneath the machine's weight. I pulled the trigger again and held firm as bullets blazed from the barrel, empty cartridge cases tumbling down in front of me. Still he came. The stutter and vibration of my gun shook me to the core. Bullets pinged and sparked as they struck the metal of the bike and one shattered its headlamp. Still he came roaring towards me . . . twenty feet . . . ten feet. As my gun's magazine emptied, the rider lurched violently backwards and upwards, as if some invisible force had grabbed him by the scruff of the neck and dragged him off his bike, but the machine kept coming. I ducked down behind the ridge just in time. The bike roared over my head and ploughed into a sandy slope behind me. I flung down my empty weapon and fled.

Up one slope and down the next, on I went,

scrambling, slipping, sliding through the dark, my legs aching, my lungs fit to burst. Although I couldn't hear anyone in pursuit, I had to assume they were there, closing in on me, spreading out in a line to make sure I didn't slip through their net. I needed to get back to civilization, to buildings, to an environment that offered possibilities for concealment. I changed direction and hobbled towards the boulevard.

I tried my best not to appear too conspicuous as I crossed the boulevard. There were plenty of people about. I didn't look back either. To avoid drawing attention I walked steadily, hands in pockets, hiding my nervousness and my limp. The dried blood from the gash on the side of my head was a worry, likely to land me in trouble if observed, as were my swollen eye and split lip. I had to rely on darkness to protect me, and so I avoided the light from streetlamps. Once beyond the boulevard, I crossed a road and slipped into a narrow gap between two buildings, sank into the gloom and took stock of my situation. I could hear shouting and the unmistakable clatter of dozens of soldiers' boots on the pavements. I prayed they were making for the beach to sweep across its length. It would take them a while to figure out I'd doubled back into town.

I had to think clearly, rationally, *calmly*. That afternoon Otto had told me that he didn't know how to contact Marieke directly. Other than as a place of refuge, his shop was of no immediate use to me. I could remember the address Marieke had whispered to me – the safe house where she'd left the airmen – but without a map it could take all night to locate. I was also bound to be apprehended trying. In any event I figured she'd probably already left, guiding the airmen to the Pols' farm. So that had to be my immediate goal: to reach the farm. As I'd only been arrested early that afternoon, it was conceivable Steiff's men hadn't raided it yet, a thought born more out of hope than anything, although I remembered that Steiff had reckoned my papers were false, so he might have supposed the address had been fabricated too. But with my escape, a raid on the farm would gain top priority: it was the only thing Steiff had to go on. I needed to beat him to it, and to do that I needed transport. Music drifted from a nearby café. There were bicycles leaning up against a wall . . . Time to borrow one.

It was pitch black as I approached the windmill on the path beside the canal. It had begun raining again too, just a light drizzle. The cool drops soothed my bruised and swollen face. Intending to head straight for the farmhouse, I halted in my tracks on hearing the door to the mill banging open and shut in the strengthening wind. Flinging my bike aside, I drew the pistol from my belt and approached the steps to the cutting floor. There were no lights, no voices, nothing.

Silently I stepped inside and began ascending the curved wooden staircase, carefully placing my feet so as not to make the treads creak under my weight. No one was there. I made for the top floor and the hiding place for Freya's transmitter. It was gone.

Was I too late? Had Steiff's men come and seized everything? Had they ransacked the place and found the incriminating radio set? Was that why the door had been left swaying in the wind? Hurrying outside as quickly as I could, I ran for my bike but hesitated on hearing voices and spotting torch beams. Whoever they were, they were coming from the direction of the farmhouse. Abandoning my bike, I made off into the nearest field and lay flat on the ground. Half a dozen Germans appeared. They stopped and gazed up at the windmill. A couple made their way inside. Scrambling to my feet and fearing the worst, I hobbled towards the farmhouse.

An army truck and a staff car were parked on the rutted track. The coast was clear. Pressing up against the farmhouse wall, I edged my way to the entrance to the yard and risked glancing around. Light was coming from the barn. The door to the house was open as well. Loki and Freya's bikes were propped up against the wall next to it. I risked looking in through the kitchen window. My stare settled on a basket containing the bread.

I slipped inside the house, grabbed the bread from the basket and began tearing it apart. A tyreburster emerged. Then another in the second loaf. Where were the grenades? I quickly discovered they'd already been removed. I'd have to make do. I placed the tyrebursters in my pocket and limped into the hall. The parlour was empty. I thought of Willem lying upstairs in the dark. Was he still there? I crept up and found his room – all the rooms – empty. The barn! They'd taken them all to the barn. A noise came from downstairs – first a clattering, and then what sounded like drawers being pulled out and cast to the floor, of stuff being swept from shelves with a rifle butt. I heard Saskia's precious collection of blue and white Delft china shatter as it fell from the dresser. I was trapped. The only way was up. I made for my room in the attic, knelt down and grabbed the rope I'd placed beneath my bed in case of emergency. Gently pushing the bed up against the wall directly beneath the dormer window, I tied the rope to the bed frame and eased the window open. I looked down. The coast was clear. I flung out the rope, climbed onto the sill and began my descent. This was becoming a habit, I realized, a very dangerous habit. Halfway down I hesitated. There was someone below, just round the corner, by the kitchen door. I froze.

'*Schnell, Hans!*'

'*Ich komme gleich, Leutnant Grüber. Ich komme gleich!*'

So Grüber was among the search party, I realized. Landing softly, I made for the cover of the SS Mercedes and crouched behind it. I watched as a spotty young private of the Wehrmacht emerged from the house carrying a long kitchen knife. He and Grüber headed back towards the barn. A blood-curdling scream emerged moments after they stepped inside. Who was being tortured? Were they all in there – Loki, Freya, Saskia and Willem? And what about Marieke and the airmen? And Father?

I dipped a hand into my pocket and removed a tyre-burster. Palm-sized, round and about an inch or so deep, it contained a small quantity of explosive triggered when a tyre ran over it by a neat little pressure switch. I twisted the lid to activate it and wedged it beneath the leading edge of one of the car's front tyres, then scurried across to the truck and placed the second device beneath one of the rear tyres. Removing my pistol, I checked that it was fully loaded and made for the large barn doors. Through a crack in the woodwork I saw the sick horror unfolding inside and the contents of my stomach churned.

Willem had been stripped to the waist and his hands tied above him to a beam supporting the hayloft. From the blood on his torso glistening in the lamplight, I could see that his suffering was well under way, his wounds being inflicted by the young SS officer who just hours earlier had acquainted me with his prized knuckleduster. Grüber and the other soldier were looking on in fascination. Crumpled in a heap on the floor to one side, a distraught Saskia sobbed un-controllably. Though I strained to look in all directions, I couldn't see Steiff or anyone else. So it was effectively three against one – poor odds, but I had two things in my favour: the element of surprise and a raging thirst for revenge.

'Tell me where the others are. We know they were here,' the SS officer hissed. Willem squirmed and shook his bloodied head. The officer pressed the point of the kitchen knife into Willem's back and twisted the blade. Willem howled like a wolf caught in the teeth of a viciously sprung trap.

'Wait!' Saskia wailed. 'No more. Please stop. I'll tell you what you want to know.'

'*Nee Moeder! Nee!*' Willem shouted defiantly.

On all fours, Saskia crawled towards the SS officer, reaching out to him, begging him to stop. 'They are at the next farm.' She pointed in the direction of the Kramers'. 'There. I've told you all we know. Now let him go. *Pleeease!*'

I had to act fast. Saskia had cracked under pressure and the remaining soldiers might return from the mill at any moment. I'd be hopelessly outnumbered. I pressed gently against the barn door and noted that with a decent shove it would swing open. Gripping my pistol tightly, I took three deep breaths, kicked the door open and leaped inside.

The young SS officer snapped his head round and glared at me. I pulled the trigger, and the force of the bullet flung him backwards. I twisted to my left and fired again, instinctively – no time to aim carefully – and the young private clutched hold of his chest and groaned as he sagged to his knees and then fell flat. That left Grüber. He darted across my field of vision towards the dangling Willem. I fired and missed. I fired again. It caught Grüber in the arm but no more than grazed him. He slipped behind Willem, grabbed him about the neck, and seemingly from nowhere produced his pistol. He pressed the barrel against Willem's temple and yelled at me to drop my gun or he'd shoot. My hand was shaking. I could see just enough of the Nazi thug's head to fire but I stood an equal chance of hitting Willem.

Grüber snarled at me again to relinquish my weapon.

Willem gazed at me intensely, his eyes narrowing. Breathing heavily, he called out to me in Norwegian, telling me to shoot, to shoot now – not to worry about him; all that mattered was putting a bullet into Grüber.

Saskia covered her face with her hands. I felt my grip on the trigger tighten. Yes, I had a shot, but it was damned difficult. An inch either way and it would be the end of Willem.

Grüber hissed, '*Halt's Maul!*' and pressed the barrel harder against Willem's head.

But Willem refused to shut his mouth. 'Shoot the bastard, Finn,' he yelled. 'On the count of three. I'll twist to my left – give you a better target. One . . .'

'*Halt's Maul!*' Grüber shouted again.

'Two . . . three . . .'

Using his formidable strength, Willem twisted to one side, revealing a slice of Grüber's torso. I pulled the trigger, a blast rang out, and Grüber's eyes widened. I fired again. The Nazi thug's grip on Willem's neck loosened and his pistol slipped from his hand. He toppled like a felled oak.

I rushed to grab the kitchen knife from the floor and set about freeing Willem. Saskia ran to support her son's bloodied body. 'Help him with his clothes,' I said, making for the barn door. 'Quickly – we don't have long.' I glanced out and saw the coast was clear. 'Can you walk?'

Willem nodded. 'But there are others . . . Jesus, Finn, your face. What did they do to you?'

'Much the same as you, Willem. I saw the other soldiers go into the mill. They'll be back soon. No way can we take them all on. Damn, if only I had one of our grenades.'

Saskia reached into the pocket of her skirt and removed one. 'I . . . I . . . took it. I . . . I . . . was going to use it if we couldn't get away.' She was trembling. 'I know I told them where the others were . . . but they'd never have lived to tell a soul.'

Willem put his arms around her and looked to me. 'Freya and Loki rounded up their gear and made for the Kramers' farm, Finn. Laura will help them.'

I was confused. 'How did they know the Germans were coming? Why didn't you go as well?'

'A girl came to the house. In a right state. Explained that she thought you'd been captured. Said she'd seen Germans heading our way.'

Marieke! 'Did she have others with her?' I imagined being just minutes from a reunion with Father.

Willem shrugged. 'She knocked on our door. I think she was alone. Loki and Freya knew her. That much I could tell. Mother said we couldn't leave the farm. She said that if Loki and Freya left, then the Germans wouldn't find anything and she thought they would go away and leave us alone. I tried to tell her it wouldn't work out like that.' He shot Saskia a look that said, *Told you so*. 'And when we saw Grüber was among that SS officer's henchmen, I knew we were in big trouble.'

'Listen, I've got some terrible news,' I said. I didn't quite know how to say it, so I just blurted it out. 'I saw a list of names at the Nazi's HQ – those who've been executed by the SS. Gottfried's name was on it.'

Saskia sank to her knees. Clutching Willem's legs, she wailed hysterically. Willem's expression hardened. 'I should have guessed. Somehow I never could quite bring myself to believe they'd simply been transported to work in German factories.' He tried to get Saskia to her feet. 'Come now, Mother, be strong.'

I ran and seized the grenade from Saskia's trembling hand. 'Right,' I said. 'We need to buy some time. And I need your help. Grab a gun. This is the plan . . .'

Having dragged the dead soldiers out of view and covered them with straw, I extinguished the oil lamp. We slipped out of the barn, crossed the yard and crouched in the gloom. There was no sign of the soldiers returning. I ran across to the SS staff car and truck to remove the tyrebursters I'd placed there minutes earlier, and then, reaching inside the car, released the hand brake. Together we pushed the car round to the side of the farm buildings, well out of sight. 'When the others return, they'll see the car's gone and no light coming from the barn. I reckon they'll figure you've been driven back to their HQ. They'll hop aboard their truck and head off back to barracks or wherever. If they spot something's wrong, we'll just have to deal with them.'

Saskia remained distraught. 'We're going to have to leave here, aren't we? For good?'

'Yes,' I said. 'I'm sorry. I was arrested and the SS saw the farm's address on my papers. It's my fault. Even if we get away, others will come. It'll be quite a while before the farm's safe again.'

Willem patted me on my back. 'You got Grüber, Finn, that's all that matters. Now, are we all set?'

Ten minutes later the soldiers returned from the mill and were indeed surprised to find the car gone. They peered at the barn and one went to look inside. He called out that it was empty. The soldiers stood around, smoking and chatting, uncertain what to do. All the while we lay just yards away from them, behind a low fence, pistols at the ready. I was poised to pull the pin of the grenade at the first sign of trouble. Eventually they got bored and clambered back into their truck. The engine started up. The headlamps came on and the driver crunched into gear. The truck turned, then bounced and rocked slowly back along the rutted track, onto the lane, and vanished into the night.

Chapter Twenty-three
A Cunning Plan

Mr Kramer, a large man with short thinning blond hair, opened the door an inch and peered out. Seeing Willem and Saskia, he relaxed and ushered us inside. Willem hurriedly told them what had happened as Mrs Kramer helped him ease down onto a chair. I leaned against the back of the door to steady myself. My foot throbbed in time with the pounding in my head. 'Where are Freya and Loki? Where's Laura?' I demanded.

Mr Kramer pointed towards the back of the house. '*Schuur!*' He was very angry about something.

Meanwhile Mrs Kramer fetched some water and cloths, and Saskia began easing off Willem's blood-stained shirt. Willem turned to me. 'He said they're in the barn, Finn. I think Mr Kramer's annoyed because he fears the Germans coming here. He's right to be worried too. Barely half a mile separates our two farms. Laura, take Finn to the others.'

We may indeed have brought trouble to their doorstep, but only if Steiff decided to search the whole area. I hobbled out of the back door and followed Laura to the Kramers' massive barn. The others were gathered around a series of straw bales on which a map had been spread out. My unannounced arrival was greeted by barrels of Sten machine guns and a yelp of fright from Freya. It took several seconds for them to realize it was me beneath all the swelling, dried blood and bruising. Freya ran over to me. 'Thank God – we thought we'd never see you again!' She gave me a hug, examined my swollen eye, split lip and bruises, and pulled a face in sympathy at my hurt.

I opened my mouth and yanked back my top lip to show the missing tooth. 'That's not the only bit missing. You wait until you see my foot.'

Loki gaped at me. 'Bloody hell, Finn!'

'I'd better fetch some cloths and antiseptic from the kitchen,' said Laura.

I told my story, finishing up with, 'Steiff knows virtually everything about Special Ops, except he has no idea that we've sussed out their little radio game. He thought I was a member of Asparagus.'

Loki began pacing anxiously. 'Yes, but as you've escaped, Finn, he'll assume you'll inform our HQ. He'll reckon his little radio charade is finished. He'll have no further use for Bram Keppel or Theo Drees or any of the others being held prisoner.'

'I'll send a message to warn the brigadier,' said Freya. 'And to tell them you're safe, Finn. Maybe van Alblas's group should try to rescue them. Target the Palace Hotel rather than the prison.'

'Where's Marieke?' I asked, looking every which way. 'Where are the airmen? And what happened to Jan?'

'Jan got away. I had to use that sleeve pistol though. Worked rather well, in fact. Marieke figured you'd been captured and so came to warn us,' Loki explained. 'Naturally, she didn't bring the airmen with her as she originally discussed with you. And because she'd told you where they were being hidden in town, she's had to move them again.'

'Where to? She said she'd run out of options.'

Loki shrugged. 'Wouldn't say. Probably for the best. She reckons you saved her life.'

'Well, one thing's for sure, Steiff knows that Falcon is among them. His whereabouts was really all Steiff wanted to know.'

Laura returned, and together with Freya began wiping the dried blood from my face, bathing my eye; they cried out in horror when I removed my boots to expose a rather bloodied foot. 'Willem's in quite a bad way too,' Laura remarked. 'Mother's telephoned for van Alblas to come. He'll need several stitches. We should discuss this mess with the doctor. The way I see it, you're going to need his help. We're all going to need it.'

'The time for games is over,' said van Alblas sternly, putting down his leather bag. His cough was no better and he looked pale and drawn. 'Everything's a shambles. I have to know what the hell's going on if my group are to assist you.'

'There are airmen being hidden by our people over here,' Freya began. 'It's our job to get them out. It's a matter of great importance.'

Van Alblas threw his hands up in the air. 'Many people have tried to escape Holland – not just airmen and agents, but Jews, peasants and politicians, hundreds of them, and most have been caught. We even have a name for them – *Engelandvaarders*. Why are these particular men so special?'

'Among them is a spy,' Freya continued, 'codenamed Falcon. Using the name Klaus Kiefer, he's been impersonating a German officer in Berlin and is in possession of documents detailing Herr Hitler's plans to invade Russia. A plane from our elite Wolf Squadron was sent to pick him up outside Berlin, but as it took off it suffered damage to one of its engines. Apparently they were spotted and a German patrol tried to shoot them down.'

I was astonished. 'How do you know all this?'

'Marieke told us, Finn. Anyway, they crash-landed in Holland. Falcon and two of the flight crew survived and managed to make contact with the Resistance. They were passed down the line until Asparagus took them under their wing. They were hidden in a safe house along with three other airmen awaiting escape to England. Then, of course, Asparagus were arrested.'

'And Father?' I asked. My question drew looks of surprise from van Alblas and Laura.

Loki shook his head at me. 'Marieke said nothing about your father, Finn.'

'Did you ask her?'

'Marieke couldn't hang around,' Freya interrupted. 'We had only minutes to get away. There simply wasn't time—'

Loki interrupted, 'Surely Marieke would've said, Finn . . . Sorry.'

It felt like a punch to my stomach. Loki was right – she would have said, wouldn't she? Maybe I *was* crazy. A cloud of depression descended over me. I wanted to kick out at everything and anything. My wounds suddenly hurt twice as much. Had my hopes and dreams all been for nothing? I felt like crawling into a corner of the barn, curling up and asking to be woken only when the war was over. Then, amid my misery, a thought occurred to me. The airmen would probably have been given false papers by the Resistance somewhere along the way, essential for moving them across occupied territory. If they had, then there was no reason why Marieke would know that Father was among them. There'd be no one with the name Gunnersen. Yes, I thought, that was possible. The inner flame that had kept me going through my interrogation and had almost extinguished itself flickered more strongly now, and I felt heaps better. Deep down I just knew he was here. *Keep the faith, Finn*, I told myself. *Don't let anyone convince you otherwise, not until you've seen the airmen with your own eyes. Only then will you know for sure.*

Van Alblas rubbed his chin thoughtfully. 'Tell me, just how were you intending to get them out?'

Between us we explained Operation Double Dutch.

'Are you mad?' he shouted. 'Right under their noses? The Palace Hotel is crawling with troops day and night. And there are bunkers beside the Kurhaus with lines of sight across the whole beach. It would be like a fairground shooting gallery. You must forget this lunacy. No, we must come up with an alternative.'

Waves of tiredness washed over me. Feeling unsteady on my feet, I lay down on the floor and closed my eyes. Laura said she'd fetch me some broth from the stove in the kitchen and hurried off. Loki came and sat down beside me. I grumbled to him, 'Well, we can't stay here for long. And we don't know how to contact Marieke directly. What a nightmare!'

'I gave Marieke a spare set of crystals for her radio set,' Freya told me, settling down between us. 'My spare set. That means we can both transmit and receive on the same set of frequencies.'

Forcing my good eye open, I turned my head to look at her. 'So you mean we can communicate directly with each other?'

'Yes, Finn. We decided that to pass all radio traffic via HQ was a waste of precious time. I've let them know. They can listen in and will be able to follow our activities.'

'And so will the enemy,' I muttered.

'No, Finn. We've agreed on a method of coding that will take the Germans a few days to crack. It'll buy us some time.'

Willem came into the barn with Laura. 'He refuses to rest,' she tutted as she handed me a bowl of soup. 'Insisted on joining us.'

'I want to help,' said Willem. 'I can handle a gun. Even with this patch over one eye, I reckon I could still put a bullet in Steiff from a hundred yards. Spent my whole life shooting vermin on our farm. It's no different.'

As I drained the dregs of my bowl, I noticed van

Alblas was doing complex mental arithmetic, counting things off on his fingers. I nudged Loki. 'Any bright ideas?' I asked the doctor.

'What?'

I'd clearly broken his train of thought.

'Oh, I was just wondering whether my group could create some sort of diversion. As I mentioned to you before, I've been planning a raid on Scheveningen prison. It could be brought forward. That would draw troops away from the hotel and coastline. Maybe you *could* get onto the beach somehow.'

'Yes, you mentioned you had a contact inside the prison,' I responded. 'But are you sure you can you trust him?'

Van Alblas detected the doubt in my voice. 'I think so. Why, do you know otherwise?'

I shrugged. 'It's just that Steiff showed me a list of prisoners, of *Todeskandidaten*. I reckon there were at least a hundred names on it. Nearly all have already been executed.'

The doctor didn't bother to disguise his fury, clenching his fists and raising his arms as if wanting to lash out. But as I witnessed his pain at the thought of losing good friends and fellow Resistance fighters and maybe misjudging the trustworthiness of others, an idea occurred to me. 'We could use your contact to our advantage, even if he is an informant,' I suggested.

'Go on, I'm listening,' said van Alblas cagily.

'Tell him the raid will go ahead. Use your team to set explosives in the area close to the prison. If I'm right,

242

Steiff will learn of the raid and will double or triple the guards. They'll cover the surrounding streets too. That'll require a lot of men. When the charges go off, it'll be mayhem. Of course, your team will be nowhere to be seen.'

'A bluff, you mean? Simply a diversion and no more.'

'Exactly. No need to risk members of your group.'

'All very good,' said Loki. 'But how does that help us?'

'Well, back at their HQ, because they know about the attempted raid they'll be expecting captured members of the Resistance to arrive for questioning. So when we turn up, they won't be surprised.'

'You intend going back inside that place? Ridiculous!' Laura Kramer snapped. 'You must be suffering from brain damage.'

Loki, however, knew me too well. He guessed there had to be more to my plan. 'Run through it for us, Finn. I'm all ears.'

I drew breath and began. 'When we first cycled into Scheveningen and reconnoitred the Palace Hotel and its surroundings, I noticed there were apartments for rent on the other side of the road, opposite the Kurhaus. We either rent one or break into one that's empty. Either way, we'll get Marieke to move the airmen there a few hours before we make our move. It's the perfect safe house. There are excellent views of our exit route from the windows.'

Van Alblas nodded. 'It could be arranged.'

I continued, 'When I visited Marieke's contact, Otto,

I saw he had a number of German uniforms, including one for a senior officer in the SS. We can make use of them. Loki and the airmen will use them as disguises. Freya and I will be your prisoners. That agent of ours, Falcon, can earn his ticket home by strutting about as the senior SS officer. It's the perfect role for him. He'll know exactly how to behave. No menial soldier will dare question his authority. And in this state I'll look just like a Resistance fighter who's been roughed up a bit.'

'Sounds good so far, Finn. Then what?'

'Once the diversion at the prison is underway, we cross from the apartment, enter the hotel and make our way down to the basement. There we overpower the guards and get Bram and the others out of their cells. Falcon and the rest of you then march us out of there and we make for the beach. As long as our dinghies are there to pick us up we'll be OK. *And* because you lot are in uniform we shouldn't get too much grief from the guards at the rear of the hotel and any others in the nearby bunker. Any sign of trouble and we simply deal with them. We have enough grenades.'

Laura Kramer turned away and cursed. 'Reckless idiots. You'll all get yourselves killed.'

Like everyone else she understood just how dangerous my plan was, and no doubt saw Loki, Freya and me as young and naive, full of crazy schemes that would end in tragedy. But she knew nothing about us or what we'd been through to escape our homeland; how we'd been trained by the best in the business; how we'd already earned our spurs in previous operations.

Freya barely looked her sixteen years but was the daughter of the great Norwegian outdoorsman, Heimar Haukelid. He'd raised her as a hunter, and she was a truly astonishingly good markswoman, the best shot Special Ops had ever seen. We were a surprisingly good team, and the enemy would often underestimate us; that's what gave us the edge. My plan was audacious, brazen even. Nobody in their right mind would step right into the enemy's lair – that was its strength. Rule number one – do what the enemy least expects. It could work, I just knew it, and it offered the possibility of rescuing Bram and the others.

Van Alblas looked thoughtful. 'Given the importance of your mission, is it worth risking the rescue of your fellow agents? Would it not be better simply to get the airmen to the beach?'

'He's raised a good point, Finn,' said Loki. 'Remember what X said to us? It's unfortunate, but rescuing Asparagus isn't our priority, or our mission. We had to accept that.'

'We should try,' I said.

I would've readily compromised except for one thing. Bram and Theo and whoever else was shut away in those hideous cells were far more to me than just vague recollections of people we'd trained with from Dovecote. I'd spoken with Theo, albeit through tapping Morse on a pipe. I'd experienced their nightmare of incarceration, their feeling of hopelessness, knowing that it was just a question of time before Steiff decided they were of no further use to him. I felt connected to them.

Abandoning them when an opportunity presented itself for an attempted rescue was out of the question. I had to try. We were their last hope. But I could also sense reluctance in the others. 'Listen, if we get there and find that we can't get to the basement, then we'll cut and run. OK?'

Van Alblas was the sort who liked to think things through, dot all the 'i's and cross all the 't's. 'And do you think the airmen will be willing to go through with it? Without their cooperation your plan's a non-starter.'

'Yes,' Loki responded, coming to my rescue. 'I think they will. Falcon has been living and breathing the life of a German officer in Berlin, so it'll be like another day at the office for him; and as for the airmen, well, those from the Wolf Squadron sound like the sort who'd be up for anything. You'd need to be, in their line of work. They fly the most hazardous missions of all. The other three airmen – who knows? – but we don't give them the choice. It's a case of taking part or staying behind.'

'I want to go with you,' Willem announced. 'To England. I want to train and do what you do.'

Laura spun round in fright. 'No!'

'I've given it a lot of thought, Laura. While lying in the dark I've had time to think. Look at our situation here. We live in fear of men like Lieutenant Grüber. They treat us like worthless dogs, beating us and taking our food. And given what's happened, we can't go back to our farm – not now, not for a long time, possibly not until the war's over. With Father dead, I want revenge. I want to hit back, hard.'

Saskia appeared at the entrance to the barn. Willem spun round to look at her. 'I'm sorry, Mother, but my mind's made up. There's nothing for me here.'

'There's me!' Laura cried, grabbing Willem's arm.

'I know but . . .' Willem's gaze returned towards his mother. 'Don't try and dissuade me, Mother.'

Saskia's shoulders sagged. 'I'm not going to,' she said. 'You must do whatever you feel is right.' Without another word she turned and walked away.

There was a silence as we watched her go. Then I turned to the others. 'There is just one problem with my plan,' I announced hesitantly. Everyone looked at me. 'I'm not sure how you'll get me into town, not in my state. I don't have any papers either. My description will undoubtedly have been circulated. There are bound to be extra patrols and checkpoints.'

An air of depression descended over us until van Alblas suddenly shot a finger into the air. 'There is a way, Finn. There is a way we can get you into town. But you'll need to play dead!'

Chapter Twenty-four
Too Many Escapees

For three painfully long and frustrating days we holed up in the Kramers' barn, forever on our guard, fearful the enemy would sweep the area. The only bright spots were when messages came in from Marieke. Van Alblas had the bodies from the Pols' farm removed and disposed of, and the SS staff car was driven away, ending up being dumped in the river. To be on the safe side, when Freya and Loki disappeared to exchange messages with Marieke by radio, they chose a different location for transmitting each time in case the Germans had their detector vans in the vicinity. As Willem and I slowly began to recover, my plan started to take shape nicely.

Van Alblas successfully rented a second-floor apartment opposite the Kurhaus, having taken steps to ensure the proprietor was trustworthy and willing to accept cash with no questions asked. Marieke prepared to move the airmen one final time on our signal. Her big problem, however, was the uniforms. According to her messages to Freya, Otto was willing to help but pointed out that the uniforms in his possession belonged to men who'd be expecting them back! He reckoned their sudden disappearance would be impossible for him to explain, and that would land him in a heap of trouble. Loki suggested that he could report a break-in and theft, but Otto was reluctant. Instead, he offered to run up some new ones for us, but it would take him a couple of days. We judged the wait worthwhile and supplied Marieke with Loki's measurements. Back at Mulberry, an increasingly anxious brigadier remained in a heightened state of alert, ready to send the high-speed MGBs across the North Sea as soon as we gave him the green light.

Each evening at around ten o'clock van Alblas came to the farm to update us. We met in the barn. He struck me as increasingly weary and I realized he'd had little sleep. I also quickly ascertained that his Undertaker network comprised more than just a handful of willing volunteers. He had small groups of determined men and women located in just about every village in the area, as well as in Scheveningen and The Hague.

'I've been giving our plan a good deal of thought,' he announced on the third night of our stay at the Kramers'. 'I confess to being somewhat worried.'

'Go on,' said Loki hesitantly.

'I have everything arranged concerning the pretend raid on Scheveningen prison. But . . .' He paused and looked at me. 'Finn had doubts about my contact there. To be honest, I can't be sure one way or the other. However, if my contact *doesn't* inform Steiff about our raid, then we're faced with two sticky problems. Firstly, Steiff's men won't be dispatched to cover the prison and surrounding streets. Secondly, when you lot go marching into their HQ, it'll come as quite a surprise to the soldiers there. What it boils down to is this – your plan will begin to unravel as soon as you set foot inside.'

'What do you suggest?' Freya asked.

Van Alblas delved into his jacket pocket and removed a map. 'That we have a night of insurrection. Not just close to the prison but lots of small raids all over the area, co-ordinated to cause chaos.' Unfolding the map, he spread it out on top of a straw bale and drew a lamp closer. We gathered round and followed his finger as he pointed to one potential target after another. 'We can derail a train here . . . Cut power lines there . . . Set fire to this building as it's close to one of their munitions stores . . .' His fingers danced about the map. A dozen different targets, all in and around Scheveningen and The Hague.

Loki whistled. 'You can do all this?'

Van Alblas looked up. 'Yes. I have sufficient volunteers and they're raring to get their teeth into direct action. Many have grown frustrated over recent months as we've avoided activities like these. Sabotage leads to reprisals, you see. The Germans make us pay dearly for even the slightest display of resistance. You saw that for yourselves at the Rembrandt. If too many innocent people are killed, I worry the local population might turn against us. We'd be in even greater danger than we are now – this time from our fellow Dutchmen! However, your mission is of such importance I think it is time to put such concerns to one side. There is a bigger picture to be considered – the future of Europe and beyond. If there are consequences for the people of Holland, then I believe that on this occasion they are worth bearing.'

We gratefully accepted his offer.

On the surface it seemed that we had everything under control. But the Kramers' farm was not a happy place. There was a growing tension in the air between Laura and Willem. Any idiot could see their feelings for one another ran deep, but I also got the impression that Laura feared being left behind. It was as if being with Willem kept her going, made her existence bearable. Saskia, however, struck me as a broken woman, bereft of all hope. She said very little from dawn to dusk, although she did keep herself busy helping Mrs Kramer with chores about the farm. I couldn't help feeling we were to blame. Since our arrival their world had been turned upside down. Had we not arrived on their doorstep they'd still be ignorant of Gottfried's fate and Saskia would still be rising each morning with a small glimmer of hope burning inside her.

'You're wrong, Finn,' Freya declared one afternoon after I'd shared my sense of guilt. We'd ventured out of the barn and into a walled garden behind the Kramers' farmhouse for some fresh air. 'I know it feels as if we've opened up Pandora's box since our arrival, but think about it. Had we not come, Willem would still have been beaten up by Grüber's men and they'd still be living in fear for their lives. The only real difference is you discovering what happened to Gottfried. Horrible, I know, but at least they know the truth. To exist from day to day on false hopes is never a good thing.'

Deep down I knew she was right, and yet her words reverberated in my brain. I pictured Father. It was only the thought that he was still alive that had kept me going during my capture and interrogation. And although I wanted to believe it, I had no absolute physical proof that he was in Holland, or even that he was still alive. I simply believed it was the case. Was I kidding myself? Had I fallen into the same trap as Saskia and Willem? Was I living on false hope? I shuddered and dispelled the idea. No, Father *was* alive. I'd seen his picture fall out of the files back at Mulberry House. Nils confessed that he may have been mistaken about what he saw during that dogfight over the North Sea. I swallowed hard. *Keep the faith, Finn*.

For much of the following day Willem hung out with us in the barn, despite van Alblas advising him to rest. He was full of questions about becoming a member of Special Ops. I could tell he was relishing the possibility of joining us and he insisted on being shown how all of our equipment worked. To pass the time Freya began teaching him rudimentary Morse code, tapping out messages on an upturned milk pail, and I showed him how to strip and clean a pistol. Willem took everything on board, absorbing it all like a sponge. I had little doubt he'd be an asset to Special Operations.

'I'm not bad with a shotgun,' Willem remarked while cradling a revolver in his hand, 'but I've never fired one of these. How long before I become a crack shot just like you, Finn?'

Loki roared with laughter. 'Finn's no marksman. Freya's by far the best among us.'

'But the way you shot Grüber, Finn. You had barely

an inch to aim at. A slight misjudgement either way, I'd have been a goner.'

'Loki's right,' I replied. 'It was a lucky shot, Willem. I pulled the trigger knowing there was a fifty–fifty chance I'd shoot you instead.'

'Really?' Willem looked genuinely astonished. Then his expression darkened as the reality of it sank in. '*Really?*'

'Yes, Willem, you're lucky to be alive.' I thought back to all the scrapes Freya, Loki and I had been through. 'Listen, Willem, I think you'd make a fine agent with Special Ops. But it's not all glory, you know. There's a good chance that you won't return from a mission; that along the way you may lose many friends – people you've come to rely on, people you love; and if you make just one wrong move, it may be your last mistake or one that leads to the capture, torture and death of others.'

Willem put down the gun and slumped onto the straw. 'All right, Finn, I understand what you're saying. It's just that, what with all that's happened, I want to—'

'I know,' I interrupted. 'You want to do your bit. But have you thought about Laura in all this?'

Willem fell silent and stared blankly at his mud-encrusted boots.

'Why doesn't she come with us as well?' Loki suggested.

Willem raised his head. 'I've thought about that. I've tried persuading her but she doesn't want to leave her parents and the farm behind. I'll keep trying though.'

'I guess that's her choice,' Loki responded unsympathetically.

'Probably just as well,' Freya added. 'I doubt it would be possible anyway.'

'What do you mean, not possible?' I asked.

'The brigadier informed me that there will only be three dinghies sent ashore. There's barely enough room for the five airmen, Kiefer and us. I guess we can squeeze Willem on board at a push. Any more might prove unworkable.'

'Get them to send a fourth dinghy.'

'I asked. He said it's out of the question.'

Alarmed, Willem sprang to his feet. 'They'll *have* to send a fourth. There's Mother as well.'

'Saskia?' Then it dawned on me. I turned and eyeballed Loki. 'You've promised to take her to England too, haven't you?'

'What else could I do, Finn? We've come here, forced ourselves upon them, made a right mess of things, ruined their lives . . . She can't go back to the farm, not now, not while Steiff is in charge. I figured it's the least we owe her.'

I buried my face in my hands. Loki was right, we did owe Saskia. I owed Saskia. But including them both in our escape filled me with dread. There were enough of us to contend with as it was: the airmen, Kiefer, the three of us, Bram and Theo and . . . '*Oh hell!*' I suddenly realized something. 'What on earth do we do with Bram and Theo and the others from Asparagus? If we manage to free them, there won't be room for them either.'

Freya swallowed hard. 'They have to stay behind, Finn. Sorry. Brigadier's orders.'

I shook my head. 'They have to send in more dinghies. They simply *must*.'

Freya groaned. 'I'll ask HQ again but I got the feeling it's non-negotiable.'

That evening van Alblas arrived at the farm as pale as a sheet. He was exhausted. 'I was stopped five times today,' he informed us wearily between fits of coughing that clearly pained him. 'Luckily, as a physician I have freedom of movement to make house calls. Others are being given a hard time at the checkpoints. The Germans are twitchy. It's as if they know we're up to something.' He coughed even more violently, holding a handkerchief to his mouth. When he removed it I saw flecks of blood. He reached out to steady himself.

'Loki, grab him — I think he's about to faint,' I shouted just as van Alblas's knees crumpled beneath him.

'What's the matter with him, Finn?' Willem ran to give Loki a hand.

'I don't know. Go and get Mrs Kramer. Freya, see what he's got in that bag of his.'

With van Alblas stretched out on the floor, I loosened his collar and tie. I felt his forehead. He was burning up. Freya came and knelt beside me with the bag. 'There's not much in here, Finn.'

Willem soon reappeared with Laura and her mother. Mrs Kramer seized the doctor's wrist and took his pulse.

'The poor man. I told him he was overdoing things. We need to get him inside. You'll have to carry him between you. The tuberculosis is gradually killing him. He must get some rest.'

Tuberculosis really was a big killer. It was difficult to treat, and the right medicines were hard to come by. Total rest and lots of fresh air were usually prescribed. Exactly what we didn't have. Recovery was possible but slow, often taking months. This was terrible. We needed van Alblas to be fit enough to deal with his side of our operation. Without his diversions we were doomed to failure.

Between us we managed to get the doctor into the house and made him comfortable on a sofa. It soon became clear, however, that he was in no state to carry on driving from village to village at all hours of the day and night to brief his network of Undertakers. He slept a while, and when he finally woke, he peered at my concerned face through watery eyes and apologized. 'I'm sorry, Finn.'

Freya nervously chewed her nails. 'Our HQ informed me that the weather's set fair for the next three nights. After that they're predicting storms coming in from the west, with quite a swell in the North Sea. That might cause them problems with the crossing. And getting Falcon back to England can't wait beyond then. We've got to make our move . . .'

With a great effort van Alblas lifted himself onto his elbows. 'A good night's sleep may give me enough strength. Everything's set my end but I need to issue final orders to each group in person. It's the only way.'

'You're not fit to drive anywhere,' Laura pronounced. 'It's impossible.'

Loki had a brainwave. 'Can either of you drive?' His question was directed to Willem and Laura. Both nodded but confessed that they hadn't driven much. 'Then we need you to take the doctor to his people. You can help make sure all the diversions go to plan.'

'But I'm coming with you,' said Willem. 'How can I do both?'

Laura didn't appear too keen on Loki's suggestion either. 'If we get stopped at a checkpoint, I'm sure the Germans will be suspicious. We haven't got the right permits for driving the car. It's too risky. We'd have to rely on telling the Germans that it's an emergency, that the doctor's sick.' She was shaking her head energetically as though already imagining being arrested.

'Loki's right,' I said. 'We need you to do this, Willem. And you, Laura. It's the only way. With both of you I'm sure you'll manage.'

'And there should be time for you to get back and join us for the rendezvous at the hotel,' Loki added.

'I'll drive.'

The voice came from behind us. We all turned and saw Saskia standing in the doorway.

'*Moeder?*' Willem frowned.

'I'll drive the doctor. You and Laura can sit in the back and deal with Dr van Alblas's contacts at each stop.'

Loki caught my eye and grinned. It was the sort of grin that said, *See, Finn? I was right about her all along.*

When the chips are down you can always rely on a Larson.

'Are you sure?' Freya asked.

Saskia nodded firmly. 'I'll make sure Dr van Alblas gets home safely once we're all done. Holland needs men like him if we're ever to win this war.'

'But you're coming to England too. With me.'

'No, Willem, I have no desire to go to England. I can be of more use here. The doctor needs looking after. I will stay with him at his house until he is well again. By then maybe I can return to the farm. If not I'll come and stay here. Mrs Kramer has kindly offered me a room for as long as I need it.'

Taking stock of our situation and aware of the deteriorating health of van Alblas, I came to a decision. 'I propose we don't hang around. We go tomorrow night. Agreed?'

Everyone agreed.

'Right, well, I'd better go and send messages to Marieke and the brigadier,' said Freya. 'Come with me, Loki.'

Van Alblas mustered his strength. 'Help me to the Kramers' telephone. I must make a call. If you're all set for tomorrow, then I need to finalize the arrangements for your funeral, Finn. With your face still looking so swollen and bruised it's the only way you'll make it into town.' He managed to laugh. 'They'll come and pick up your corpse tomorrow morning.'

I swallowed hard. This was one part of our plan that I really wasn't looking forward to.

Chapter Twenty-five
Journey of the Dead

That night I had trouble sleeping. Loki was restless too. The barn was draughty and our blankets coarse and itchy.

'You awake, Finn?'

'Uh-huh.'

'Scared about tomorrow?'

'Uh-huh.'

'Don't be. Freya and I will be right there with you all the way. I overheard van Alblas on the phone. First we'll be taking you to the cemetery. It's near Scheveningen. There's a chapel there. As soon as you're inside van Alblas's family burial vault in the crypt, we'll get you out of the coffin.'

'Sounds good to me.'

'I'll stay with you until it gets dark and then we'll make our way to the apartment. Freya will go on ahead to await Marieke and the airmen. Now, is there anything we've not thought of?'

When I failed to respond, he added, 'You all right, Finn?'

'Uh-huh.'

Unconvinced, he crawled across to where I was lying on a makeshift bed of straw. 'Listen, Finn, I know you've been praying that your father's among those airmen, but he almost certainly isn't. I mean, I know how fantastic it would be if he was — after all this time, you thinking he was dead, him hiding out in a crawlspace in some Dutchman's house or barn. It would be wonderful. But . . .'

'I just have this feeling that he is here, Loki. I can't get it out of my head.'

'It's a million-to-one chance—'

'I know, but it's kept me going,' I interrupted irritably. 'I'm not sure I'd have survived if I didn't believe.'

'Yes you would have, Finn.' Freya sat up and rubbed the sleep from her eyes. 'And I'll tell you why. You're too much like him. You're as determined and bloody-minded as he was. My dad was just the same. He would simply never have entertained the idea of giving up. I know he made the ultimate sacrifice but he would have accepted it as a price worth paying. His dream was *our* dream, Finn: for our homeland to be free again, our people to be free again.'

'She's right.' Loki sounded bullish. 'It's in your blood too, Freya. In all our blood. I think it's why we're cut out for this work.'

Freya huddled up to Loki and put her arms around him. 'It's all right for us. If all goes to plan, this time tomorrow we'll be heading back to England. Marieke, Jan and the others will still be in this hell hole. Will this war never end?'

'It will one day,' Loki replied. 'And I've been thinking. If this Falcon's intelligence is correct, and

Hitler's going to invade Russia, that'll keep him busy, which will buy us time to prepare an invasion. The Third Reich's days may well be numbered.'

'Let's hope so,' said Freya, yawning so wide her jaw cracked. 'Now we've worked out how to win this war, can we get some sleep?'

When I awoke, three things struck me simultaneously: it was light, there was a noise coming from outside, and I still hurt like hell all over. I struggled to my feet and hobbled over to the large barn doors. Blinded by the sun, I squinted through my good eye at the strange scene in the yard.

A huge black horse stood there, its coat so glossy it gleamed in the morning sun, its mane and tail neatly plaited. The beast was hitched up to a cart, but it was no ordinary cart: it was black and shiny too. A smartly dressed man was sitting on top, reins in one hand, long whip in the other. He looked down at me and said in a rather grim, funereal tone, 'Goede morgen.'

Freya hurried across the yard. 'You're awake, Finn. Willem and Laura are just about to leave with van Alblas and Saskia. They've got a busy day ahead of them.'

'How is van Alblas?'

'Not good. Fingers crossed they can get the job done between them. Now, Loki needs you to give him a hand. He's round the back.'

Sleeves rolled up and sweat glistening on his forehead, Loki beamed at me. 'Mr Kramer and I went over to the windmill before sun-up, Finn. We picked the best of the bunch. I need a hand lifting it onto the hearse. What do you think?'

Seeing him next to one of the coffins we'd made at the mill, I was suddenly filled with a renewed sense of dread. In truth, I didn't fancy the idea of being cooped up in the dark, unable to flex my arms, maybe unable to breathe. But I had no choice. Together, we shifted the coffin into the yard and slid it onto the back of the cart.

'I've got to go and change,' Loki announced. 'After all, I have to look smart for my best friend's funeral.' He laughed. 'Mr Kramer said he'd lend me a decent shirt.'

I followed him inside and was confronted by Mrs Kramer in the kitchen. Although readying herself to leave for work in the fields, she took a moment to peer at me closely. Shaking her head, she tutted. 'Not convincing enough. Too much colour. Quick, come and sit down on this stool,' she ordered. 'I need to make you look dead.'

Some face cream and talc soon provided me with a wonderfully pasty complexion. The bruising on my face showed through in places, as if I were beginning to rot on the inside. The swelling about my eye added to the overall effect.

Freya appeared and raised a hand to her mouth. 'God, you don't look at all well, Finn.'

'Very funny. Is this all really necessary?'

'Yes,' Mrs Kramer replied while inspecting her handiwork and applying the finishing touches. 'You may be stopped on the way into town. It's highly likely they'll want to look inside the coffin.'

'*Look inside?*' Now I was genuinely worried.

'Yes. If they do, remember to try not to breathe. Keep your eyes shut and stay perfectly still. I've instructed the driver to tell them that you died of typhus. With any luck they'll not want to get too close. Also, the smell should put them off.'

'Smell?' I didn't like the sound of that.

Mrs Kramer handed me a bottle, and before I'd even unscrewed the cap I caught a whiff of an indescribably foul pong.

'That's the thing about living in the country,' she said. 'There are always dead things lying around. There, I'm done. You'd better all make a move.' She grabbed my shoulder and stared at me hard. 'Ready?'

In the yard I climbed onto the cart and lay down in the coffin.

'Cross your hands on your chest,' Freya instructed. 'That's how you should be. We've drilled several holes in the end nearest your head to let in air. Here, take this just in case there's trouble. Wedge it behind you.' She handed me a pistol.

Mrs Kramer passed Loki her bottle of putrefied semi-liquid disgustingness and instructed him to dribble a little into the coffin. 'Take some deep breaths, Finn. And try not to vomit,' she said. 'Your nose will soon become accustomed to it. You'll barely be able to smell it in five minutes.'

The stench did indeed make me nauseous, but it was the coffin lid being placed on top that made me feel ten times worse. And it wasn't the total darkness that caused my guts to clench but the loud blows of the nails being driven home. I heard muffled voices. Loki was asking if I was all right, telling me to knock twice for 'yes' and three times for 'no'. Tempted to rap my knuckle against the lid a third time, I stopped after the second strike. Horrid though this was, it was for the best.

With a jolt we set off. I could faintly hear the clop of horseshoes and was rocked wildly as we trundled over ruts on the track. Then the ride grew smoother. We were on the road.

I'd never been frightened of spiders or snakes, heights, deep water or thunder and lightning. Phobias always struck me as silly and irrational. I thought girls who shrieked at seeing a big furry insect or ran a mile on spotting a rat were just being stupid. But I had to confess I wasn't too keen on confined spaces – not ones this cramped; not when I couldn't get out. The coffin grew unbearably hot and stuffy too. I began to panic, certain they'd not drilled enough holes. It got harder and harder to breathe. I felt the sweat drip from me and my heart pounded. I suddenly wanted out. I tried pushing up the lid. It wouldn't budge. I thumped it and began shouting. The cart stopped so rapidly that it made me slide and bang my head against the end of the coffin. 'Stop that, or you'll get us all killed,' a voice called out. 'There's a checkpoint round the next corner so play dead or you'll be dead for real.'

Minutes later we drew to a halt again and I heard muffled German being spoken. Then nothing. Then more voices. It seemed like we'd stopped for an age. I had no idea what was happening but feared some sort of problem, maybe with Loki or Freya's papers. I could feel my gun sticking into my ribs beneath me. Should I try reaching for it, just in case? Would I make a noise trying?

The next thing I was aware of was the coffin sliding off the cart, ending up at an angle of about sixty degrees. Luckily my head was at the upturned end. Then the sound I dreaded – the sound of wood splintering. They were opening the coffin. I forced myself to stop shaking, willed myself to relax, and slowed my breathing until it was so shallow my chest barely moved. I kept my eyes shut, but not too firmly in case my eyelids twitched, and then the pitch blackness I'd grown accustomed to was suddenly replaced by an astonishing brightness. The lid had been removed. Fresh air flooded in and I desperately wanted to take in a deep lungful. I heard Freya weeping sorrowfully and Loki complaining bitterly at the top of his voice. The driver shouted, '*Vlektyfus! Vlektyfus!*' I presumed he was saying *typhus*.

A German snapped, '*Scheisse! Mein Gott! Er stinkt fürchterlich!*'

Quickly the lid was replaced and hammered down again. I was slid back on top of the cart and we were on our way. I thanked God. I owed van Alblas and the Kramers my life – especially Mrs Kramer. *Clever*, I thought. *Very clever*. I began wondering what assortment of really vile things she had put in that awful-smelling concoction of hers, and rapidly decided it was probably best not to dwell on it.

Chapter Twenty-six
The Crypt

Opening my eyes, I blinked. The coffin lid had been removed and a lit oil lamp appeared above me. 'We're here, Finn. The nightmare's over. Jesus, you smell rank.'

I clambered out, and Freya, covering her nose, handed me some damp cloths. 'Wipe as much of that make-up off as you can, Finn. Right, I'm off to check out the apartment and wait for Marieke. Van Alblas said the key had been left beneath the doormat. Remember it's on the second floor – number twenty-three.'

Once my eyes had adjusted I looked about me. Freya had rested the oil lamp on top of a nearby sarcophagus. It bathed the stone walls in an eerie yellow flickering light. Dusty cobwebs dangled from the ceiling. The crypt was surprisingly large but possessed a strange stillness and silence that gave me the feeling that few people ever ventured down the stone steps from the chapel above. That was reassuring. I wiped Mrs Kramer's make-up off as best I could but couldn't rid myself of the terrible stink until I realized that most of the contents of her foul concoction sprinkled over me had ended up on my shirtsleeve. I grabbed hold of it and was about to rip it off when Loki presented me with one of Mr Kramer's shirts. 'Thought you might need this, Finn. I grabbed it at the last minute.'

'Thanks.' I tore my shirt off and stuffed it back inside my coffin, relieved to close the lid. I took a deep breath. 'That's better. Good thinking, Loki.'

'Hah! I couldn't stand the idea of being cooped up in here with you stinking the place out.'

'I really must go,' Freya repeated anxiously.

Loki seized her tightly and they hugged. 'Are you sure you're all right going on alone?'

Freya nodded. 'The driver of the hearse is going to give me a lift to within a hundred yards or so of the boulevard.' She took from her pocket a tiny scent bottle, opened it and dabbed a little of its contents into each eye. 'Vinegar,' she said as the tears streamed down her cheeks. She rubbed her eyes, slapped her cheeks to redden them and then looked at us. 'Well, do I look suitably upset, as if I've just buried a loved one?'

We both nodded.

'Good,' she continued. 'Now, I doubt Marieke will move all the airmen at once. It would look too suspicious. In her last message she said she'd get Jan to follow her in case she encounters a problem. If that happens he'll come here to the crypt. He knows you'll be hiding out here until sunset. Jan hasn't been told the exact address of the apartment in case he gets stopped. Marieke doubts he'd hold out for long during questioning, so the less he knows the better.'

'But he knows where we are. Oh great, we're expendable then?' Loki complained.

'It's not that, you fool.' Freya looked at him in exasperation. 'It's just that we don't have our wireless set now. It was too dangerous to risk bringing it on the hearse. That means from now on we can't communicate with Marieke. If she gets caught or needs urgent help, Jan needs to know how to find you.'

'Freya's right,' I said.

'Thank you, Finn. Now, repeat the timings to me one more time. I need to be sure you've got it all straight.'

'Van Alblas said he'd stagger his various diversions to start from about twenty-three hundred hours, detonating the explosives close to the prison at twenty-three forty-five,' Loki began. 'If all goes to plan, Saskia will drop Willem off close to the apartment in good time: Laura too if Willem's managed to persuade her. If they're delayed for any reason, we won't wait. It's up to them to make it. Saskia will then return van Alblas to his house. By midnight Steiff should have dispatched all the troops he's likely to. We'll aim to reach you as soon after dusk as we dare. Hopefully we can get there before all hell breaks loose. I don't fancy wandering about once the alert's been sounded. Anyway, it shouldn't take us long and we'll try to avoid the roads as much as possible. Caught in a streetlamp, Finn's face might still draw some unwelcome attention.'

I continued, 'The dinghies should reach the shore at exactly o-o-thirty tomorrow morning. Our signal is three flashes from our torches. We're aiming to enter the hotel at o-o-fifteen, so we don't need to leave the apartment until a minute or so before that. It'll give us fifteen minutes to free Bram and the others and get down to the beach. Any longer and we'd be standing around twiddling our thumbs – not something you want to do inside one of the Nazis' HQs.'

Freya smiled and hugged us both goodbye. Loki watched her leave. 'She'll be fine,' I said. 'Don't worry.'

The airless crypt smelled mouldy and damp, of death and decay. We turned the wick of our oil lamp down to conserve it. We were in for a long wait, so we rested, lying on top of cold stone sarcophagi. I traced the inscriptions with the tips of my fingers. 'I'm lying on top of van Alblas's mother,' I said, and Loki laughed so loud it echoed and gave him a stitch.

'Shush, Loki! You never know, someone might be upstairs in the chapel, paying their last respects. If they hear a voice from down here they'll wet themselves. They'll figure the place is haunted.'

Loki stifled his laughter but got a fit of the giggles. It was the first time we'd relaxed since we arrived in Holland. An hour went by, then another, and another. Time seemed to slow, morning crawling into afternoon, and then staggering into evening. We'd been buzzing, but the wait grew unbearably frustrating. We wanted to get on with Operation Double Dutch, to head home – I was almost looking forward to seeing Smithy's ugly face and hearing his cheerful shout – *All right, lads?*

'What do you think will happen to Saskia?' I asked Loki after a prolonged period of silence. 'Do you reckon she'll be able to return to her farm once everything's died down? Or will she have to remain at the Kramers'?'

'The way I see it, if we succeed, Steiff will blow a fuse. There'll be reprisals, round-ups, executions, and dozens of searches. The Kramers' farm might not be safe for her. She might be better off staying with van Alblas – unless, of course, Steiff ends up suspecting him as well. I suppose it all depends on whether any of the doctor's Resistance group are captured tonight and subsequently talk under interrogation.'

'She's taking quite a risk staying behind. Maybe we should have tried to get her out as well as Willem.'

'She made up her own mind, Finn. She knows the risks.'

My thoughts turned to Marieke. How could she stay behind to build the new Aardappel network if she was now compromised? She'd have to live through the threat of reprisals too. Just the thought made me feel sick to the stomach. I wanted her safe. I wanted her to return to England with us. I wanted us to be together.

'My aunt's got courage, I'll say that for her,' Loki continued.

'Listen,' I said. 'I'm sorry that I misjudged her. You were right. She's a Larson through and through. She just didn't appear to want to help us at first. After all, you're family.'

'Tell you the truth, I was beginning to have my doubts too, Finn. I guess finding out that Gottfried had been executed changed everything. Now she wants revenge.'

'You really think so?'

'Yes. But before we knew about Gottfried it occurred to me that maybe we were expecting too much from her. Not everyone has the same convictions as we do,

Finn. Not everyone is willing to lay their lives on the line in order to defeat Herr Hitler. It's easy to forget that sometimes. Some people just want to protect whatever they have left. And I don't mean that they're collaborators or bad people or cowards: when presented with seemingly impossible odds, they simply react differently.'

'Maybe you're right. I guess we're all different.'

Suddenly Loki shot bolt upright. 'Quiet, Finn. I thought I heard something.'

We listened out. The silence seemed to hiss in our ears. Footsteps: light but hurried.

'Someone's up there, Finn.'

We rolled off the stone sarcophagi and drew our pistols. I lifted the lamp and blew out the flame. Loki pressed himself against the wall next to the door leading to the stone steps. It was the only way out of the crypt; the only way up into the chapel.

The patter of boots against flagstones continued, one moment growing louder, the next fading. I couldn't fathom it, but imagined someone running to and fro as if flummoxed, uncertain which way to go. I heard someone call out tentatively, 'Finn? Loki?'

'It's Jan!' I said. 'I'm going up. Cover me.'

To describe Jan as distraught would have been an understatement. Hands on knees, he was bent double and breathing so hard his dribbled spittle was hanging from his mouth. He saw us emerge from the crypt, shouted something in Dutch and pointed towards the door. 'You must come. All wrong. Marieke in danger.'

'Calm down,' I said, guiding him to the nearest pew. 'Sit down, put your head between your knees and breathe steadily ... That's it ... Now explain what's happened ... Take it slow.'

'Marieke take three men to apartment. I follow. All go well. She return and we go for others. I wait outside. Then Germans come. SS officer go inside.'

'Jesus, Finn, they must've received a tip-off.'

'Wait, Loki,' I said. 'Just where exactly is Marieke hiding the airmen, Jan?'

'A shop – Brueghels.'

'But that's Otto's place!' cried Loki in alarm.

I realized that, having run out of safe houses, in desperation Marieke had moved the airmen to her grandfather's. She'd taken a huge risk. I recalled seeing the senior SS officer's uniform there, and I began to wonder. 'It may not be as bad as you think, Jan,' I said. 'Maybe that officer was just picking up his uniform.'

Jan shook his head violently. 'I think so too. At first. But more soldiers come. They block street. Both ends.'

'Sounds like big trouble, Finn. What on earth can we do?'

'Who did Marieke take to the apartment first, Jan?' I asked.

'A man she call Falcon and two she say from Wolf something.'

'Wolf Squadron?'

Jan nodded.

'Listen, Finn,' said Loki. 'It's getting dark outside. We

ought to be heading for the apartment too. The important men are safe. Our mission can still proceed. That's our priority – to get Falcon out. The others will have to take their chances. Think what's at stake! We daren't risk screwing it all up trying to fashion some sort of crazy rescue.'

'No!' Jan's eyes widened with horror. 'We must help Marieke.'

My brain was in turmoil. All I could think about was Father and Marieke. They needed my help. I had to try to do something. 'Jan's right. You two go on to the apartment and update the others. If I'm not back by the time you need to make your move, then proceed without me. Get Falcon out.' I snapped open my revolver and checked it was fully loaded.

Loki grabbed hold of me. 'This is madness, Finn. What on earth do you think you'll be able to do?'

'I don't know. But Marieke's in trouble and we're her only hope. And if I was right all along, then Father's there too. I simply *have* to go.'

Loki clenched his fists and howled – a mix of anger, anxiety and frustration. His voice bounced and echoed around the darkening chapel. 'This is lunacy – you'll get yourself killed, Finn.' He grabbed me and tried to shake sense into me. But I was immovable. Seeing I couldn't be persuaded, his shoulders wilted. 'All right. *All right!* We stick together, no matter what, Finn. I'm coming with you.' He turned to Jan. 'I'm going to give you the address where Marieke took Falcon and the others. Freya will be there. Tell her what's happened and that we'll do our best to reach her before midnight. Understand?'

Jan nodded. 'You go help Marieke, come to apartment, and then we help my brother, Bram. Yes?'

At that moment the idea of rescuing Bram and others from Asparagus in the cells in the basement of the Palace Hotel seemed a long way off, little more than a wishful dream. But I said yes to Jan and it made him happy. 'Lend me your cap,' I said, snatching it from his head. 'I need to hide my face.'

The Nieuwe Siegelstraat was barricaded at both ends. Through the gloom of a fading dusk we saw two soldiers standing guard outside Otto's shop. This wasn't going to be easy. Loki dipped a hand into his jacket pocket and handed me a silencer for my revolver. I attached it, then we made our way into the next street, one running parallel to the rear of Otto's. Somehow we had to find a way to get to the workshop. I figured this was our best bet. There had to be some sort of yard and back entrance.

'This is hopeless, Finn. I can't see any way through. There's no alleyway or path,' Loki muttered angrily.

Several premises were boarded up. Others had the word JUDEN painted in big letters on their dusty windows. From their appearance it struck me that the owners and their families had long since gone, either into hiding or out of the country, or been arrested. 'About here,' I said, stopping. 'Otto's is right behind this place. We'll have to break in.'

Nervously Loki looked up and down the street. 'Better make it quick then.'

I tried the door of what looked like a bookshop. It was locked. Loki took hold of my arm and yanked me aside. 'No time for fannying around, Finn.' He lifted his right foot and kicked the door with all his might. It crashed open and we hurried inside.

The place had been shut up for some while, the air still and stale, and thick with the aroma of sun-bleached paper and leather. We trod through a sea of books that had been swept from shelves, through another door into a storeroom full of upturned boxes. Faded paperwork lay strewn across the floor amid broken glass. The place had been ransacked. The only things intact were a couple of rickety old chairs and a paraffin stove. I made for a small window and gently used the sleeve of my shirt to wipe a peephole in the grime. There was a tiny back yard surrounded by a brick boundary wall about six feet high. Beyond it, I could see the outline of Otto's cutting room. Space was so tight it had been built hard up against the wall. There was light emerging from the skylights in the roof.

Outside, I gestured for Loki to give me a leg up. From the top of the wall I saw that there was a side door to the cutting room that gave access to Otto's back yard, but neither the door nor the wall to the building had any windows. The only way I was going to see what was going on inside was to get onto the roof and look down through the skylights. I turned and reached down to give Loki a hand scrambling up. 'Help me up onto the roof,' I whispered. 'Before we go in, we need to see what we're up against.'

I needed to be light-footed, agile and as silent as a cat on the prowl. The slightest sound would undoubtedly end in disaster. With Loki supporting my legs, I took a firm hold of the cast-iron guttering and pulled myself up. The pitch of the roof was quite steep and I lay flat against it and edged my way along until I could peer down through one of the glass panes.

The sight that greeted me made me shudder. Otto lay motionless in a pool of blood to one side of the cutting table. Three men in German uniform were tied to chairs. The airmen! They had their backs to me and two further soldiers stood behind them. Was Father one of those seated? I couldn't see their faces. The one on the left was too tall, the one on the right too short and fat. The one in the middle? I squinted. Could be. He was the right build. I felt my pulse race. *Yes*, I thought, *a definite maybe*. The excitement and sense of anticipation was almost overwhelming, dizzying. Edging an inch or two to my left, I strained to see what else was happening. And I got such a fright I almost lost my footing. Marieke was sitting on another chair on the opposite side of the room. Major Steiff was pacing about her waving something in the air. He looked angry. I guessed it was the photograph of Falcon that he kept shoving before Marieke's eyes. He'd found three of the airmen but not the one man he really wanted – Falcon, aka Klaus Kiefer, enemy spy. Marieke looked calm despite having a riled Steiff shouting in her face. Then, her eyes wandering about the room, she glanced up and spotted me. Luckily she didn't gasp or react in any way. Instead, she looked away. Then, as Steiff turned his back on her, she glanced up again and repeatedly jerked her head towards the cutting table. Was she trying to tell me something? There was cloth and chalk, needles and thread and a large pair of scissors. *Scissors!* It dawned on me what she was indicating. I saw she'd not been tied to the chair. I nodded to her. When we made our move, she'd reach for the scissors and give Steiff something nasty and sharp to think about. It would buy us a precious second or two. I edged away and slid back down to rejoin Loki.

'We go in through the side door. The airmen are tied to chairs to our left. There are two guards behind them. Marieke's to our right. She's sitting down but not bound. She saw me. When we burst in she'll distract Steiff.'

'*He's* in there?' Loki was astonished but then grinned. 'Payback time! What about Otto?'

'Dead.'

Loki swallowed hard. 'Right. Best get on with it then.'

Chapter Twenty-seven
Shattered Dreams

Gently, ever so gently, I turned the handle. The door was unlocked. I nodded the OK to Loki, and on the count of three we burst in. We didn't shout or yell or scream. We simply pointed our pistols and pulled the triggers. The air filled with pops as bullets flew from the silencers. The two guards never stood a chance. Marieke spun off her chair, snatched the scissors from the table and sank them into Steiff's leg. He let out a cry and dropped to his knees. Recognizing me, he cried out, '*Sie!*' a split second before Loki placed a bullet in him.

Marieke turned to me, her face filled with joy. 'Finn, I just knew you'd come.'

I suddenly felt in a daze, my head a whirl. My stare fixed on the middle of the three airman. I'd waited so long, said so many prayers, willed with every ounce of strength for this moment to come. Feeling giddy, I dropped my gun and froze.

'Finn, are you all right? *Finn?*' Marieke seized my arm and shook it.

I blinked and then blinked again. The man sitting in the middle chair seemed puzzled and mildly unsettled by my gaze. He was in his early twenties and close up looked nothing like Father. I felt crushed; utterly, utterly crushed. Loki finished untying them and saw I was in a trance. He ran and gave me a shove. 'Snap out of it, Finn. I'm sorry, but I did warn you.'

'Warn him about what?' asked Marieke.

'He thought his father was among the airmen. I told him he was crazy but he wouldn't listen. Now, let's get the hell out of here.'

Marieke's mouth opened in astonishment. 'Y-your father! Oh God, I'm so sorry, Finn. I had no idea.'

Luckily for all of us Loki took control of the moment. I wasn't in a fit state to think straight about anything. Distributing weapons from the guards to the airmen, he led them outside and got them climbing over the wall into the yard of the bookshop.

Marieke let go of me, turned and knelt beside the body of her grandfather. She leaned forward, removed his broken spectacles and kissed him on the forehead. 'Forgive me,' she whispered and then looked up. 'I had nowhere else to go, Finn. I had to risk bringing the airmen here. Grandfather said they could hide in the attic. Steiff came this afternoon to collect his uniform. He must've heard noises coming from upstairs. He knew Otto lived alone and probably became suspicious – must have thought he was hiding Jews or something. It's all my fault.' Her eyes glistened with tears. 'Grandfather always said he wasn't a courageous man. But when Steiff returned he stood between us. He refused to let me be harmed. He stood up to him, Finn; he stood up to that Nazi pig. But Steiff simply took out his pistol and shot him.' The tears streamed down her cheeks. 'He always said he wished he was brave enough to stand up to them.'

I lifted Marieke to her feet. 'He was, Marieke. He was as brave as any of us.'

An agitated Loki appeared at the door. 'For pity's sake,' he hissed. 'Get a bloody move on.'

Making for the apartment was a case of dodging soldiers on patrol and keeping to poorly lit streets. Somehow we made it. For me the journey was all a blur. I'd been wrong. Completely wrong. The despair of it hammered away inside my skull. Father wasn't here, and that meant Nils had probably been right all along. Father was dead. It *was* his plane Nils had seen corkscrewing down into the sea, flames leaping from a burning fuel tank. And Father didn't bale out, wasn't rescued, and hadn't been hiding out with the Resistance all this time. How could I have been so blind? I'd imagined him alive and embellished it with such detail that it felt too real to be anything other than true. It was one big lie – a lie I'd told myself, a lie I'd all too willingly believed, especially after seeing that photograph in the files at Mulberry.

Clutching a Sten machine gun, a relieved Freya greeted us at the door to the second-floor apartment. She ushered us inside, into dark rooms devoid of furniture. 'Best not to use the lights,' she said. 'This place hasn't even got curtains, so don't go too close to the windows unless you're really careful and keep down low.'

Jan ran and gave Marieke a hug. 'You did it, Finn. You save them.'

'I couldn't have done it without Loki, Jan. Where's Willem?'

'No sign of him yet, Finn, but there's still time.' Freya did her best to sound hopeful.

While Loki set about briefing the second group of three airmen we'd brought from Otto's on our escape plan, I slumped down on the floor, rested my head against the wall and closed my eyes. I wanted to remain strong but I struggled to hold back the tears. Freya knelt beside me. 'Come on, Finn. I know it's a letdown, but we're all safe. That's the most important thing. We have a job to do. The next bit is going to be the most difficult. I need you to be focused. We all need you to be focused.'

'Just because he's not here doesn't mean he's not alive.'

The voice was unfamiliar. Perfect English and yet clipped with an accent that was definitely German. I looked up to see a tall man in SS uniform holding out a hand towards me.

'You can call me Falcon. I must take this opportunity to thank you for all that you've done. Freya told me about your father. You know, there's inevitably much chaos in times of war. Often it's unclear what's happened to those lost in action or stranded behind enemy lines. My advice to you is simple. Don't give up. Not until you know for certain.'

'He's right.' A chubby, moustached man in his late

forties appeared at Falcon's shoulder. 'Group Captain
Wolfie Collins at your service.' He gestured about the
room, to his comrade, Jenkins, and the other airmen,
who I learned were the surviving crew from a Lancaster
bomber that never reached its target in the Rühr,
Germany's industrial heartland. 'All of us here have
families back home,' Collins continued. 'They too
have no idea whether we're dead or alive. They probably
fear the worst, but I'll bet my life that none of them have
given up hope, not completely, even when weeks and
months have passed without any news.' He saw that I
remained unconvinced. 'The point I'm trying to make
is that we're all still alive. And so your father might be as
well. At least, us lot are living and breathing at present.
This plan of yours sounds barmy. Is it really the only way
out of here?'

'Yes,' Loki replied from the other side of the room.
'It's the only stretch of coast not mined.'

'Then so be it. You can rely on us to put up a fight if
it all goes pear-shaped.'

I studied Falcon, who looked every bit the German
officer. I rose to my feet and approached him. 'So you're
the cause of all this trouble, are you? I suppose the
intelligence you have in your possession is worth all this
sacrifice?'

'Not for me to judge, young man, but London
believes so. There have been rumours for months that
Herr Hitler intends to invade Russia but many remain
unconvinced, and even those willing to entertain
the notion can't agree on how he'll go about it.' He

tapped his breast pocket. 'It's all here. Codenamed Operation Barbarossa. Due to kick off any day now. Between you and me, this war's about to get a whole lot nastier.'

Loki moved closer to the window to keep a watchful eye on the Palace Hotel across the road. Eleven o'clock came and went. Eventually trucks, cars and motorcycles began leaving. 'Looks like van Alblas's people have done their bit.'

Freya had a question for Loki and me. 'Have you noticed that the airmen are all wearing their RAF uniforms beneath their German ones?' she whispered. 'It makes them look a little odd – sort of unnaturally padded. It's summer, for God's sake. Should we try to persuade them to abandon them?'

'We can ask, but if I were them I'd want to keep them on,' I replied. 'If they get caught wearing their RAF uniforms they'll only be looking forward to a spell in a prisoner-of-war camp. Without them they'll be facing torture and a firing squad, like us from Special Ops, shot as enemy spies.'

'He's right,' said Loki. 'We can't ask them to do that. It's a step too far.'

Feeling weary, I slumped back down on the floor and leaned my back against the wall. Marieke came and sat next to me, resting her head on my shoulder. 'Thank you for saving my life. That's twice now: first outside that shop in The Hague and then at Grandfather's. Both times I really thought I was done for.' She twisted round and peered into my face, reaching up as if wanting to touch the swelling about my eye. 'Did they hurt you badly?'

I shook my head. 'Managed to escape before Steiff really turned the screw.'

She sighed. 'I'm glad. I had no idea you thought your father was alive, Finn. I wish you'd said because I know exactly how you must feel. I've not told many people this, but I have a brother somewhere in Holland. No idea where, but I'm sure he's still alive and I intend to find him.'

'What's his name?'

'Karel. He's three years older than me. I just know he's out there somewhere. I can feel it.' She drew her fingers through her hair to cover her scar and then reached up and kissed me. 'We are two of the same, you and me, Finn. Both of us have a guiding light inside us, a light that says while there's even the faintest glimmer of hope we simply cannot give up our search.'

'There's no need to cover it up,' I said, pushing her hair back behind her ear. I ran my finger softly down the scar, from her temple to her neck. For what felt like for ever we sat together in each other's arms.

Freya eventually approached, leaned down and whispered to us, 'Still no sign of Willem. It looks like we'll have to leave him behind. We go in five minutes. It's best you say your goodbyes now as there won't be time later.'

Our goodbyes. The moment I was dreading. I wished it wasn't true. Just the thought of possibly never setting eyes on Marieke again made me feel desperate, angry, frustrated. 'Come with us,' I said. 'Come back to England.'

'I . . . I . . . I can't,' she said, her voice shaky. 'I have to lead Bram and the others to safety, and then there's much work to be done rebuilding our network.'

I cursed. 'But how can you continue now?'

She rose onto her knees and turned to face me. 'Someday we'll win this war and our countries will be free once again. We will all be free to follow our dreams. I'll be able to set up that flower shop I've always wanted. And you, Finn, what's your dream?'

'To fly,' I said without a moment's hesitation. 'I want to fly.'

'Well, when that day comes I'd like us to meet again. Promise me, Finn. Promise we'll be together again one day. *Please*. I need to hear you to say it.'

I held her tightly. 'I promise.'

'Time we were off,' said Loki, smacking home a full clip of ammo into his Sten machine gun. 'How do I look, Finn?'

He'd changed into his German uniform. As far as I could tell in the pale moonlight filtering through the windows, Otto had done a fine job. But Loki's boots were old and scruffy, and wouldn't convince anyone. About to point it out, I thought better of it. As we were unable to rectify the problem, mentioning it was only likely to dent Loki's confidence.

As we quietly filed down the staircase of the apartment block, praying we wouldn't meet anyone coming up, I realized what a motley bunch we were. Freya,

Marieke and I were supposedly captured partisans. At least we looked the part. Falcon was a tall man, and when he stiffened up, he'd convince anyone that he was an SS colonel. In fact, I learned from Wolfie Collins that beneath Falcon's layers of disguise and deception was an Englishman who'd grown up near Heidelberg and considered the Germans his people but who also hated the Nazis with venom. His German was perfect too, brimming with arrogant authority, and having spent a good deal of time in Berlin among the enemy, he'd adopted their mannerisms: to behave as if he ruled the world, to treat everyone else as if they were dirt. It was the others who worried me: five airmen, all looking slightly overweight, all nervous and sweaty from wearing two uniforms in the middle of summer. And Loki with his cracked and worn boots. My heart sank. I had the feeling our escape would not go as smoothly and un-noticed as I'd hoped.

With us all assembled by the entrance to the apart-ment block, Marieke turned to Jan. 'Wait here and remember to keep your eyes peeled. All being well, Bram and the others will be here within the next fifteen minutes or so. If I don't make it, take them to that address I gave you. The people there can be trusted. They'll look after you. Here, take this.' She handed Jan a pistol. 'Do your best to cover us if the need arises.'

'Take good care of yourself, Jan,' I said. 'Without your help we'd probably not have got this far.' He reached out and shook my hand.

'We can't wait any longer,' Loki observed after taking

a quick peek outside. 'Marieke, try to get in touch with the Kramers if you can. They'll be able to assist you with the new Aardappel network. Send us a message to let us know they're OK.'

She nodded.

With one final round of nervous goodbyes, Loki grabbed the door handle and puffed out his cheeks. 'Here goes. Good luck, everyone.'

Chapter Twenty-eight
The Great Escape

We needed to move fast. Falcon led us across the road towards the Palace Hotel, his pistol drawn. Loki had a firm grasp of the scruff of Freya's neck, Collins of mine, and Jenkins guided Marieke, having twisted her arm firmly behind her back. The other three airmen dressed as Wehrmacht soldiers marched behind us shoulder to shoulder, machine guns at the ready. Straight ahead lay our first obstacle: a guard house and barrier blocking the entranceway to the hotel. On we marched, our bellies full of butterflies, our hearts in our mouths. Falcon waved his gun and yelled for the barrier to be lifted. The guards peered at us for a moment. I dreaded it was all about to end in disaster. Then, through the darkness, one of them spotted the SS flashes on Falcon's uniform and hurriedly lifted the barrier. On we went, eyes forward, pushed and shoved, Falcon leading the way with un-rivalled confidence.

Two sentries guarded the side entrance of the hotel. Their somewhat slouched, lazy demeanour quickly changed as Falcon strode towards them. Snapping to attention, they clacked their heels and saluted. '*Heil Hitler!*' they barked in unison. Falcon knew better than to salute back. Instead he ignored such lowly privates of the Wehrmacht, as any brute of an SS colonel would, and stormed past them, thumping open the door. Bundled in on his heels, I heard a scuffle behind me and realized the two guards had been silenced. Once inside, I shuddered at becoming reacquainted with the hallway that held memories − bad memories − of my last capture. The light was bright and the place reeked of polish.

En masse we abruptly turned left and came to a stop in front of the large mahogany desk. I peered up at a clock behind it: twenty minutes past twelve. Ten minutes to go. So far so good. I glanced over my shoulder. To my relief the hall was empty apart from the middle-aged administrator who, startled by all the commotion and the squeak of boots against polished stone floor, looked up at us over the top of his glasses. Registering that an SS colonel was glaring at him, he rose sharply from his chair and shot an arm into the air. '*Heil Hitler, Herr Oberst!*' His eyes darted towards Freya, Marieke and then settled on me. He couldn't conceal his delight. '*Herr Gunnersen. Da wären wir wieder! Bravo, Herr Oberst, bravo!*' Excitedly he reached for his telephone.

'*Nein!*' Falcon shouted.

The man behind the desk paused, telephone receiver in hand. '*Warum? Was ist los?*'

'This is what's the matter,' Falcon replied. He raised his pistol and shot him, a tiny wisp of smoke emerging from the end of the silencer as the blast flung the man back against the wall. He slid to the floor.

Loki turned to Jenkins. 'Grab him and follow us. Where are the stairs, Finn?'

Down the stone steps we sped, in single file, boots clattering, pistols and machine guns poised. The guards in the basement never knew what hit them. As Loki and Wolfie Collins hurried along the basement corridor, sliding bolts and heaving open the doors to cells, Freya and I began undressing two of the guards, hurriedly yanking on their trousers and tunics. While I was buttoning mine up, Jenkins arrived dragging the administrator's body. 'What do we do with him?' he called out.

'Put him in the nearest empty cell. Then move these oafs too. Get the others to check all the cells.'

Moments later I looked up and gulped. The skinny figure of Theo Drees was being shouldered towards me by one of the airmen, who called out, 'This one's in pretty bad shape, but you should see the other poor sod. Right mess. Those bastards have really gone to town on him.'

Between them, Loki and Collins dragged another boy out of a cell. I hardly recognized him, but it was definitely Bram Keppel. His clothes were in tatters, his head limp, his feet bare. As he came closer, I saw the trails of blood on the floor left by his feet – long smears like snail tracks. He'd lost far more than one toenail. 'He's barely conscious, Finn,' Loki spat in disgust.

Theo Drees had fared better and, although weak, could at least stand up without support. A third emerged from another cell, a boy I didn't recognize. 'Is that it?' I said, horrified. 'Are you all that remains of Asparagus?'

They were indeed all that was left of what had once been Special Ops' largest network of agents. Marieke was alarmed at the state of them. 'How am I going to get them away from here? Can't you take them with you, Finn?'

'No. There's no room in the dinghies. And, anyway, we'd never get them down the beach.' I grabbed hold of Theo. 'I'm Finn – remember me? I was here too. I tapped the message on the pipes.'

Despite his bewilderment, Theo nodded.

'Good. Right, listen to me. You two are going to have to drag or carry Bram across the street to an apartment block. It's not far but you'll have to be quick and pray to God no soldiers spot you. There's someone covering you from the opposite side of the street, and Marieke will cover you from this side. All right?'

Again he nodded.

'Finn!' Loki called out. 'There's no time. We must get down to the shore. We've got less than five minutes. And what about those sentries at the barrier? They're bound to see Theo and Bram.'

'I've not finished,' I said, turning to Falcon. 'When we get outside, I want you to call over all the guards at the barrier. Say there's an emergency or something. As soon as they approach we deal with them. That should buy the others a few precious seconds.' Everyone just stared at me. 'Well, anybody got any better ideas?' My question was met with blank faces. 'That's settled then.'

Up the steps we went, and in twos and threes we crossed the hall and exited the hotel, crouching down in the dark. Falcon took my signal and strode purposefully a few paces towards the front of the building, just so that he was illuminated by the light from a window. There he called out, bellowing orders at the sentries. Waving his pistol, he gestured for them all to follow him. '*Folgen Sie mir. Schnell!*'

They raced towards him. They couldn't see us crouching in the shadows, silencers poised, fingers on the triggers. As they reached him, Falcon flung himself out of the way, pressing hard up against the wall. A volley of pops was followed by the heavy sounds of bodies crashing onto the path.

'Go, go, go!' I said in a loud whisper to Theo and the other boy, who had Bram strung between them. I pushed them forward. Together they began dragging Bram in the direction of the apartment. Clutching a Sten gun, Marieke followed.

'You two get everyone down onto the beach,' I said to Freya and Loki. 'Remember to walk nice and slow, as if you've just finished dinner and are taking a stroll down to the water's edge. You're all in uniform so you should be fine.'

'What about you, Finn?'

'Just get going,' I snapped through clenched teeth. 'I'll be right behind you.'

Crouching low, I instead scurried back after Marieke. Although she was going to cover Theo and the others in case something went wrong, I was asking myself who was going to cover *her* back?

At the corner of the hotel I reached Marieke's shoulder. She turned sharply. 'Finn! Go. Otherwise you'll never get away.'

'I wanted to see that you're safe,' I said as we watched a trio of rather forlorn figures hobble, drag and stagger across the road.

'I think it's all right for me to try and follow now. They've almost made it to the other side.' She turned and gave me a kiss. 'Goodbye, Finn. Go. Please go. Now!'

As she edged forward, I reached out and grabbed hold of her. 'Wait! Something's not right.'

Out of the corner of my eye I'd spotted a car moving swiftly in our direction along the road from The Hague. It was a black saloon, and as it was lit by a streetlamp I suddenly realized that it was identical to van Alblas's car. 'Bloody hell, they've cut it fine. It's Willem.'

The car swerved and screeched to a halt outside the front of the Kurhaus, about twenty yards away from us. The rear doors swung open. Willem and Laura leaped out and looked around.

'Over here,' I shouted, waving frantically. 'Get a move on.'

'Laura's coming too,' Willem called out.

'Yes, yes, just get the hell over here.'

Marieke drew a sharp breath and pointed. 'Look, Finn, they're being followed.'

From the direction of The Hague a column of motorcycles streamed along the road towards us. I could hear the roar of their engines and see their headlamps flickering as they bounced over ruts. Were they in pursuit? Or were they just returning to HQ? It was impossible to tell. One thing was certain, however. They were travelling at speed and would be on top of us far too soon for comfort. We had maybe thirty seconds at best. I rushed over to the car and saw Saskia at the wheel.

She opened the window and poked her head out. 'Roadblocks, Finn. We had to make a detour. Sorry.' She threw a fretful glance in the rear-view mirror. 'I didn't think we were being followed. We thought we'd avoided them. They just came out of nowhere.'

Realizing Saskia's situation was desperately perilous and that she had little chance of avoiding being apprehended, I yelled, 'You've got to come with us. Quickly, or else you'll be caught.' I grabbed the door handle.

'No, Finn.' She shook her head.

'But—'

Having checked that Willem and Laura had disappeared into the gloom beside the hotel, Saskia threw van Alblas's car into gear and revved the engine.

'No, there's still time. Abandon the car,' I pleaded.

'No, Finn. I've got some scores to settle.' She picked up a pistol from her lap and I realized she was deadly serious. 'I'll buy you all as much time as I can. Say goodbye to Willem for me.'

'But—'

She tore off, turning round in as tight a circle as she could, tyres squealing, and then accelerated hard back towards the road to The Hague, directly into the path of the enemy.

I stood there for a moment, glued to the spot, utterly dumbfounded. Freya and Loki arrived at my shoulder. 'For Christ's sake, what's happening?'

I pointed at the car heading directly into the path of the German motorcycles. Such was my horror I could barely bring myself to speak. 'Saskia's trying to buy us some time.'

'The others got across the boulevard OK and are making their way down the beach,' Loki said breathlessly. 'Probably at the water's edge by now, with any luck. I gave Falcon my torch. He knows the signal.'

I was transfixed by van Alblas's car. I had to see what happened; I just had to. Saskia drove straight into the line of motorcycles at top speed. The absence of brake lights told me she had no intention of slowing down or avoiding them. I saw some of the motorcycles swerve out of her path; others went crashing in a screech of metal on tarmac; yet others turned sharply to pursue her. Then machine-gun fire. Lots of gunfire. The car began zigzagging, and then under a hail of bullets swung to the side of the road and came to a stop. More shooting. The car burst into flames. Motorcycles cut past the wreckage and headed our way.

'Oh my God!' Loki cried.

'Run!' I shouted, taking hold of Marieke's arm. 'You're coming with us. It's too dangerous to stay here. There's no time for you to get to the apartment.'

Briefly she tried to resist.

'Look, Jan's taken Bram and the others inside. They've not been seen. They're safe.'

'All right, Finn. You're right.'

The four of us charged down the road separating the Palace Hotel from the Kurhaus and headed for the boulevard and beach. With all hell breaking loose, any cover we'd had was blown. And there was the small matter of the bunker at the corner of the Kurhaus to deal with. 'Grenade,' I called out as I ran, reaching out and taking one from Loki's hand, as if I were the final leg in a relay race. With the cracks, pops and rat-a-tat-tats of gunfire coming from the streets behind us, there was no going back. The bunker lay straight ahead. I remembered seeing it during my escape from Steiff's office. I calculated the timings in my head, pulled the pin and six strides later found myself on the bunker's concrete roof overlooking the beach. I fell flat onto my belly, reached down over the front and flung the grenade in through one of the narrow slits. Loki hauled me to my feet and we jumped off the side. I heard shouts of panic, saw a flash and was briefly deafened by the blast. Smoke and dust billowed out from the remains.

Together we ran across the boulevard, jumped over the wall, and dropped down, landing on the soft sand. My sore toe sent shooting pains through me but I had little choice but to curse out loud and scramble to my feet. 'Which way? Where are the dinghies?'

Freya set off without a moment's hesitation. 'I saw them earlier. They're waiting on the far side of the pier. About a hundred yards or so beyond the breakers. There are soldiers patrolling the pier, so get ready to fire at the walkway.'

We ran as fast as we could, cutting diagonally down the beach, aiming to reach the wooden supports of the pier where they met the water's edge. Two guards on the walkway spotted us. They shouted the alarm, lifted their rifles to their shoulders and let off a couple of rounds. Freya dropped onto one knee, steadied her Sten and let rip with a sweeping arc of fire. Her marksmanship stood us all in good stead as the figures above us crumpled to their knees, their weapons spilling over the railings and dropping down onto the sand some twenty yards in front of us. Loki, Marieke and I sped past Freya and dipped beneath the pier. Briefly we had cover. Freya joined us and, as the waves crashed about our legs, we paused for a moment to catch our breaths and to figure out just exactly where the dinghies were waiting for us.

'I can't see them,' Loki gasped. 'Where the hell are they?'

'They've got to be there. Surely one's remained behind for us,' I replied. In truth I was beginning to panic. What if they'd given up on us? They had Falcon. That's who they'd come for. His escape to England would mean Operation Double Dutch had been a success. Were we the price of that success?

The commotion drew soldiers from their HQ. Loads of soldiers. From their vantage point on the boulevard they began shooting. I didn't reckon they could see us as many were firing wildly, blindly in the direction of the water. Few had their weapons trained on the area beneath the pier. Nevertheless, we were effectively trapped.

'There!' Marieke pointed.

In the moonlight the sea glistened, sparkled and

shimmered. Far out a tiny, barely discernible black shape bobbed up and down. It looked like a lump of flotsam being washed ashore. But it was enough to lift our spirits – it was our way home. One dinghy had remained behind.

'We're going to have to risk it,' Loki announced. 'It won't be long before those soldiers make their way along the pier. They'll be able to see us swimming out. It's now or never. Into the water!'

We waded in, clutching our Stens above our heads. Two-foot waves crashed into us. The cold stole our breaths, making us gasp. Deeper and deeper we went, the swell reaching our waists, then our shoulders, the power of each surge sufficient to lift us off our feet. I slung my Sten over my shoulder and began to swim. I could hear splashing and kicking all around me, amid encouraging shouts from Loki. 'Swim steadily and don't panic. The tide's on the way out so it'll help draw us away from the beach.'

I crawled and kicked with all my strength. I felt the strap of my Sten slip from my shoulder and suddenly it was gone. I trod water and turned. About to dive under to retrieve my weapon, I realized there was little point. The flashes from small-arms fire were coming from the beach now, and not just the boulevard. Marieke caught me up, spluttering and coughing violently. I realized she wasn't a great swimmer. 'Keep going, we're halfway there. Need a hand?'

She swallowed another mouthful of brine and shook her head. 'No, Finn, I can manage.'

We now heard a noise that sounded like pebbles skimming or breaking the surface. They made tiny splashes too. That's how I could tell what they were — bullets. We weren't out of range yet.

Our clothes soaked up the sea and wanted to drag us under. It was like having blocks of concrete tied about your waist. As I flung my arms forward in the best crawl I could muster, I kept my eyes open, looking out for the others. Having grown up swimming in the glacier-fed fjords of our homeland, Loki, Freya and I were strong swimmers and could withstand the cold. Loki was way ahead of me, Freya not far behind. Marieke worried me though. She seemed to be slowing down. I swam over to her and kept alongside her. Still the bullets came. All around us they plunged, making their strange deadly noise, almost like whispers of death.

'Nearly there,' I called out encouragingly. 'That's the dinghy ahead of us. See it? That black shape.'

'Yes, Finn, I can see it. You go on. You're quicker than me. I'll be OK.'

About to press on with renewed determination, I heard Marieke let out a strange cry. Her whole body seemed to lift slightly out of the water. Then she rolled over and slipped under, with just her arms above the surface.

Frantically I reached out and took hold of her. 'I've got you. Don't worry. It's not far now. Don't struggle.'

I kicked with both legs and sculled with my one free arm. Marieke was wounded but I had no idea how badly. She groaned. At least she was still conscious. That was the most important thing. 'Hang on, Marieke. Almost there.'

Gritting my teeth and cursing every energy-sapping stroke, I struggled towards the dinghy. I could see figures on board. Loki got there first and waited for Freya to catch up before helping her aboard. I still had twenty yards to go and felt as if I had only enough energy left for ten. Loki saw me struggling with Marieke and returned to help. 'You all right, Finn?'

'Yes, but Marieke's been shot,' I yelled.

Loki snatched hold of the collar of my jacket and helped drag both of us towards safety. 'We're out of range now,' he cried triumphantly. 'We're going to make it, Finn. We're bloody well going to make it.'

Clutching Marieke with one hand, I reached out with my other and grabbed hold of a rope thrown to me by someone on board the dinghy. A figure dressed all in black, face darkened with burned cork, pulled on the rope, then leaned over the side and hauled us both into the dinghy. 'You took your bleedin' time. Killer and me was wondering whether you'd ever bother turning up.'

'Good to see you too, Smithy,' I shouted. 'Marieke's been shot.'

'Right-o, Finn.' He let go of me and set about rescuing Loki. 'You'll be pleased to learn that the others have all made it safely, including a couple of additional unexpected guests.'

I nodded.

'You lie still and rest. Our turn now – Killer and me

are going to get us to the MGB before she leaves. Sit tight and we'll soon get you all home.'

My teeth chattered, the cold penetrating my bones, as I watched Smithy and Killer paddle furiously into deeper water. Our dinghy rocked and bobbed in the swell. It was hellishly cramped – barely room for all six of us – and every few seconds waves crashed over us, inundating the boat with spray. I cradled Marieke tightly in my arms to keep her warm. Loki and Freya huddled together too. It was all over. Nearly.

'Finn . . .' Marieke whispered to me so softly I could barely hear her.

'Yes?'

'I'm so cold, Finn.'

'I know. So am I. Let's keep each other warm.' I tightened my grip on her.

'That's it, Finn,' Smithy called out. 'Keep her awake. Keep her talking.'

'Does it hurt?'

I felt Marieke shake her head. 'But I feel so tired, Finn. I just want to sleep.'

'No! Stay awake. Talk to me, Marieke. Keep talking to me.'

I felt her summoning her strength. 'I hope your father is alive. That he's somewhere out there, safe and sound. Don't give up on him. Please, Finn. Promise me.'

'I'll promise, but only if you do too. About your brother, I mean. One day you'll be reunited with Karel . . . *Marieke!*' I shook her. 'Get a move on, Smithy – we're losing her.'

'Killer and me are doing the best we can, lad. Not far now.'

'Listen, Finn. If I don't make it . . .' Marieke mumbled.

'Don't talk rubbish. Of course you'll make it.'

'But if I don't, will you try to find Karel for me? Tell him I was always thinking of him. That I never gave up hope. Please.' She pressed her head into my shoulder. 'He helped me to keep going through the really dark times, Finn. Every day I imagine us at home again, free to live our lives, Karel one day heading off to study medicine, me living in Scheveningen with my flower shop . . .' Her voice trailed off. She sounded sleepy, distant.

'What will you call your shop, Marieke?' I shook her again. 'What will you call it?' I suddenly felt really frightened. She was slipping away and I was helpless.

'Margo's, Finn,' she whispered so softly I barely heard.

'But there's already a flower shop with that name. Remember? That's where you left the card in the window for us. *Remember?*'

I felt her nod. 'I know, Finn. That was once my mother's shop. Her name was Margo.'

'That's a wonderful dream, Marieke. You hang onto it. One day it'll come true. I'm sure of it.'

'I shall, Finn. A life without hopes and dreams is no life at all, is it?'

'I think you're right, Marieke. Want to know a secret? I kept that pressed flower you sent to me at Mulberry. Got it safely tucked between the pages of a book. They last for ever, don't they?'

The thump and splutter of an idling diesel engine together with the unmistakable gurgling of a bilge pump gave me renewed hope. The MGB! I pressed my eyes shut and finally let the waves of tiredness wash over me. We'd soon be speeding home, skimming the waves, going so fast the enemy stood no chance of catching us up. Our nightmare was over. I felt the dinghy clatter into the hull of the gunboat and heard voices.

'Time to let go of her, Finn . . . Come on now, let go of her,' said Smithy softly, trying to prise Marieke from my grasp. 'She's dead, Finn. There's nothing we can do for her now.'

Postscript

The successful escape of Allied aircrews shot down over enemy territory proved a great morale booster during the Second World War. The total number who escaped or evaded capture was remarkable. For France, Belgium and Holland combined, a reasonable estimate is about three thousand airmen shot down prior to D-Day (June 1944).

Much of the effort was co-ordinated by the then newly formed, top secret MI9, based at the War Office in London. Escape routes out of occupied Europe were numerous and varied, some leading to neutral countries like Switzerland, Sweden, Portugal and Spain, others more direct, as described in this book.

The majority of locations in *Wolf Squadron* are fictional, such as the Pols' farm, the shops Margo's and Breughel's, and the Rembrandt cafe in The Hague. The Palace Hotel and the Kurhaus in Scheveningen, however, are real. Today, Scheveningen remains a vibrant Dutch seaside resort, with long sandy beaches and dunes. During the Nazi occupation of Holland the magnificent Palace Hotel on Scheveningen's beachside boulevard served for a time as the regional headquarters of the German navy's (Kriegsmarine) coastal security division. A small stretch of sand behind it was kept free of mines and other defences so that German officers could bathe. Astonishingly, despite the many obvious dangers, this weakness in the coastal defences was exploited: on a few especially dark nights, Royal Navy MGBs raced across the North Sea to try and drop off agents and pick up waiting escapees from the beach right under the enemy's nose, just as in *Wolf Squadron*. According to published accounts, these operations did not always go smoothly! Some years after the war, the Palace Hotel was demolished. The adjacent Kurhaus, however, has been fully restored to its former splendour and is now a famous hotel. The wooden pier offering Finn and the others much-needed cover during their escape was eventually destroyed by the Germans by fire in 1943. Today, Scheveningen has a splendid new pier that is quite a tourist attraction.

Finn Gunnersen's world of Special Operations is inspired by the activities of a real wartime clandestine organization known as the Special Operations Executive, or SOE. Over the course of the war several thousand young men and women of more than fifteen different nationalities were recruited and trained as secret agents in great secrecy at various locations throughout Great Britain. Many ended up at what became known as the 'Finishing School', a series of houses near Beaulieu in the New Forest in southern England, the setting for Mulberry House in Finn's adventures.

Training was extensive, covering subjects such as sabotage, armed and unarmed combat, survival skills, radio operating and ciphers, disguise, evasion and intelligence-gathering. The SOE evolved at about the same time as Britain's newly created Special Forces, the SAS (Special Air Service) and SBS (Special Boat Service), and many of the techniques taught and equipment used were similar.

Agents were also supplied with various 'gadgets', a section within the SOE being dedicated to dreaming up useful things for an agent to take on a mission. It was this group that inspired the writer Ian Fleming to create 'Q' and his gadgets in the famous James Bond stories. The equipment and devices described in *Wolf Squadron*, like the parachutists' striptease suits, silk maps, sickness-inducing and lethal L-pills, sleeve pistols, tyrebursters and incendiary cigarettes, are all real and were available to agents at the time (see pages 311–313).

Many who successfully completed their training were subsequently sent behind enemy lines on highly dangerous missions to sabotage enemy targets or to establish and coordinate Resistance networks. Their campaigns of dirty tricks were to cause the Nazis a great deal of trouble.

What is extraordinary about the SOE is that recruits were often ordinary people with civilian backgrounds, and not highly trained military personnel. Frequently, it was simply their excellent local knowledge or linguistic skills that led to them being recruited. The heroism and sacrifice of some agents are well documented, including those awarded the George Cross, the highest civilian award for courage. There are numerous other unsung heroes and heroines, though, whose stories have not been told so fully. Nevertheless, we owe them all a great debt of gratitude for the work they did in the name of freedom and the fight against tyranny. Many did not survive to tell their tales.

Although a work of fiction, *Wolf Squadron* is inspired by the darkest episode in the true story of the SOE. In 1942 a wireless operator in the Dutch section operating in The Hague was betrayed by a *V-Mann* (informant) and captured along with his wireless set and ciphers. The Germans 'persuaded' him to continue sending messages home as if all was well. Although the agent included faulty security checks in his transmissions to indicate his terrible predicament, these were repeatedly overlooked at SOE headquarters. Soon more agents and supplies were being dropped by parachute right into the enemy's arms. The Germans codenamed the operation *Nordpol* (North Pole). It also became known as the *England Spiel* (England game). They learned a great deal about the SOE organisation and employed their own expert signalmen to work captured radio sets. Sadly, the operation proved incredibly successful – in the end the Germans had acquired and used fourteen different SOE radio sets and had captured over fifty Dutch SOE agents, most of whom were subsequently executed, along with others. The episode led to recriminations, including claims that the Germans had a spy high up in the SOE organization. Such claims, however, have never been proven.

Wolf Squadron is set during May and June 1941, at a time when Britain's cities were suffering many harrowing night-time bombing raids by the Luftwaffe (the Blitz) and much of Europe had been occupied. The question was – what would Adolf Hitler do next? Early on the morning of 22 June 1941 the world found out. Seven German infantry armies led by four Panzer divisions invaded the Soviet Union, beginning the largest land war in history, codenamed Barbarossa. Hitler hoped to destroy the Russian army and seize vast territories in the east, his so-called *Lebensraum* (living space) – industrial and agricultural land he believed would ensure Germany's survival as a great power. As his armed forces became thinly stretched and bogged down, meeting fierce resistance on multiple fronts, it was to prove a significant blunder.

Equipment

Parachute Suit

Made of canvas, these parachute suits are also known as *striptease suits* because two-way zip fasteners fitted on each side enable rapid removal upon landing. Contain pockets for dagger, pistol, spade and handle, emergency rations etc.

Available in four sizes based upon parachutist's height, they are large enough to allow the user to wear two overcoats underneath. Also available in white canvas.

Note: Model shown here carrying Sten machine gun, a favourite among agents.

Suitcase Radio (Transceiver)

This is similar to the replacement suitcase radio set Freya carries into Holland in *Wolf Squadron*.

It comprises a transmitter, receiver and combination power pack, and is supplied with a box containing aerial wire, Morse transmitting key, headset, spare fuses, spare valves and screwdriver.

Set can be operated via mains electricity (AC) or 6-volt accumulator.

Silk Maps

Printed on silk, these maps are the size of handkerchiefs and can be hidden in the lining of coats, cuffs and collars. The one shown here is of France.

Special Operations: Unlocking the Secrets of Book Codes

In *Wolf Squadron* the Dutch Special Ops group led by Bram Keppel used so-called Book Codes to encipher their messages. In the early years of clandestine wartime missions, Book Codes were frequently utilized. Almost any book can be used, even this one!

If you wanted to encipher a message so that only your friends could read it, one of the simplest ways of doing this is to change each letter into another by a fixed rule – for example, change each to the next letter of the alphabet, i.e. A becomes B, B becomes C, etc., all the way to Z. You could of course choose to *shift* or *transpose* by, say, three letters instead, so that A becomes D, B becomes E, and so on. If your friends know by how much you've *transposed* the letters it is easy for them to decode your message by doing the operation in reverse.

The problem with this method, however, is that because every letter is transposed by the same rule, the coding is easy to crack simply by trial and error. With 26 letters in the alphabet, there are only 25 possible variations to try out. A far more effective version would be to transpose each letter by a *different* amount, and to make it seem as random as possible. For example, the first letter of your message might be shifted five places through the alphabet, the second by twelve places, the third by eight, and so on. This makes it much, much harder to crack. Naturally, the person receiving your message needs to know how you've done the transposing in order to decode it. This is called a *KEY*, and is where a book can be used. This is how it is done:

Firstly, it is useful to write out the alphabet, numbering each letter:

A	B	C	D	E	F	G	H	I	J	K	L	M
1	2	3	4	5	6	7	8	9	10	11	12	13
N	O	P	Q	R	S	T	U	V	W	X	Y	Z
14	15	16	17	18	19	20	21	22	23	24	25	26

Now, suppose you want to send your friends the following message in coded form so no one else can read it:

Meet you outside the cinema at nine o'clock tonight. Don't be late. I've got to be home by midnight.

To select our code KEY we need a book. Let's use this one, *Wolf Squadron*. The next step is to select an extract at random. I've chosen the first sentence of Chapter Nine in this instance:

Our Whitley roared into the night, thundering eastwards across the coast and over the North Sea.

This forms the basis of our KEY. Each letter in the extract now needs to be numbered according to its position in the alphabet.

O	U	R	W	H	I	T	L	E	Y	R	O	A	R	E
15	21	18	23	8	9	20	12	5	25	18	15	1	18	5
D	I	N	T	O	T	H	E	N	I	G	H	T	T	H
4	9	14	20	15	20	8	5	14	9	7	8	20	20	8
U	N	D	E	R	I	N	G	E	A	S	T	W	A	R
21	14	4	5	18	9	14	7	5	1	19	20	23	1	18
D	S	A	C	R	O	S	S	T	H	E	C	O	A	S
4	19	1	3	18	15	19	19	20	8	5	3	15	1	19
T	A	N	D	O	V	E	R	T	H	E	N	O	R	T
20	1	14	4	15	22	5	18	20	8	5	14	15	18	20
H	S	E	A											
8	19	5	1											

This gives us the following sequence of numbers:

15-21-18-23-8-9-20-12-5-25-18-15-1-18-5-4-9-14-
20-15-20-8-5-14, etc.

Each of these numbers is used to determine by how
many places we transpose each letter of our message.
The first word of our message is *MEET*. Following the
sequence above, the *M* is transposed 15 places, *E* by 21,
the second *E* by 18, and the *T* by 23 spaces, and so on
for the complete message. Doing this, *MEET* becomes
BZWQ. (Note: think of the alphabet as a circle or
wheel, so once you get to Z, you count on to A, B, C,
etc.). Coding all our message gives rise to the following:

EQUIPMENT

BZWQ GXO AZSKXEW YLN QCCYUF OC
UQHY W'XZSHC CCUNHAN. APF'X UF OSIX.
B'PM LRI UH VF VSBA GQ GQIBXYBB.

This coded message would be pretty hard to decipher
if it got into the wrong hands! However, if your friends
know that the KEY is based on the first sentence of
Chapter Nine of *Wolf Squadron*, they can simply do the
above in reverse – i.e. using the same sequence of numbers
(the KEY) and applying it again to the coded message, this
time counting *backwards* through the alphabet rather than
forwards. So, the first coded letter *B* is *transposed backwards*
by 15 letters to become M again, and so on.

When Book Codes were used, it was vital that both
the secret agent and his HQ had identical copies of the
books (same edition etc.) so there could be no confusion. The agent (or HQ) would begin a message with
a page and line reference so the other knew where to get
the KEY from. As you will see if you try it out, it takes a
while to code and decode even short messages, and it's
quite easy to make a mistake. Agents had to take great care,
often in difficult circumstances. Generally the messages
were safe provided the enemy didn't discover which book
was being used. Such information was, however, sometimes revealed under interrogation, as happened to
members of Asparagus in *Wolf Squadron*, thus triggering
Finn's mission into Holland. So-called 'checks' or 'bluff-
checks' were often used by agents in the field (deliberate
errors or additional phrases, or use of specific words) that
if present or missing would alert HQ that something was

317

wrong. Occasionally such 'alerts' were overlooked, most probably because some agents forgot to include them so frequently that HQ grew used to their failings and assumed they'd simply been careless.

Have a go at using the book code with your friends. Perhaps pick your favourite bit of *Wolf Squadron* as your KEY.

For fun, also have a go at decoding the following message written by Finn. It describes his favourite food – something he's not eaten since leaving his homeland of Norway. He's used the same KEY as I have above. To help you, I've written out the *transposing* sequence beneath the message and left space for you to fill in the decoded letters. *Don't forget* – as you're 'decoding' you count *backwards* through the alphabet (use the alphabet wheel printed opposite to help you if it's easier).

Finn's favourite food is:

BZSQ JJFXX HF QSGBR BOORY. EJ Q JST NBMH YNTWCHRFLXL.

B	Z	S	Q	J	J	F	X	X	H	F	Q	S	G
15	21	18	23	8	9	20	12	5	25	18	15	1	18

B	R	B	O	O	R	Y	E	J	Q	J	S	T	N
5	4	9	14	20	15	20	8	5	14	9	7	8	20

B	M	H	Y	N	T	W	C	H	R	F	L	X	L
20	8	21	14	4	5	18	9	14	7	5	1	19	20

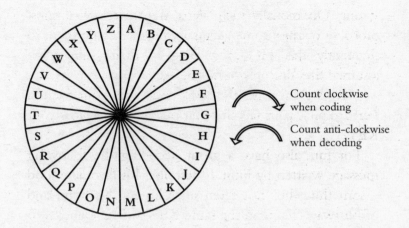

Count clockwise
when coding

Count anti-clockwise
when decoding

Alphabet Code Wheel – use it to help count the letter transpositions.

If you'd like to learn more about the coding methods used by the real Special Operations Executive, I have included information about another method called the 'Playfair Code' in Finn's second adventure, *Special Operations: Death Ray*.

JOIN FINN GUNNERSEN IN HIS FIRST SPECIAL OPERATION

Eighty miles per hour . . .
'Now, Loki!' I said, seizing the other column in front of me.
We both pulled back. The plane lurched like a runaway
train about to derail. Then, suddenly, the pounding ceased
and everything seemed mighty smooth.
My God, I thought, we're flying!

A teenage boy and his best friend, obsessed
with fighter planes . . .

A country invaded by the enemy . . .

One daring mission that might just save the day . . .

Get ready for take-off and a full-throttle action-adventure!

HIGH-OCTANE EXCITEMENT, PERFECT FOR FANS OF
ANDY MCNAB, ROBERT MUCHAMORE AND CHRIS RYAN

978 0 552 55674 3

**'TO ALL INTENTS AND PURPOSES THE THREE OF
US DIDN'T EXIST, NOT OFFICIALLY . . . '**

Completing their Special Operations training,
Finn, Loki and Freya head into enemy territory.
Britain is staring at defeat and Bomber Command
is experiencing horrendous losses . . .

Suspicion falls on a Nazi installation
close to the French coast . . .

Something deadly has been built there . . .

The obvious thing would be to destroy it . . .

Better still would be to go in and steal it!

978 0 552 55675 0

Also by Craig Simpson

RESISTANCE

Following their father's arrest by the Nazis,
Marek and Olaf are forced to seek refuge in
the frozen Norwegian wilderness . . .

Saved from an icy grave by the Resistance, the
quick-thinking Marek sees an opportunity for revenge . . .

But can he keep his nerve when his actions threaten
the safety of his family and friends . . . ?

978 0 552 55674 3

READY FOR YOUR NEXT SPECIAL OPERATION?

Log on to

www.finngunnersen.co.uk

for competitions, an interview with
Craig Simpson and updates about Finn's adventures!